Why Didn't They Ask Evans?

HarperCollins*Publishers*

HarperCollins*Publishers* Ltd
1 London Bridge Street
London SE1 9GF
www.harpercollins.co.uk

HarperCollins*Publishers*
1st Floor, Watermarque Building, Ringsend Road
Dublin 4, Ireland

This paperback edition 2022
1

First published in Great Britain by
Collins, The Crime Club 1934

A catalogue record for this book is available from the British Library

ISBN 978-0-00-852135-6

Set in Sabon LT Std by Palimpsest Book Production Limited, Falkirk, Stirlingshire
Printed and bound in the UK using
100% Renewable Electricity at CPI Group (UK) Ltd

MIX
Paper from
responsible sources
FSC™ C007454

This book is produced from independently certified FSC™ paper
to ensure responsible forest management.

For more information visit: www.harpercollins.co.uk/green

*To Christopher Mallock
in memory of Hinds*

CONTENTS

WHY DIDN'T THEY
ASK EVANS?

ALSO BY AGATHA CHRISTIE

Mysteries
The Man in the Brown
Suit
The Secret of Chimneys
The Seven Dials Mystery
The Mysterious Mr
Quin
The Sittaford Mystery
The Hound of Death
The Listerdale Mystery
Why Didn't They Ask
Evans?
Parker Pyne Investigates
Murder Is Easy
And Then There Were
None
Towards Zero
Death Comes as the End
Sparkling Cyanide
Crooked House
They Came to Baghdad
Destination Unknown
Spider's Web *
The Unexpected Guest *
Ordeal by Innocence
The Pale Horse
Endless Night
Passenger To Frankfurt
Problem at Pollensa Bay
While the Light Lasts

Poirot
The Mysterious Affair at
Styles
The Murder on the
Links
Poirot Investigates
The Murder of Roger
Ackroyd
The Big Four
The Mystery of the Blue
Train
Black Coffee *
Peril at End House

Lord Edgware Dies
Murder on the Orient
Express
Three-Act Tragedy
Death in the Clouds
The ABC Murders
Murder in Mesopotamia
Cards on the Table
Murder in the Mews
Dumb Witness
Death on the Nile
Appointment with Death
Hercule Poirot's
Christmas
Sad Cypress
One, Two, Buckle My
Shoe
Evil Under the Sun
Five Little Pigs
The Hollow
The Labours of Hercules
Taken at the Flood
Mrs McGinty's Dead
After the Funeral
Hickory Dickory Dock
Dead Man's Folly
Cat Among the Pigeons
The Adventure of the
Christmas Pudding
The Clocks
Third Girl
Hallowe'en Party
Elephants Can
Remember
Poirot's Early Cases
Curtain: Poirot's Last
Case

Marple
The Murder at the
Vicarage
The Thirteen Problems
The Body in the Library
The Moving Finger

A Murder Is Announced
They Do It with Mirrors
A Pocket Full of Rye
4.50 from Paddington
The Mirror Crack'd
from Side to Side
A Caribbean Mystery
At Bertram's Hotel
Nemesis
Sleeping Murder
Miss Marple's Final Cases

Tommy & Tuppence
The Secret Adversary
Partners in Crime
N or M?
By the Pricking of My
Thumbs
Postern of Fate

**Published as Mary
Westmacott**
Giant's Bread
Unfinished Portrait
Absent in the Spring
The Rose and the Yew
Tree
A Daughter's a Daughter
The Burden

Memoirs
An Autobiography
Come, Tell Me How You
Live
The Grand Tour

Plays and Stories
Akhnaton
The Floating Admiral †
Star Over Bethlehem
Hercule Poirot and the
Greenshore Folly

* novelized by Charles Osborne   † contributor

CHAPTER 1

The Accident

Bobby Jones teed up his ball, gave a short preliminary waggle, took the club back slowly, then brought it down and through with the rapidity of lightning.

Did the ball fly down the fairway straight and true, rising as it went and soaring over the bunker to land within an easy mashie shot of the fourteenth green?

No, it did not. Badly topped, it scudded along the ground and embedded itself firmly in the bunker!

There were no eager crowds to groan with dismay. The solitary witness of the shot manifested no surprise. And that is easily explained—for it was not the American-born master of the game who had played the shot, but merely the fourth son of the Vicar of Marchbolt—a small seaside town on the coast of Wales.

Bobby uttered a decidedly profane ejaculation.

He was an amiable-looking young man of about eight and twenty. His best friend could not have said that he was handsome, but his face was an eminently likeable one, and his eyes had the honest brown friendliness of a dog's.

'I get worse every day,' he muttered dejectedly.

'You press,' said his companion.

Dr Thomas was a middle-aged man with grey hair and a red cheerful face. He himself never took a full swing. He played short straight shots down the middle, and usually beat more brilliant but more erratic players.

Bobby attacked his ball fiercely with a niblick. The third time was successful. The ball lay a short distance from the green which Dr Thomas had reached with two creditable iron shots.

'Your hole,' said Bobby.

They proceeded to the next tee.

The doctor drove first—a nice straight shot, but with no great distance about it.

Bobby sighed, teed his ball, reteed it, waggled his club a long time, took back stiffly, shut his eyes, raised his head, depressed his right shoulder, did everything he ought not to have done—and hit a screamer down the middle of the course.

He drew a deep breath of satisfaction. The well-known golfer's gloom passed from his eloquent face to be succeeded by the equally well-known golfer's exultation.

'I know now what I've been doing,' said Bobby—quite untruthfully.

A perfect iron shot, a little chip with a mashie and Bobby lay dead. He achieved a birdie four and Dr Thomas was reduced to one up.

Full of confidence, Bobby stepped on to the sixteenth tee. He again did everything he should not have done, and this time no miracle occurred. A terrific, a magnificent, an almost superhuman slice happened! The ball went round at right angles.

'If that had been straight—whew!' said Dr Thomas.

'*If*,' said Bobby bitterly. 'Hullo, I thought I heard a shout! Hope the ball didn't hit anyone.'

He peered out to the right. It was a difficult light. The sun was on the point of setting, and, looking straight into it, it was hard to see anything distinctly. Also there was a slight mist rising from the sea. The edge of the cliff was a few hundred yards away.

'The footpath runs along there,' said Bobby. 'But the ball can't possibly have travelled as far as that. All the same, I did think I heard a cry. Did you?'

But the doctor had heard nothing.

Bobby went after his ball. He had some difficulty in finding it, but ran it to earth at last. It was practically unplayable—embedded in a furze bush. He had a couple of hacks at it, then picked it up and called out to his companion that he gave up the hole.

The doctor came over towards him since the next tee was right on the edge of the cliff.

The seventeenth was Bobby's particular bugbear. At it you had to drive over a chasm. The distance was not actually so great, but the attraction of the depths below was overpowering.

They had crossed the footpath which now ran inland to their left, skirting the very edge of the cliff.

The doctor took an iron and just landed on the other side.

Bobby took a deep breath and drove. The ball scudded forward and disappeared over the lip of the abyss.

'Every single dashed time,' said Bobby bitterly. 'I do the same dashed idiotic thing.'

He skirted the chasm, peering over. Far below the sea sparkled, but not every ball was lost in its depths. The drop was sheer at the top, but below it shelved gradually.

Bobby walked slowly along. There was, he knew, one place where one could scramble down fairly easily. Caddies did so, hurling themselves over the edge and reappearing triumphant and panting with the missing ball.

Suddenly Bobby stiffened and called to his companion.

'I say, doctor, come here. What do you make of that?'

Some forty feet below was a dark heap of something that looked like old clothes.

The doctor caught his breath.

'By Jove,' he said. 'Somebody's fallen over the cliff. We must get down to him.'

Side by side the two men scrambled down the rock, the more athletic Bobby helping the other. At last they reached the ominous dark bundle. It was a man of about forty, and he was still breathing, though unconscious.

The doctor examined him, touching his limbs, feeling his pulse, drawing down the lids of his eyes. He knelt down beside him and completed his examination. Then he looked up at Bobby, who was standing there feeling rather sick, and slowly shook his head.

'Nothing to be done,' he said. 'His number's up, poor fellow. His back's broken. Well, well. I suppose he wasn't familiar with the path, and when the mist came up he walked over the edge. I've told the council more than once there ought to be a railing just here.'

4

He stood up again.

'I'll go off and get help,' he said. 'Make arrangements to have the body got up. It'll be dark before we know where we are. Will you stay here?'

Bobby nodded.

'There's nothing to be done for him, I suppose?' he asked.

The doctor shook his head.

'Nothing. It won't be long—the pulse is weakening fast. He'll last another twenty minutes at most. Just possible he may recover consciousness before the end; but very likely he won't. Still—'

'Rather,' said Bobby quickly. 'I'll stay. You get along. If he does come to, there's no drug or anything—' he hesitated.

The doctor shook his head.

'There'll be no pain,' he said. 'No pain at all.'

Turning away, he began rapidly to climb up the cliff again. Bobby watched him till he disappeared over the top with a wave of his hand.

Bobby moved a step or two along the narrow ledge, sat down on a projection in the rock and lit a cigarette. The business had shaken him. Up to now he had never come in contact with illness or death.

What rotten luck there was in the world! A swirl of mist on a fine evening, a false step—and life came to an end. Fine healthy-looking fellow too—probably never known a day's illness in his life. The pallor of approaching death couldn't disguise the deep tan of the skin. A man who had lived an out-of-door life—abroad, perhaps. Bobby studied him more closely—the crisp curling chestnut hair just touched with grey at the temples, the big nose, the strong jaw, the white teeth just showing through the parted lips. Then the broad shoulders and the fine sinewy hands. The legs were twisted at a curious angle. Bobby shuddered and brought his eyes up again to the face. An attractive face, humorous, determined, resourceful. The eyes, he thought, were probably blue—

And just as he reached that point in his thoughts, the eyes suddenly opened.

They *were* blue—a clear deep blue. They looked straight at Bobby. There was nothing uncertain or hazy about them. They seemed completely conscious. They were watchful and at the same time they seemed to be asking a question.

Bobby got up quickly and came towards the man. Before he got there, the other spoke. His voice was not weak—it came out clear and resonant.

'*Why didn't they ask Evans?*' he said.

And then a queer little shudder passed over him, the eyelids dropped, the jaw fell . . .

The man was dead.

CHAPTER 2

Concerning Fathers

Bobby knelt down beside him, but there was no doubt. The man was dead. A last moment of consciousness, that sudden question, and then—the end.

Rather apologetically, Bobby put his hand into the dead man's pocket and, drawing out a silk handkerchief, he spread it reverently over the dead face. There was nothing more he could do.

Then he noticed that in his action he had jerked something else out of the pocket. It was a photograph and in the act of replacing it he glanced at the pictured face.

It was a woman's face, strangely haunting in quality. A fair woman with wide-apart eyes. She seemed little more than a girl, certainly under thirty, but it was the arresting quality of her beauty rather than the beauty itself that seized upon the boy's imagination. It was the kind of face, he thought, not easy to forget.

Gently and reverently, he replaced the photograph in the pocket from which it had come, then he sat down again to wait for the doctor's return.

The time passed very slowly—or at least so it seemed to the waiting boy. Also, he had just remembered something. He had promised his father to play the organ at the evening service at six o'clock and it was now ten minutes to six. Naturally, his father would understand the circumstances, but all the same he wished that he had remembered to send a message by the doctor. The Rev. Thomas Jones was a man of extremely nervous temperament. He was, *par excellence*, a fusser, and when he fussed, his digestive apparatus collapsed and he suffered agonizing pain. Bobby, though he considered his father a pitiful old ass, was nevertheless extremely fond of him. The Rev. Thomas, on the other hand, considered his fourth son a pitiful *young* ass, and with less tolerance than Bobby sought to effect improvement in the young man.

'The poor old gov'nor,' thought Bobby. 'He'll be ramping up and down. He won't know whether to start the service or not. He'll work himself up till he gets that pain in the tummy, and then he won't be able to eat his supper. He won't have the sense to realize that I wouldn't let him down unless it were quite unavoidable—and, anyway, what does it matter? But he'll never see it that way. Nobody over fifty has got any sense—they worry themselves to death about tuppenny-ha'penny things that don't matter. They've been brought up all wrong, I suppose, and now they can't help themselves. Poor old Dad, he's got less sense than a chicken!'

He sat there thinking of his father with mingled affection and exasperation. His life at home seemed to him to be one long sacrifice to his father's peculiar ideas. To Mr Jones, the same time seemed to be one long sacrifice on *his* part, ill understood or appreciated by the younger generation. So may ideas on the same subject differ.

What an age the doctor was! Surely he might have been back by this time?

Bobby got up and stamped his feet moodily. At that moment he heard something above him and looked up, thankful that help was at hand and his own services no longer needed.

But it was not the doctor. It was a man in plus fours whom Bobby did not know.

'I say,' said the newcomer. 'Is anything the matter? Has there been an accident? Can I help in any way?'

He was a tall man with a pleasant tenor voice. Bobby could not see him very clearly for it was now fast growing dusk.

He explained what had happened whilst the stranger made shocked comments.

'There's nothing I can do?' he asked. 'Get help or anything?'

Bobby explained that help was on the way and asked if the other could see any signs of its arriving.

'There's nothing at present.'

'You see,' went on Bobby, 'I've got an appointment at six.'

'And you don't like to leave—'

'No, I don't quite,' said Bobby. 'I mean, the poor chap's dead and all that, and of course one can't do anything, but all the same—'

He paused, finding it, as usual, difficult to put confused emotions into words.

The other, however, seemed to understand.

'I know,' he said. 'Look here, I'll come down—that is, if I can see my way—and I'll stay till these fellows arrive.'

'Oh, would you?' said Bobby gratefully. 'You see, it's my father. He's not a bad sort really, and things upset him. Can you see your way? A bit more to the left—now to the right—that's it. It's not really difficult.'

He encouraged the other with directions until the two men were face to face on the narrow plateau. The newcomer was a man of about thirty-five. He had a rather indecisive face which seemed to be calling for a monocle and a little moustache.

'I'm a stranger down here,' he explained. 'My name's Bassington-ffrench, by the way. Come down to see about a house. I say, what a beastly thing to happen! Did he walk over the edge?'

Bobby nodded.

'Bit of mist got up,' he explained. 'It's a dangerous bit of path. Well, so long. Thanks very much. I've got to hurry. It's awfully good of you.'

'Not at all,' the other protested. 'Anybody would do the same. Can't leave the poor chap lying—well, I mean, it wouldn't be decent somehow.'

Bobby was scrambling up the precipitous path. At the top he waved his hand to the other then set off at a brisk run across country. To save time, he vaulted the churchyard wall instead of going round to the gate on the road—a proceeding observed by the Vicar from the vestry window and deeply disapproved of by him.

It was five minutes past six, but the bell was still tolling.

Explanations and recriminations were postponed until after the service. Breathless, Bobby sank into his seat and manipulated the stops of the ancient organ. Association of ideas led his fingers into Chopin's funeral march.

Afterwards, more in sorrow than in anger (as he expressly pointed out), the Vicar took his son to task.

'If you cannot do a thing properly, my dear Bobby,' he said, 'it is better not to do it at all. I know that you and all your young friends seem to have no idea of time, but there is One whom we should not keep waiting. You offered to play the organ of your own accord. I did not coerce you. Instead, faint-hearted, you preferred playing a game—'

Bobby thought he had better interrupt before his father got too well away.

'Sorry, Dad,' he said, speaking cheerfully and breezily as was his habit no matter what the subject. 'Not my fault this time. I was keeping guard over a corpse.'

'You were what?'

'Keeping guard over a blighter who stepped over the cliff. You know—the place where the chasm is—by the seventeenth tee. There was a bit of mist just then, and he must have gone straight on and over.'

'Good heavens,' cried the Vicar. 'What a tragedy! Was the man killed outright?'

'No. He was unconscious. He died just after Dr Thomas had gone off. But of course I felt I had to squat there—couldn't just push off and leave him. And then another

11

fellow came along so I passed the job of chief mourner on to him and legged it here as fast as I could.'

The Vicar sighed.

'Oh, my dear Bobby,' he said. 'Will nothing shake your deplorable callousness? It grieves me more than I can say. Here you have been brought face to face with death—with sudden death. And you can joke about it! It leaves you unmoved. Everything—everything, however solemn, however sacred, is merely a joke to your generation.'

Bobby shuffled his feet.

If his father couldn't see that, of course, you joked about a thing because you had felt badly about it—well, he couldn't see it! It wasn't the sort of thing you could explain. With death and tragedy about you had to keep a stiff upper lip.

But what could you expect? Nobody over fifty understood anything at all. They had the most extraordinary ideas.

'I expect it was the War,' thought Bobby loyally. 'It upset them and they never got straight again.'

He felt ashamed of his father and sorry for him.

'Sorry, Dad,' he said with a clear-eyed realization that explanation was impossible.

The Vicar felt sorry for his son—he looked abashed—but he also felt ashamed of him. The boy had no conception of the seriousness of life. Even his apology was cheery and impenitent.

They moved towards the Vicarage, each making enormous efforts to find excuses for the other.

The Vicar thought: 'I wonder when Bobby will find something to do . . .?'

Bobby thought: 'Wonder how much longer I can stick it down here . . .?'

Yet they were both extremely fond of each other.

CHAPTER 3

A Railway Journey

Bobby did not see the immediate sequel of his adventure. On the following morning he went up to town, there to meet a friend who was thinking of starting a garage and who fancied Bobby's co-operation might be valuable.

After settling things to everybody's satisfaction, Bobby caught the 11.30 train home two days later. He caught it, true, but only by a very narrow margin. He arrived at Paddington when the clock announced the time to be 11.28, dashed down the subway, emerged on No. 3 Platform just as the train was moving and hurled himself at the first carriage he saw, heedless of indignant ticket collectors and porters in his immediate rear.

Wrenching open the door, he fell in on his hands and knees, picked himself up. The door was shut with a slam by an agile porter and Bobby found himself looking at the sole occupant of the compartment.

It was a first-class carriage and in the corner facing the engine sat a dark girl smoking a cigarette. She had on a red skirt, a short green jacket and a brilliant blue beret, and despite a certain resemblance to an organ grinder's monkey (she had long sorrowful dark eyes and a puckered-up face) she was distinctly attractive.

In the midst of an apology, Bobby broke off.

'Why, it's you, Frankie!' he said. 'I haven't seen you for ages.'

'Well, I haven't seen you. Sit down and talk.'

Bobby grinned.

'My ticket's the wrong colour.'

'That doesn't matter,' said Frankie kindly. 'I'll pay the difference for you.'

'My manly indignation rises at the thought,' said Bobby. 'How could I let a lady pay for me?'

'It's about all we seem to be good for these days,' said Frankie.

'I will pay the difference myself,' said Bobby heroically as a burly figure in blue appeared at the door from the corridor.

'Leave it to me,' said Frankie.

She smiled graciously at the ticket collector, who touched his hat as he took the piece of white cardboard from her and punched it.

'Mr Jones has just come in to talk to me for a bit,' she said. 'That won't matter, will it?'

'That's all right, your ladyship. The gentleman won't be staying long, I expect.' He coughed tactfully. 'I shan't be round again till after Bristol,' he added significantly.

'What can be done with a smile,' said Bobby as the official withdrew.

Lady Frances Derwent shook her head thoughtfully.

'I'm not so sure it's the smile,' she said. 'I rather think it's father's habit of tipping everybody five shillings whenever he travels that does it.'

'I thought you'd given up Wales for good, Frankie.'

Frances sighed.

'My dear, you know what it is. You know how mouldy parents can be. What with that and the bathrooms in the state they are, and nothing to do and nobody to see—and people simply won't come to the country to stay nowadays! They say they're economizing and they can't go so far. Well, I mean, what's a girl to do?'

Bobby shook his head, sadly recognizing the problem.

'However,' went on Frankie, 'after the party I went to last night, I thought even home couldn't be worse.'

'What was wrong with the party?'

'Nothing at all. It was just like any other party, only more so. It was to start at the Savoy at half-past eight. Some of us rolled up about a quarter-past nine and, of course, we got entangled with other people, but we got sorted out about ten. And we had dinner and then after a bit we went on to the Marionette—there was a rumour it was going to be raided, but nothing happened—it was just moribund, and we drank a bit and then we went on to the Bullring and that was even deader, and then we went to a coffee stall, and then we went to a fried-fish place, and then we thought we'd go and breakfast with Angela's uncle and see if he'd be shocked, but he wasn't—only bored, and then we sort of fizzled home. Honestly, Bobby, it isn't good enough.'

'I suppose not,' said Bobby, stifling a pang of envy.

Never in his wildest moments did he dream of being able to be a member of the Marionette or the Bullring.

His relationship with Frankie was a peculiar one.

As children, he and his brothers had played with the children at the Castle. Now that they were all grown up, they seldom came across each other. When they did, they still used Christian names. On the rare occasions when Frankie was at home, Bobby and his brothers would go up and play tennis. But Frankie and her two brothers were not asked to the Vicarage. It seemed to be tacitly recognized that it would not be amusing for them. On the other hand, extra men were always wanted for tennis. There may have been a trace of constraint in spite of the Christian names. The Derwents were, perhaps, a shade more friendly than they need have been as though to show that 'there was no difference'. The Jones, on their side, were a shade formal, as though determined not to claim more friendship than was offered them. The two families had now nothing in common save certain childish memories. Yet Bobbie was very fond of Frankie and was always pleased on the rare occasions when Fate threw them together.

'I'm so tired of everything,' said Frankie in a weary voice. 'Aren't you?'

Bobby considered.

'No, I don't think I am.'

'My dear, how wonderful,' said Frankie.

'I don't mean I'm hearty,' said Bobby, anxious not to create a painful impression. 'I just can't stand people who are hearty.'

Frankie shuddered at the mere mention of the word.

'I know,' she murmured. 'They're dreadful.'

They looked at each other sympathetically.

'By the way,' said Frankie suddenly. 'What's all this about a man falling over the cliffs?'

'Dr Thomas and I found him,' said Bobby. 'How did you know about it, Frankie?'

'Saw it in the paper. Look.'

She indicated with her finger a small paragraph headed: 'Fatal Accident in Sea Mist.'

The victim of the tragedy at Marchbolt was identified late last night by means of a photograph which he was carrying. The photograph proved to be that of Mrs Leo Cayman. Mrs Cayman was communicated with and journeyed at once to Marchbolt, where she identified the deceased as her brother, Alex Pritchard. Mr Pritchard had recently returned from Siam. He had been out of England for ten years and was just starting upon a walking tour. The inquest will be held at Marchbolt tomorrow.

Bobby's thoughts flew back to the strangely haunting face of the photograph.

'I believe I shall have to give evidence at the inquest,' he said.

'How thrilling. I shall come and hear you.'

'I don't suppose there will be anything thrilling about it,' said Bobby. 'We just found him, you know.'

'Was he dead?'

'No, not then. He died about a quarter of an hour later. I was alone with him.'

He paused.

'Rather grim,' said Frankie with that immediate understanding that Bobby's father had lacked.

'Of course he didn't feel anything—'

'No?'

'But all the same—well—you see, he looked awfully alive—that sort of person—rather a rotten way to finish—just stepping off a cliff in a silly little bit of mist.'

'I get you, Steve,' said Frankie, and again the queer phrase represented sympathy and understanding.

'Did you see the sister?' she asked presently.

'No. I've been up in town two days. Had to see a friend of mine about a garage business we're going in for. You remember him. Badger Beadon.'

'Do I?'

'Of course you do. You must remember good old Badger. He squints.'

Frankie wrinkled her brows.

'He's got an awfully silly kind of laugh—haw haw haw—like that,' continued Bobby helpfully.

Still Frankie wrinkled her brows.

'Fell off his pony when we were kids,' continued Bobby. 'Stuck in the mud head down, and we had to pull him out by the legs.'

'Oh!' said Frankie in a flood of recollection. 'I know now. He stammered.'

'He still does,' said Bobby proudly.

'Didn't he run a chicken farm and it went bust?' inquired Frankie.

'That's right.'

19

'And then he went into a stockbroker's office and they fired him after a month?'

'That's it.'

'And then they sent him to Australia and he came back?'

'Yes.'

'Bobby,' said Frankie. 'You're not putting any money into this business venture, I hope?'

'I haven't got any money to put,' said Bobby.

'That's just as well,' said Frankie.

'Naturally,' went on Bobby. 'Badger has tried to get hold of someone with a little capital to invest. But it isn't so easy as you'd think.'

'When you look round you,' said Frankie, 'you wouldn't believe people had any sense at all—but they have.'

The point of these remarks seemed at last to strike Bobby.

'Look here, Frankie,' he said. 'Badger's one of the best— one of the very best.'

'They always are,' said Frankie.

'Who are?'

'The ones who go to Australia and come back again. How did he get hold of the money to start this business?'

'An aunt or something died and left him a garage for six cars with three rooms over and his people stumped up a hundred pounds to buy second-hand cars with. You'd be surprised what bargains there are to be had in second-hand cars.'

'I bought one once,' said Frankie. 'It's a painful subject. Don't let's talk of it. What did you want to leave the Navy for? They didn't axe you, did they? Not at your age.'

Bobby flushed.

'Eyes,' he said gruffly.

'You always had trouble with your eyes, I remember.'

'I know. But I just managed to scrape through. Then foreign service—the strong light, you know—that rather did for them. So—well—I had to get out.'

'Grim,' murmured Frankie, looking out of the window. There was an eloquent pause.

'All the same, it's a shame,' burst out Bobby. 'My eyes aren't really bad—they won't get any worse, they say. I could have carried on perfectly.'

'They look all right,' said Frankie.

She looked straight into their honest brown depths.

'So you see,' said Bobby, 'I'm going in with Badger.'

Frankie nodded.

An attendant opened the door and said, 'First luncheon.'

'Shall we?' said Frankie.

They passed along to the dining car.

Bobby made a short strategic retreat during the time when the ticket collector might be expected.

'We don't want him to strain his conscience too much,' he said.

But Frankie said she didn't expect ticket collectors had any consciences.

It was just after five o'clock when they reached Sileham, which was the station for Marchbolt.

'The car's meeting me,' said Frankie. 'I'll give you a lift.'

'Thanks. That will save me carrying this beastly thing for two miles.'

He kicked his suitcase disparagingly.

'Three miles, not two,' said Frankie.

'Two miles if you go by the footpath over the links.'

'The one where—'

'Yes—where that fellow went over.'

'I suppose nobody pushed him over, did they?' asked Frankie as she handed her dressing-case to her maid.

'Pushed him over? Good Lord, no. Why?'

'Well, it would make it much more exciting, wouldn't it?' said Frankie idly.

CHAPTER 4

The Inquest

The inquest on the body of Alex Pritchard was held on the following day. Dr Thomas gave evidence as to the finding of the body.

'Life was not then extinct?' asked the coroner.

'No, deceased was still breathing. There was, however, no hope of recovery. The—'

Here the doctor became highly technical. The coroner came to the rescue of the jury:

'In ordinary everyday language, the man's back was broken?'

'If you like to put it that way,' said Dr Thomas sadly.

He described how he had gone off to get help, leaving the dying man in Bobby's charge.

'Now as to the cause of this disaster, what is your opinion, Dr Thomas?'

'I should say that in all probability (failing any evidence as to his state of mind, that is to say) the deceased stepped inadvertently over the edge of the cliff. There was a mist rising from the sea, and at that particular point the path turns abruptly inland. Owing to the mist the deceased may not have noticed the danger and walked straight on—in which case two steps would take him over the edge.'

'There were no signs of violence? Such as might have been administered by a third party?'

'I can only say that all the injuries present are fully explained by the body striking the rocks fifty or sixty feet below.'

'There remains the question of suicide?'

'That is, of course, perfectly possible. Whether the deceased walked over the edge or threw himself over is a matter on which I can say nothing.'

Robert Jones was called next.

Bobby explained that he had been playing golf with the doctor and had sliced his ball towards the sea. A mist was rising at the time and it was difficult to see. He thought he heard a cry, and for a moment wondered if his ball could have hit anybody coming along the footpath. He had decided, however, that it could not possibly have travelled so far.

'Did you find the ball?'

'Yes, it was about a hundred yards short of the footpath.'

He then described how they had driven from the next tee and how he himself had driven into the chasm.

Here the coroner stopped him since his evidence would have been a repetition of the doctor's. He questioned him closely, however, as to the cry he had heard or thought he heard.

'It was just a cry.'

'A cry for help?'

'Oh, no. Just a sort of shout, you know. In fact I wasn't quite sure I heard it.'

'A startled kind of cry?'

'That's more like it,' said Bobby gratefully. 'Sort of noise a fellow might let out if a ball hit him unexpectedly.'

'Or if he took a step into nothingness when he thought he was on a path?'

'Yes.'

Then, having explained that the man actually died about five minutes after the doctor left to get help, Bobby's ordeal came to an end.

The coroner was by now anxious to get on with a perfectly straightforward business.

Mrs Leo Cayman was called.

Bobby gave a gasp of acute disappointment. Where was the face of the photo that had tumbled from the dead man's pocket? Photographers, thought Bobby disgustedly, were the worst kind of liars. The photo obviously must have been taken some years ago, but even then it was hard to believe that that charming wide-eyed beauty could have become this brazen-looking woman with plucked eyebrows and obviously dyed hair. Time, thought Bobby suddenly, was a very frightening thing. What would Frankie, for instance, look like in twenty years' time? He gave a little shiver.

Meanwhile, Amelia Cayman, of 17 St Leonard's Gardens, Paddington, was giving evidence.

Deceased was her only brother, Alexander Pritchard. She had last seen her brother the day before the tragedy when he had announced his intention of going for a walking tour in Wales. Her brother had recently returned from the East.

'Did he seem in a happy and normal state of mind?'

'Oh, quite. Alex was always cheerful.'

'So far as you know, he had nothing on his mind?'

'Oh! I'm sure he hadn't. He was looking forward to his trip.'

'There have been no money troubles—or other troubles of any kind in his life recently?'

'Well, really I couldn't say as to that,' said Mrs Cayman. 'You see, he'd only just come back, and before that I hadn't seen him for ten years and he was never one much for writing. But he took me out to theatres and lunches in London and gave me one or two presents, so I don't think he could have been short of money, and he was in such good spirits that I don't think there could have been anything else.'

'What was your brother's profession, Mrs Cayman?'

The lady seemed slightly embarrassed.

'Well, I can't say I rightly know. Prospecting—that's what he called it. He was very seldom in England.'

'You know of no reason which should cause him to take his own life?'

'Oh, no; and I can't believe that he did such a thing. It must have been an accident.'

'How do you explain the fact that your brother had no luggage with him—not even a knapsack?'

'He didn't like carrying a knapsack. He meant to post

parcels alternate days. He posted one the day before he left with his night things and a pair of socks, only he addressed it to Derbyshire instead of Denbighshire, so it only got here today.'

'Ah! That clears up a somewhat curious point.'

Mrs Cayman went on to explain how she had been communicated with through the photographers whose name was on the photo her brother had carried. She had come down with her husband to Marchbolt and had at once recognized the body as that of her brother.

As she said the last words she sniffed audibly and began to cry.

The coroner said a few soothing words and dismissed her.

Then he addressed the jury. Their task was to state how this man came by his death. Fortunately, the matter appeared to be quite simple. There was no suggestion that Mr Pritchard had been worried or depressed or in a state of mind where he would be likely to take his own life. On the contrary, he had been in good health and spirits and had been looking forward to his holiday. It was unfortunately the case that when a sea mist was rising the path along the cliff was a dangerous one and possibly they might agree with him that it was time something was done about it.

The jury's verdict was prompt.

'We find that the deceased came to his death by mis-adventure and we wish to add a rider that in our opinion the Town Council should immediately take steps to put a fence or rail on the sea side of the path where it skirts the chasm.'

The coroner nodded approval.

The inquest was over.

CHAPTER 5

Mr and Mrs Cayman

On arriving back at the Vicarage about half an hour later, Bobby found that his connection with the death of Alex Pritchard was not yet quite over. He was informed that Mr and Mrs Cayman had called to see him and were in the study with his father. Bobby made his way there and found his father bravely making suitable conversation without, apparently, much enjoying his task.

'Ah!' he said with some slight relief. 'Here is Bobby.'

Mr Cayman rose and advanced towards the young man with outstretched hand. Mr Cayman was a big florid man with a would-be hearty manner and a cold and somewhat shifty eye that rather belied the manner. As for Mrs Cayman, though she might be considered attractive in a bold, coarse fashion, she had little now in common with that early photograph of herself, and no trace of that wistful expression remained. In fact, Bobby reflected, if she had not recognized her own photograph, it seemed doubtful if anyone else would have done so.

Agatha Christie

'I came down with the wife,' said Mr Cayman, enclosing Bobby's hand in a firm and painful grip. 'Had to stand by, you know; Amelia's naturally upset.'

Mrs Cayman sniffed.

'We came round to see you,' continued Mr Cayman. 'You see, my poor wife's brother died, practically speaking, in your arms. Naturally, she wanted to know all you could tell her of his last moments.'

'Absolutely,' said Bobby unhappily. 'Oh, absolutely.'

He grinned nervously and was immediately aware of his father's sigh—a sigh of Christian resignation.

'Poor Alex,' said Mrs Cayman, dabbing her eyes. 'Poor, poor Alex.'

'I know,' said Bobby. 'Absolutely grim.'

He wriggled uncomfortably.

'You see,' said Mrs Cayman, looking hopefully at Bobby, 'if he left any last words or messages, naturally I want to know.'

'Oh, rather,' said Bobby. 'But as a matter of fact he didn't.'

'Nothing at all?'

Mrs Cayman looked disappointed and incredulous. Bobby felt apologetic.

'No—well—as a matter of fact, nothing at all.'

'It was best so,' said Mr Cayman solemnly. 'To pass away unconscious—without pain—why, you must think of it as a mercy, Amelia.'

'I suppose I must,' said Mrs Cayman. 'You don't think he felt any pain?'

'I'm sure he didn't,' said Bobby.

Mrs Cayman sighed deeply.

'Well, that's something to be thankful for. Perhaps I did hope he'd left a last message, but I can see that it's best as it is. Poor Alex. Such a fine out-of-door man.'

'Yes, wasn't he?' said Bobby. He recalled the bronze face, the deep blue eyes. An attractive personality, that of Alex Pritchard, attractive even so near death. Strange that he should be the brother of Mrs Cayman and the brother-in-law of Mr Cayman. He had been worthy, Bobby felt, of better things.

'Well, we're very much indebted to you, I'm sure,' said Mrs Cayman.

'Oh, that's all right,' said Bobby. 'I mean—well, couldn't do anything else—I mean—'

He floundered hopelessly.

'We shan't forget it,' said Mr Cayman. Bobby suffered once more that painful grip. He received a flabby hand from Mrs Cayman. His father made further adieus. Bobby accompanied the Caymans to the front door.

'And what do you do with yourself, young man?' inquired Cayman. 'Home on leave—something of that kind?'

'I spend most of my time looking for a job,' said Bobby. He paused. 'I was in the Navy.'

'Hard times—hard times nowadays,' said Mr Cayman, shaking his head. 'Well, I wish you luck, I'm sure.'

'Thank you very much,' said Bobby politely.

He watched them down the weed-grown drive.

Standing there, he fell into a brown study. Various ideas flashed chaotically through his mind—confused reflections—the photograph—that girl's face with the wide-apart eyes and the misty hair—and ten or fifteen years later Mrs Cayman with her heavy make-up, her plucked eyebrows, those wide-apart eyes sunk in between folds of flesh till they looked like pig's eyes, and her violent henna-tinted hair. All traces of youth and innocence had vanished. The pity of things! It all came, perhaps, of marrying a hearty bounder like Mr Cayman. If she had married someone else she might possibly have grown older gracefully. A touch of grey in her hair, eyes still wide apart looking out from a smooth pale face. But perhaps anyway—

Bobby sighed and shook his head.

'That's the worst of marriage,' he said gloomily.

'What did you say?'

Bobby awoke from meditation to become aware of Frankie, whose approach he had not heard.

'Hullo,' he said.

'Hullo. Why marriage? And whose?'

'I was making a reflection of a general nature,' said Bobby.

'Namely—?'

'On the devasting effects of marriage.'

'Who is devastated?'

Bobby explained. He found Frankie unsympathetic.

'Nonsense. The woman's exactly like her photograph.'

'When did you see her? Were you at the inquest?'

'Of course I was at the inquest. What do you think? There's little enough to do down here. An inquest is a perfect godsend. I've never been to one before. I was thrilled to the teeth. Of course, it would have been better if it had been a mysterious poisoning case, with the analyst's reports

32

and all that sort of thing; but one mustn't be too exacting when these simple pleasures come one's way. I hoped up to the end for a suspicion of foul play, but it all seemed most regrettably straightforward.'

'What blood-thirsty instincts you have, Frankie.'

'I know. It's probably atavism (however do you pronounce it?—I've never been sure). Don't you think so? I'm sure I'm atavistic. My nickname at school was Monkey Face.'

'Do monkeys like murder?' queried Bobby.

'You sound like a correspondence in a Sunday paper,' said Frankie. 'Our correspondents' views on this subject are solicited.'

'You know,' said Bobby, reverting to the original topic, 'I don't agree with you about the female Cayman. Her photograph was lovely.'

'Touched up—that's all,' interrupted Frankie.

'Well, then, it was so much touched up that you wouldn't have known them for the same person.'

'You're blind,' said Frankie. 'The photographer had done all that the art of photography could do, but it was still a nasty bit of work.'

'I absolutely disagree with you,' said Bobby coldly. 'Anyway, where did you see it?'

'In the local *Evening Echo*.'

'It probably reproduced badly.'

'It seems to me you're absolutely batty,' said Frankie crossly, 'over a painted-up raddled bitch—yes, I said *bitch*— like the Cayman.'

'Frankie,' said Bobby, 'I'm surprised at you. In the Vicarage drive, too. Semi-holy ground, so to speak.'

'Well, you shouldn't have been so ridiculous.'

There was a pause, then Frankie's sudden fit of temper abated.

'What *is* ridiculous,' she said, 'is to quarrel about the damned woman. I came to suggest a round of golf. What about it?'

'OK, chief,' said Bobby happily.

They set off amicably together and their conversation was of such things as slicing and pulling and how to perfect a chip shot on to the green.

The recent tragedy passed quite out of mind until Bobby, holing a long putt at the eleventh to halve the hole, suddenly gave an exclamation.

'What is it?'

'Nothing. I've just remembered something.'

'What?'

'Well, these people, the Caymans—they came round and asked if the fellow had said anything before he died—and I told them he hadn't.'

'Well?'

'And now I've just remembered that he did.'

'Not one of your brightest mornings, in fact.'

'Well, you see, it wasn't the sort of thing they meant. That's why, I suppose, I didn't think of it.'

'What did he say?' asked Frankie curiously.

'He said: "*Why didn't they ask Evans?*"'

'What a funny thing to say. Nothing else?'

'No. He just opened his eyes and said that—quite suddenly—and then died, poor chap.'

'Oh, well,' said Frankie, turning it over in her mind. 'I don't see that you need worry. It wasn't important.'

'No, of course not. Still, I wish I'd just mentioned it. You see, I said he'd said nothing at all.'

'Well, it amounts to the same thing,' said Frankie. 'I mean, it isn't like—"Tell Gladys I always loved her", or "The will is in the walnut bureau", or any of the proper romantic Last Words there are in books.'

'You don't think it's worth writing about it to them?'

'I shouldn't bother. It couldn't be important.'

'I expect you're right,' said Bobby and turned his attention with renewed vigour to the game.

But the matter did not really dismiss itself from his mind. It was a small point but it fretted him. He felt very faintly uncomfortable about it. Frankie's point of view was, he felt sure, the right and sensible one. The thing was of no importance—let it go. But his conscience continued to reproach him faintly. He had said that the dead man had said nothing. That wasn't true. It was all very trivial and silly but he couldn't feel quite comfortable about it. Finally, that evening, on an impulse, he sat down and wrote to Mr Cayman.

Dear Mr Cayman, I have just remembered that your brother-in-law did actually say something before he died. I think the exact words were, 'Why didn't they ask Evans?' I apologize for not mentioning this this morning, but I attached no importance to the words at the time and so, I suppose, they slipped my memory.

Yours truly,

Robert Jones.

On the next day but one he received a reply:

> *Dear Mr Jones* (wrote Mr Cayman), *Your letter of 6th instant to hand. Many thanks for repeating my poor brother-in-law's last words so punctiliously in spite of their trivial character. What my wife hoped was that her brother might have left her some last message. Still, thank you for being so conscientious.*
>
> *Yours faithfully,*
> *Leo Cayman.*

Bobby felt snubbed.

CHAPTER 6

End of a Picnic

On the following day Bobby received a letter of quite a different nature:

It's all fixed, old boy, (wrote Badger in an illiterate scrawl which reflected no credit on the expensive public school which had educated him). *Actually got five cars yesterday for fifteen pounds the lot—an Austin, two Morrises and a couple of Rovers. At the moment they won't actually go, but we can tinker them up sufficiently, I think. Dash it all, a car's a car, after all. So long as it takes the purchaser home without breaking down, that's all they can expect. I thought of opening up Monday week and am relying on you, so don't let me down, will you, old boy? I must say old Aunt Carrie was a sport. I once broke the window of an old boy next door to her who'd been rude to her about her cats and she never got over it. Sent me a fiver every Christmas—and now this.*

We're bound to succeed. The thing's a dead cert. I mean, a car's a car after all. You can pick 'em up for nothing. *Put a lick of paint on and that's all the ordinary fool notices. The thing will go with a Bang. Now don't forget. Monday week. I'm relying on you.*

Yours ever,

Badger.

Bobby informed his father that he would be going up to town on Monday week to take up a job. The description of the job did not rouse the Vicar to anything like enthusiasm. He had, it may be pointed out, come across Badger Beadon in the past. He merely treated Bobby to a long lecture on the advisability of not making himself liable for anything. Not an authority on financial or business matters, his advice was technically vague, but its meaning unmistakable.

On the Wednesday of that week Bobby received another letter. It was addressed in a foreign slanting handwriting. Its contents were somewhat surprising to the young man.

It was from the firm of Henriquez and Dallo in Buenos Aires and, to put it concisely, it offered Bobby a job in the firm with a salary of a thousand a year.

For the first minute or two the young man thought he must be dreaming. A thousand a year. He reread the letter more carefully. There was mention of an ex-Naval man being preferred. A suggestion that Bobby's name had been put forward by someone (someone not named). That acceptance must be immediate, and that Bobby must be prepared to start for Buenos Aires within a week.

'Well, I'm damned!' said Bobby, giving vent to his feelings in a somewhat unfortunate manner.

'Bobby!'

'Sorry, Dad. Forgot you were there.'

Mr Jones cleared his throat.

'I should like to point out to you—'

Bobby felt that this process—usually a long one—must at all costs be avoided. He achieved this course by a simple statement:

'Someone's offered me a thousand a year.'

The Vicar remained open-mouthed, unable for the moment to make any comment.

'That's put him off his drive all right,' thought Bobby with satisfaction.

'My dear Bobby, did I understand you to say that someone had offered you a thousand a year? *A thousand?*'

'Holed it in one, Dad,' said Bobby.

'It's impossible,' said the Vicar.

Bobby was not hurt by this frank incredulity. His estimate of his own monetary value differed little from that of his father.

'They must be complete mutts,' he agreed heartily.

'Who—er—are these people?'

Bobby handed him the letter. The Vicar, fumbling for his pince-nez, peered at it suspiciously. Finally he perused it twice.

'Most remarkable,' he said at last. '*Most* remarkable.'

'Lunatics,' said Bobby.

'Ah! my boy,' said the Vicar. 'It is after all, a great thing to be an Englishman. Honesty. That's what we stand for. The Navy has carried that ideal all over the world. An Englishman's world! This South American firm realizes the value of a young man whose integrity will be unshaken and on whose fidelity his employers will be assured. You can always depend on an Englishman to play the game—'

'And keep a straight bat,' said Bobby.

The Vicar looked at his son doubtfully. The phrase, an excellent one, had actually been on the tip of his tongue, but there was something in Bobby's tone that struck him as not quite sincere.

The young man, however, appeared to be perfectly serious.

'All the same, Dad,' he said, 'why me?'

'What do you mean—why you?'

'There are a lot of Englishmen in England,' said Bobby. 'Hearty fellows, full of cricketing qualities. Why pick on me?'

'Probably your late commanding officer may have recommended you.'

'Yes, I suppose that's true,' said Bobby doubtfully. 'It doesn't matter, anyway, since I can't take the job.'

'Can't take it? My dear boy, what do you mean?'

'Well, I'm fixed up, you see. With Badger.'

'Badger? Badger Beadon. Nonsense, my dear Bobby. This is serious.'

'It's a bit hard, I own,' said Bobby with a sigh.

'Any childish arrangement you have made with young Beadon cannot count for a moment.'

'It counts with me.'

'Young Beadon is completely irresponsible. He has already, I understand, been a source of considerable trouble and expense to his parents.'

'He's not had much luck. Badger's so infernally trusting.'

'Luck—luck! I should say that young man had never done a hand's turn in his life.'

'Nonsense, Dad. Why, he used to get up at five in the morning to feed those beastly chickens. It wasn't his fault they all got the roop or the croup, or whatever it was.'

'I have never approved of this garage project. Mere folly. You must give it up.'

'Can't sir. I've promised. I can't let old Badger down. He's counting on me.'

The discussion proceeded. The Vicar, biased by his views on the subject of Badger, was quite unable to regard any promise made to that young man as binding. He looked on Bobby as obstinate and determined at all costs to lead an idle life in company with one of the worst of possible companions. Bobby, on the other hand, stolidly repeated without originality that he 'couldn't let old Badger down'.

The Vicar finally left the room in anger and Bobby then and there sat down to write to the firm of Henriquez and Dallo, refusing their offer.

He sighed as he did so. He was letting a chance go here which was never likely to occur again. But he saw no alternative.

Later, on the links, he put the problem to Frankie. She listened attentively.

'You'd have had to go to South America?'

'Yes.'

'Would you have liked that?'

'Yes, why not?'

Frankie sighed.

41

'Anyway,' she said with decision. 'I think you did quite right.'

'About Badger, you mean?'

'Yes.'

'I couldn't let the old bird down, could I?'

'No, but be careful the old bird, as you call him, doesn't let you in.'

'Oh! I shall be careful. Anyway, I shall be all right. I haven't got any assets.'

'That must be rather fun,' said Frankie.

'Why?'

'I don't know why. It just sounded rather nice and free and irresponsible. I suppose, though, when I come to think of it, that I haven't got any assets much, either. I mean, Father gives me an allowance and I've got lots of houses to live in and clothes and maids and some hideous family jewels and a good deal of credits at shops; but that's all the family really. It's not *me*.'

'No, but all the same—' Bobby paused.

'Oh, it's quite different, I know.'

'Yes,' said Bobby. 'It's quite different.'

He felt suddenly very depressed.

They walked in silence to the next tee.

'I'm going to town tomorrow,' said Frankie, as Bobby teed up his ball.

'Tomorrow? Oh—and I was going to suggest you should come for a picnic.'

'I'd have liked to. However, it's arranged. You see, Father's got the gout again.'

'You ought to stay and minister to him,' said Bobby.

'He doesn't like being ministered to. It annoys him frightfully. He likes the second footman best. He's sympathetic and doesn't mind having things thrown at him and being called a damned fool.'

Bobby topped his drive and it trickled into the bunker.

'Hard lines,' said Frankie and drove a nice straight ball that sailed over it.

'By the way,' she remarked. 'We might do something together in London. You'll be up soon?'

'On Monday. But—well—it's no good, is it?'

'What do you mean—no good?'

'Well, I mean I shall be working as a mechanic most of the time. I mean—'

'Even then,' said Frankie, 'I suppose you're just as capable of coming to a cocktail party and getting tight as any other of my friends.'

Bobby merely shook his head.

'I'll give a beer and sausage party if you prefer it,' said Frankie encouragingly.

'Oh, look here, Frankie, what's the good? I mean, you can't mix your crowds. Your crowd's a different crowd from mine.'

'I assure you,' said Frankie, 'that my crowd is a very mixed one.'

'You're pretending not to understand.'

'You can bring Badger if you like. There's friendship for you.'

'You've got some sort of prejudice against Badger.'

'I daresay it's his stammer. People who stammer always make me stammer, too.'

'Look here, Frankie, it's no good and you know it isn't. It's all right down here. There's not much to do and I suppose I'm better than nothing. I mean you're always awfully decent to me and all that, and I'm grateful. But I mean I know I'm just nobody—I mean—'

'When you've quite finished expressing your inferiority complex,' said Frankie coldly, 'perhaps you'll try getting out of the bunker with a niblick instead of a putter.'

'Have I—oh! damn!' He replaced the putter in his bag and took out the niblick. Frankie watched with malicious satisfaction as he hacked at the ball five times in succession. Clouds of sand rose round them.

'Your hole,' said Bobby, picking up the ball.

'I think it is,' said Frankie. 'And that gives me the match.'

'Shall we play the bye?'

'No, I don't think so. I've got a lot to do.'

'Of course. I suppose you have.'

They walked together in silence to the clubhouse.

'Well,' said Frankie, holding out her hand. 'Goodbye, my dear. It's been too marvellous to have you to make use of while I've been down here. See something of you again, perhaps, when I've nothing better to do.'

'Look here, Frankie—'

'Perhaps you'll condescend to come to my coster party. I believe you can get pearl buttons quite cheaply at Woolworth's.'

'Frankie—'

His words were drowned in the noise of the Bentley's engine which Frankie had just started. She drove away with an airy wave of her hand.

44

'Damn!' said Bobby in a heartfelt tone.

Frankie, he considered, had behaved outrageously. Perhaps he hadn't put things very tactfully, but, dash it all, what he had said was true enough.

Perhaps, though, he shouldn't have put it into words.

The next three days seemed interminably long.

The Vicar had a sore throat which necessitated his speaking in a whisper when he spoke at all. He spoke very little and was obviously bearing his fourth son's presence as a Christian should. Once or twice he quoted Shakespeare to the effect that a serpent's tooth, etc.

On Saturday Bobby felt that he could bear the strain of home life no longer. He got Mrs Roberts, who, with her husband, 'ran' the Vicarage, to give him a packet of sandwiches, and, supplementing this with a bottle of beer which he bought in Marchbolt, he set off for a solitary picnic.

He had missed Frankie abominably these last few days. These older people were the limit . . . They harped on things so.

Bobby stretched himself out on a brackeny bank and debated with himself whether he should eat his lunch first and go to sleep afterwards, or sleep first and eat afterwards.

While he was cogitating, the matter was settled for him by his falling asleep without noticing it.

When he awoke it was half-past three! Bobby grinned as he thought how his father would disapprove of this way of spending a day. A good walk across country—twelve miles or so—that was the kind of thing that a healthy young man should do. It led inevitably to that famous remark: 'And now, I think, I've earned my lunch.'

'Idiotic,' thought Bobby. 'Why earn lunch by doing a lot of walking you don't particularly want to do? What's the merit in it? If you enjoy it, then it's pure self-indulgence, and if you don't enjoy it you're a fool to do it.'

Whereupon he fell upon his unearned lunch and ate it with gusto. With a sigh of satisfaction he unscrewed the bottle of beer. Unusually bitter beer, but decidedly refreshing . . .

He lay back again, having tossed the empty beer bottle into a clump of heather.

He felt rather god-like lounging there. The world was at his feet. A phrase, but a good phrase. He could do anything—anything if he tried! Plans of great splendour and daring initiative flashed through his mind.

Then he grew sleepy again. Lethargy stole over him.

He slept . . .

Heavy, numbing sleep . . .

CHAPTER 7

An Escape from Death

Driving her large green Bentley, Frankie drew up to the kerb outside a large old-fashioned house over the doorway of which was inscribed 'St Asaph's'.

Frankie jumped out and, turning, extracted a large bunch of lilies. Then she rang the bell. A woman in nurse's dress answered the door.

'Can I see Mr Jones?' inquired Frankie.

The nurse's eyes took in the Bentley, the lilies and Frankie with intense interest.

'What name shall I say?'

'Lady Frances Derwent.'

The nurse was thrilled and her patient went up in her estimation.

She guided Frankie upstairs into a room on the first floor.

'You've a visitor to see you, Mr Jones. Now, who do you think it is? Such a nice surprise for you.'

All this is the 'bright' manner usual to nursing homes.

'Gosh!' said Bobby, very much surprised. 'If it isn't Frankie!'

'Hullo, Bobby, I've brought the usual flowers. Rather a graveyard suggestion about them, but the choice was limited.'

'Oh, Lady Frances,' said the nurse, 'they're lovely. I'll put them into water.'

She left the room.

Frankie sat down in an obvious visitor's chair.

'Well, Bobby,' she said. 'What's all this?'

'You may well ask,' said Bobby. 'I'm the complete sensation of this place. Eight grains of morphia, no less. They're going to write about me in the *Lancet* and the *BMJ*.'

'What's the *BMJ*?' interrupted Frankie.

'The *British Medical Journal*.'

'All right. Go ahead. Rattle off some more initials.'

'Do you know, my girl, that half a grain is a fatal dose? I ought to be dead about sixteen times over. It's true that recovery has been known after sixteen grains—still, eight is pretty good, don't you think? I'm the hero of this place. They've never had a case like me before.'

'How nice for them.'

'Isn't it? Gives them something to talk about to all the other patients.'

The nurse re-entered, bearing lilies in vases.

'It's true, isn't it, nurse?' demanded Bobby. 'You've never had a case like mine?'

'Oh! you oughtn't to be here at all,' said the nurse. 'In the churchyard you ought to be. But it's only the good die young, they say.' She giggled at her own wit and went out.

'There you are,' said Bobby. 'You'll see, I shall be famous all over England.'

He continued to talk. Any signs of inferiority complex

that he had displayed at his last meeting with Frankie had now quite disappeared. He took a firm and egotistical pleasure in recounting every detail of his case.

'That's enough,' said Frankie, quelling him. 'I don't really care terribly for stomach pumps. To listen to you one would think nobody had ever been poisoned before.'

'Jolly few have been poisoned with eight grains of morphia and got over it,' Bobby pointed out. 'Dash it all, you're not sufficiently impressed.'

'Pretty sickening for the people who poisoned you,' said Frankie.

'I know. Waste of perfectly good morphia.'

'It was in the beer, wasn't it?'

'Yes. You see, someone found me sleeping like the dead, tried to wake me and couldn't. Then they got alarmed, carried me to a farmhouse and sent for a doctor—'

'I know all the next part,' said Frankie hastily.

'At first they had the idea that I'd taken the stuff deliberately. Then when they heard my story, they went off and looked for the beer bottle and found it where I'd thrown it and had it analysed—the dregs of it were quite enough for that, apparently.'

'No clue as to how the morphia got in the bottle?'

'None whatever. They've interviewed the pub where I bought it and opened other bottles and everything's been quite all right.'

'Someone must have put the stuff in the beer while you were asleep?'

'That's it. I remember that the paper across the top wasn't still sticking properly.'

Agatha Christie

Frankie nodded thoughtfully.

'Well,' she said. 'It shows that what I said in the train that day was quite right.'

'What did you say?'

'That that man—Pritchard—had been pushed over the cliff.'

'That wasn't in the train. You said that at the station,' said Bobby feebly.

'Same thing.'

'But why—'

'Darling—it's obvious. Why should anyone want to put *you* out of the way? You're not the heir to a fortune or anything.'

'I may be. Some great aunt I've never heard of in New Zealand or somewhere may have left me all her money.'

'Nonsense. Not without knowing you. And if she didn't know you, why leave money to a fourth son? Why, in these hard times even a clergyman mightn't have a fourth son! No, it's all quite clear. No one benefits by your death, so that's ruled out. Then there's revenge. You haven't seduced a chemist's daughter, by any chance?'

'Not that I can remember,' said Bobby with dignity.

'I know. One seduces so much that one can't keep count. But I should say offhand that you've never seduced anyone at all.'

'You're making me blush, Frankie. And why must it be a chemist's daughter, anyway?'

'Free access to morphia. It's not so easy to get hold of morphia.'

'Well, I haven't seduced a chemist's daughter.'

'And you haven't got any enemies that you know of?'

Bobby shook his head.

'Well, there you are,' said Frankie triumphantly. 'It must be the man who was pushed over the cliff. What do the police think?'

'They think it must have been a lunatic.'

'Nonsense. Lunatics don't wander about with unlimited supplies of morphia looking for odd bottles of beer to put it into. No, somebody pushed Pritchard over the cliff. A minute or two later you come along and he thinks you saw him do it and so determines to put you out of the way.'

'I don't think that will hold water, Frankie.'

'Why not?'

'Well, to begin with, I didn't see anything.'

'Yes, but he didn't know that.'

'And if I had seen anything, I should have said so at the inquest.'

'I suppose that's so,' said Frankie unwillingly.

She thought for a minute or two.

'Perhaps he thought you'd seen something that you didn't think was anything but which really was something. That sounds pure gibberish, but you get the idea?'

Bobby nodded.

'Yes, I see what you mean, but it doesn't seem very probable, somehow.'

'I'm sure that cliff business had something to do with this. You were on the spot—the first person to be there—'

'Thomas was there, too,' Bobby reminded her. 'And nobody's tried to poison him.'

'Perhaps they're going to,' said Frankie cheerfully. 'Or perhaps they've tried and failed.'

'It all seems very far-fetched.'

'I think it's logical. If you get two out of the way things happening in a stagnant pond like Marchbolt—wait—there's a third thing.'

'What?'

'That job you were offered. That, of course, is quite a small thing, but it was odd, you must admit. I've never heard of a foreign firm that specialized in seeking out undistinguished ex-Naval officers.'

'Did you say undistinguished?'

'You hadn't got into the *BMJ*, then. But you see my point. You've seen something you weren't meant to see—or so they (whoever they are) think. Very well. They first try to get rid of you by offering you a job abroad. Then, when that fails, they try to put you out of the way altogether.'

'Isn't that rather drastic? And anyway a great risk to take?'

'Oh! but murderers are always frightfully rash. The more murders they do, the more murders they want to do.'

'Like *The Third Bloodstain*,' said Bobby, remembering one of his favourite works of fiction.

'Yes, and in real life, too—Smith and his wives and Armstrong and people.'

'Well, but, Frankie, what on earth is it I'm supposed to have seen?'

'That, of course, is the difficulty,' admitted Frankie. 'I agree that it can't have been the actual pushing, because you would have told about that. It must be something about the man himself. Perhaps he had a birthmark or double-jointed fingers or some strange physical peculiarity.'

'Your mind is running on Dr Thorndyke, I see. It couldn't be anything like that because whatever I saw the police would see as well.'

'So they would. That was an idiotic suggestion. It's very difficult, isn't it?'

'It's a pleasing theory,' said Bobby. 'And it makes me feel important, but all the same, I don't believe it's much more than a theory.'

'I'm sure I'm right.' Frankie rose. 'I must be off now. Shall I come and see you again tomorrow?'

'Oh! Do. The arch chatter of the nurses gets very monotonous. By the way, you're back from London very soon?'

'My dear, as soon as I heard about you, I tore back. It's most exciting to have a romantically poisoned friend.'

'I don't know whether morphia is so very romantic,' said Bobby reminiscently.

'Well, I'll come tomorrow. Do I kiss you or don't I?'

'It's not catching,' said Bobby encouragingly.

'Then I'll do my duty to the sick thoroughly.'

She kissed him lightly.

'See you tomorrow.'

The nurse came in with Bobby's tea as she went out.

'I've seen her pictures in the papers often. She's not so very like them, though. And, of course, I've seen her driving about in her car, but I've never seen her before close to, so to speak. Not a bit haughty, is she?'

'Oh, no!' said Bobby. 'I should never call Frankie haughty.'

'I said to Sister, I said, she's as natural as anything. Not a bit stuck up. I said to Sister, she's just like you or me, I said.'

Silently dissenting violently from this view, Bobby returned no reply. The nurse, disappointed by his lack of response, left the room.

Bobby was left to his own thoughts.

He finished his tea. Then he went over in his mind the possibilities of Frankie's amazing theory, and ended by deciding reluctantly against it. He then cast about for other distractions.

His eye was caught by the vases of lilies. Frightfully sweet of Frankie to bring him all these flowers, and of course they were lovely, but he wished it had occurred to her to bring him a few detective stories instead. He cast his eye over the table beside him. There was a novel of Ouida's and a copy of *John Halifax, Gentleman* and last week's *Marchbolt Weekly Times*. He picked up *John Halifax, Gentleman*.

After five minutes he put it down. To a mind nourished on *The Third Bloodstain, The Case of the Murdered Archduke* and *The Strange Adventure of the Florentine Dagger, John Halifax, Gentleman*, lacked pep.

With a sigh he picked up last week's *Marchbolt Weekly Times*.

A moment or two later he was pressing the bell beneath his pillow with a vigour which brought a nurse into the room at a run.

'Whatever's the matter, Mr Jones? Are you taken bad?'

'Ring up the Castle,' cried Bobby. 'Tell Lady Frances she must come back here at once.'

'Oh, Mr Jones. You can't send a message like that.'

'Can't I?' said Bobby. 'If I were allowed to get up from this blasted bed you'd soon see whether I could or couldn't. As it is, you've got to do it for me.'

'But she'll hardly be back.'

'You don't know that Bentley.'

'She won't have had her tea.'

'Now look here, my dear girl,' said Bobby, 'don't stand there arguing with me. Ring up as I tell you. Tell her she's got to come here at once because I've got something very important to say to her.'

Overborne, but unwilling, the nurse went. She took some liberties with Bobby's message.

If it was no inconvenience to Lady Frances, Mr Jones wondered if she would mind coming as he had something he would like to say to her, but, of course, Lady Frances was not to put herself out in any way.

Lady Frances replied curtly that she would come at once.

'Depend upon it,' said the nurse to her colleagues, 'she's sweet on him! That's what it is.'

Frankie arrived all agog.

'What's this desperate summons?' she demanded.

Bobby was sitting up in bed, a bright red spot in each cheek. In his hand he waved the copy of the *Marchbolt Weekly Times*.

'Look at this, Frankie.'

Frankie looked.

'Well?' she demanded.

'This is the picture you meant when you said it was touched up but quite like the Cayman woman.'

Bobby's finger pointed to a somewhat blurred reproduction of a photograph. Underneath it were the words: 'PORTRAIT FOUND ON THE DEAD MAN AND BY WHICH HE WAS IDENTIFIED. MRS AMELIA CAYMAN, THE DEAD MAN'S SISTER.'

'That's what I said, and it's true, too. I can't see anything to rave over in it.'

'No more than I.'

'But you said—'

'I know I said. But you see, Frankie'—Bobby's voice became very impressive—'*this isn't the photograph that I put back in the dead man's pocket . . .*'

They looked at each other.

'Then in that case,' began Frankie slowly.

'Either there must have been two photographs—'

'—Which isn't likely—'

'Or else—'

They paused.

'*That man*—what's his name?' said Frankie.

'Bassington-ffrench!' said Bobby.

CHAPTER 8

Riddle of a Photograph

They stared at each other as they tried to adjust themselves to the altered situation.

'It couldn't be anyone else,' said Bobby. 'He was the only person who had the chance.'

'Unless, as we said, there were *two* photographs.'

'We agreed that that wasn't likely. If there had been two photographs they'd have tried to identify him by means of both of them—not only one.'

'Anyway, that's easily found out,' said Frankie. 'We can ask the police. We'll assume for the moment that there was just the one photograph, the one you saw that you put back again in his pocket. It was there when you left him, and it wasn't there when the police came, therefore the only person who *could* have taken it away and put the other one in its place was this man Bassington-ffrench. What was he like, Bobby?'

Bobby frowned in the effort of remembrance.

'A sort of nondescript fellow. Pleasant voice. A gentleman and all that. I really didn't notice him particularly. He said

57

that he was a stranger down here—and something about looking for a house.'

'We can verify that, anyway,' said Frankie. 'Wheeler & Owen are the only house agents.' Suddenly she gave a shiver. 'Bobby, have you thought? If Pritchard was pushed over—*Bassington-ffrench must be the man who did it . . .*'

'That's pretty grim,' said Bobby. 'He seemed such a nice pleasant sort of fellow. But you know, Frankie, we can't be sure he really was pushed over.'

'*I*'m quite sure!'

'You have been all along.'

'No, I just wanted it to be that way because it made things more exciting. But now it's more or less proved. If it was murder everything fits in. Your unexpected appearance which upsets the murderer's plans. Your discovery of the photograph and, in consequence, the need to put you out of the way.'

'There's a flaw there,' said Bobby.

'Why? You were the only person who saw that photograph. As soon as Bassington-ffrench was left alone with the body he changed the photograph which only you had seen.'

But Bobby continued to shake his head.

'No, that won't do. Let's grant for the moment that that photograph was so important that I had to be "got out of the way", as you put it. Sounds absurd but I suppose it's just possible. Well, then, whatever was going to be done would have to be done *at once*. The fact that I went to London and never saw the *Marchbolt Weekly Times* or the other papers with the photograph in it was just pure chance—a thing nobody could count on. The probability was that I should say at once, "That isn't the photograph I saw." Why wait till after the inquest when everything was nicely settled?'

'There's something in that,' admitted Frankie.

'And there's another point. I can't be absolutely sure, of course, but I could almost swear that when I put the photograph back in the dead man's pocket Bassington-ffrench wasn't there. He didn't arrive till about five or ten minutes later.'

'He might have been watching you all the time,' argued Frankie.

'I don't see very well how he could,' said Bobby slowly. 'There's really only one place where you can see down to exactly the spot we were. Farther round, the cliff bulges and then recedes underneath, so that you can't see over. There's just the one place and when Bassington-ffrench did arrive there I heard him at once. Footsteps echo down below. He may have been near at hand, but he wasn't looking over till then—that I'll swear.'

'Then you think that he didn't know about your seeing the photograph?'

'I don't see how he could have known.'

'And he can't have been afraid you'd seen him doing it—the murder, I mean—because, as you say, that's absurd. You'd never have held your tongue about it. It looks as though it must have been something else altogether.'

'Only I don't see what it could have been.'

'Something they didn't know about till after the inquest. I don't know why I say "*they*".'

'Why not? After all, the Caymans must have been in it, too. It's probably a gang. I like gangs.'

'That's a low taste,' said Frankie absently. 'A single-handed murder is much higher class. Bobby!'

'Yes?'

'What was it Pritchard said—just before he died? You know, you told me about it that day on the links. That funny question?'

'"*Why didn't they ask Evans?*"'

'Yes. Suppose *that* was it?'

'But that's ridiculous.'

'It sounds so, but it might be important, really. Bobby, I'm *sure* it's that. Oh, no, I'm being an idiot—you never told the Caymans about it?'

'I did, as a matter of fact,' said Bobby slowly.

'You *did*?'

'Yes. I wrote to them that evening. Saying, of course, that it was probably quite unimportant.'

'And what happened?'

'Cayman wrote back, politely agreeing, of course, that there was nothing in it, but thanking me for taking the trouble. I felt rather snubbed.'

'And two days later you got this letter from a strange firm bribing you to go out to South America?'

'Yes.'

'Well,' said Frankie, 'I don't know what more you want. They try that first; you turn it down, and the next thing is that they follow you round and seize a good moment to empty a lot of morphia into your bottle of beer.'

'Then the Caymans *are* in it?'

'Of course the Caymans are in it!'

'Yes,' said Bobby thoughtfully. 'If your reconstruction is correct, they must be in it. According to our present theory, it goes like this. Dead man X is deliberately pushed over cliff—presumably by BF (pardon these initials). It is important that X should not be correctly identified, so portrait of Mrs C is put in his pocket and portrait of fair unknown removed. (Who was she, I wonder?)'

'Keep to the point,' said Frankie sternly.

'Mrs C waits for photographs to appear and turns up as grief-stricken sister and identifies X as her brother from foreign parts.'

'You don't believe he could really have been her brother?'

'Not for a moment! You know, it puzzled me all along. The Caymans were a different class altogether. The dead man was—well, it sounds a most awful thing to say and just like some deadly old retired Anglo-Indian, but the dead man was a pukka sahib.'

'And the Caymans most emphatically weren't?'

'*Most* emphatically.'

'And then, just when everything has gone off well from the Caymans' point of view—body successfully identified, verdict of accidental death, everything in the garden lovely—*you* come along and mess things up,' mused Frankie.

'"*Why didn't they ask Evans?*"' Bobby repeated the phrase thoughtfully. 'You know, I can't see what on earth there can be in that to put the wind up anybody.'

'Ah! that's because you don't know. It's like making crossword puzzles. You write down a clue and you think it's too idiotically simple and that everyone will guess it straight off, and you're frightfully surprised when they simply can't get it in the least. "*Why didn't they ask Evans?*" must have been a most frightfully significant phrase to them, and they couldn't realize that it meant nothing at all to you.'

'More fools they.'

'Oh, quite so. But it's just possible they thought that if Pritchard said that, he might have said something more which would also recur to you in due time. Anyway, they weren't going to take chances. You were safer out of the way.'

'They took a lot of risk. Why didn't they engineer another "accident"?'

'No, no. That would have been stupid. Two accidents within a week of each other? It might have suggested a connection between the two, and then people would have begun inquiring into the first one. No, I think there's a kind of bald simplicity about their method which is really rather clever.'

'And yet you said just now that morphia wasn't easy to get hold of.'

'No more it is. You have to sign poison books and things. Oh! of course, that's a clue. Whoever did it had easy access to supplies of morphia.'

'A doctor, a hospital nurse, or a chemist,' suggested Bobby.

'Well, I was thinking more of illicitly imported drugs.'

'You can't mix up too many different sorts of crime,' said Bobby.

'You see, the strong point would be the absence of motive. Your death doesn't benefit anyone. So what will the police think?'

'A lunatic,' said Bobby. 'And that's what they do think.'

'You see? It's awfully simple, really.'

Bobby began to laugh suddenly.

'What's amusing you?'

'Just the thought of how sick-making it must be for them! All that morphia—enough to kill five or six people— and here I am still alive and kicking.'

'One of Life's little ironies that one can't foresee,' agreed Frankie.

'The question is—what do we do next?' said Bobby practically.

'Oh! lots of things,' said Frankie promptly.

'Such as . . .?'

'Well—finding out about the photograph—that there was only one, not two. And about Bassington-ffrench's house hunting.'

'That will probably be quite all right and above board.'

'Why do you say that?'

'Look here, Frankie, think a minute. Bassington-ffrench *must* be above suspicion. He *must* be all clear and above board. Not only must there be nothing to connect him in any way with the dead man, but he must have a proper reason for being down here. He may have invented house hunting on the spur of the moment, but I bet he carried out something of the kind. There must be no suggestion of a "mysterious stranger seen in the neighbourhood of the accident". I fancy that Bassington-ffrench is his own name and that he's the sort of person who would be quite above suspicion.'

'Yes,' said Frankie thoughtfully. 'That's a very good deduction. There will be nothing whatever to connect Bassington-ffrench with Alex Pritchard. Now, if we knew who the dead man really was—'

'Ah! then it might be different.'

'So it was very important that the body should not be recognized—hence all the Cayman camouflage. And yet it was taking a big risk.'

'You forget that Mrs Cayman identified him as soon as was humanly possible. After that, even if there had been pictures of him in the papers (you know how blurry these things are) people would only say: "Curious, this man Pritchard, who fell over a cliff, is really extraordinarily like Mr X."'

'There must be more to it than that,' said Frankie shrewdly. 'X must have been a man who wouldn't easily be missed. I mean, he couldn't have been the sort of family man whose wife or relations would go to the police at once and report him missing.'

'Good for you, Frankie. No, he must have been just going abroad or perhaps just come back (he was marvellously tanned—like a big-game hunter—he looked that sort of person) and he can't have had any very near relations who knew all about his movements.'

'We're deducing beautifully,' said Frankie. 'I hope we're not deducing all wrong.'

'Very likely,' said Bobby. 'But I think what we've said

so far is fairly sound sense—granted, that is, the wild improbability of the whole thing.'

Frankie waved away the wild improbability with an airy gesture.

'The thing is—what to do next,' she said. 'It seems to me we've got three angles of attack.'

'Go on, Sherlock.'

'The first is *you*. They've made one attempt on your life. They'll probably try again. This time we might get what they call "a line" on them. Using you as a decoy, I mean.'

'No thank you, Frankie,' said Bobby with feeling. 'I've been very lucky this time, but I mightn't be so lucky again if they changed the attack to a blunt instrument. I was thinking of taking a great deal of care of myself in the future. The decoy idea can be washed out.'

'I was afraid you'd say that,' said Frankie with a sigh. 'Young men are sadly degenerate nowadays. Father says so. They don't enjoy being uncomfortable and doing dangerous and unpleasant things any longer. It's a pity.'

'A great pity,' said Bobby, but he spoke with firmness. 'What's the second plan of campaign?'

'Working from the "*Why didn't they ask Evans?*" clue,' said Frankie. 'Presumably the dead man came down here to see Evans, whoever he was. Now, if we could find Evans—'

'How many Evanses,' Bobby interrupted, 'do you think there are in Marchbolt?'

'Seven hundred, I should think,' admitted Frankie.

'At least! We might do something that way, but I'm rather doubtful.'

'We could list all the Evanses and visit the likely ones.'

'And ask them—what?'

'That's the difficulty,' said Frankie.

'We need to know a little more,' said Bobby. 'Then that idea of yours might come in useful. What's No. 3?'

'This man Bassington-ffrench. There we *have* got something tangible to go upon. It's an uncommon name. I'll ask Father. He knows all these county family names and their various branches.'

'Yes,' said Bobby. 'We might do something that way.'

'At any rate, we are going to do something?'

'Of course we are. Do you think I'm going to be given eight grains of morphia and do nothing about it?'

'That's the spirit,' said Frankie.

'And besides that,' said Bobby, 'there's the indignity of the stomach pump to be washed out.'

'That's enough,' said Frankie. 'You'll be getting morbid and indecent again if I don't stop you.'

'You have no true womanly sympathy,' said Bobby.

CHAPTER 9

Concerning Mr Bassington-ffrench

Frankie lost no time in setting to work. She attacked her father that same evening.

'Father,' she said, 'do you know any Bassington-ffrenches?'

Lord Marchington, who was reading a political article, did not quite take in the question.

'It's not the French so much as the Americans,' he said severely. 'All this tomfoolery and conferences—wasting the nation's time and money—'

Frankie abstracted her mind until Lord Marchington, running like a railway train along an accustomed line, came, as it were, to a halt at a station.

'The Bassington-ffrenches,' repeated Frankie.

'What about 'em?' said Lord Marchington.

Frankie didn't know what about them. She made a statement, knowing well enough that her father enjoyed contradiction.

'They're a Yorkshire family, aren't they?'

'Nonsense—Hampshire. There's the Shropshire branch, of course, and then there's the Irish lot. Which are your friends?'

'I'm not sure,' said Frankie, accepting the implication of friendship with several unknown people.

'Not sure? What do you mean? You must be sure.'

'People drift about so nowadays,' said Frankie.

'Drift—drift—that's about all they do. In my days we asked people. Then one knew where one was—fellow said he was the Hampshire branch—very well, your grandmother married my second cousin. It made a link.'

'It must have been too sweet,' said Frankie, 'But there really isn't time for genealogical and geographical research nowadays.'

'No—you've no time nowadays for anything but drinking these poisonous cocktails.'

Lord Marchington gave a sudden yelp of pain as he moved his gouty leg, which some free imbibing of the family port had not improved.

'Are they well off?' asked Frankie.

'The Bassington-ffrenches? Couldn't say. The Shropshire lot have been hard hit, I believe—death duties, and one thing or another. One of the Hampshire ones married an heiress. An American woman.'

'One of them was down here the other day,' said Frankie. 'Looking for a house, I believe.'

'Funny idea. What should anyone want with a house down here?'

That, thought Frankie, was the question.

On the following day she walked into the office of Messrs. Wheeler & Owen, House and Estate Agents.

Mr Owen himself sprang up to receive her. Frankie gave him a gracious smile and dropped into a chair.

'And what can we have the pleasure of doing for you, Lady Frances? You don't want to sell the Castle, I suppose. Ha! Ha!' Mr Owen laughed at his own wit.

'I wish we could,' said Frankie. 'No, as a matter of fact, I believe a friend of mine was down here the other day—a Mr Bassington-ffrench. He was looking for a house.'

'Ah! yes, indeed. I remember the name perfectly. Two small f's.'

'That's right,' said Frankie.

'He was making inquiries about various small properties with a view to purchase. He was obliged to return to town the next day, so could not view many of the houses, but I understand he is in no great hurry. Since he left, one or two suitable properties have come into the market and I have sent him on particulars, but have had no reply.'

'Did you write to London—or to the—er—country address?' inquired Frankie.

'Let me see now.' He called to a junior clerk. 'Frank, Mr Bassington-ffrench's address.'

'Roger Bassington-ffrench, Esq., Merroway Court, Staverley, Hants,' said the junior clerk glibly.

'Ah!' said Frankie. 'Then it wasn't my Mr Bassington-ffrench. This must be his cousin. I thought it was odd his being here and not looking me up.'

'Quite so—quite so,' said Mr Owen intelligently.

'Let me see, it must have been the Wednesday he came to see you.'

'That's right. Just before six-thirty. We close at six-thirty. I remember particularly because it was the day when that sad accident happened. Man fell over the cliff. Mr

69

Bassington-ffrench had actually stayed by the body till the police came. He looked quite upset when he came in here. Very sad tragedy, that, and high time something was done about that bit of path. The Town Council have been criticized very freely, I can tell you, Lady Frances. Most dangerous. Why we haven't had more accidents than we have I can't imagine.'

'Extraordinary,' said Frankie.

She left the office in a thoughtful mood. As Bobby had prophesied, all Mr Bassington-ffrench's actions seemed clear and above aboard. He was one of the Hampshire Bassington-ffrenches, he had given his proper address, he had actually mentioned his part in the tragedy to the house agent. Was it possible that, after all, Mr Bassington-ffrench was the completely innocent person he seemed?

Frankie had a qualm of doubt. Then she refuted it.

'No,' she said to herself. 'A man who wants to buy a little place would either get here earlier in the day, or else stay over the next day. You wouldn't go into a house agent's at six-thirty in the evening and go up to London the following day. Why make the journey at all? Why not write?'

No, she decided, Bassington-ffrench was the guilty party.

Her next call was the police station.

Inspector Williams was an old acquaintance, having succeeded in tracking down a maid with a false reference who had absconded with some of Frankie's jewellery.

'Good afternoon, Inspector.'

'Good afternoon, your Ladyship. Nothing wrong, I hope.'

'Not as yet, but I'm thinking of holding up a bank soon, because I'm getting so short of money.'

The inspector gave a rumbling laugh in acknowledgement of this witticism.

'As a matter of fact, I've come to ask questions out of sheer curiosity,' said Frankie.

'Is that so, Lady Frances?'

'Now do tell me this, Inspector—the man who fell over the cliff—Pritchard, or whatever his name was—'

'Pritchard, that's right.'

'He had only *one* photograph on him, didn't he? Somebody told me he had *three*!'

'One's right,' said the inspector. 'Photograph of his sister it was. She came down and identified him.'

'How absurd to say there were three!'

'Oh! That's easy, your Ladyship. These newspaper reporters don't mind how much they exaggerate and as often as not they get the whole thing wrong.'

'I know,' said Frankie. 'I've heard the wildest stories.' She paused a moment then drew freely on her imagination. 'I've heard that his pockets were stuffed with papers proving him to be a Bolshevik agent, and there's another story that his pockets were full of dope, and another again about his having pockets full of counterfeit bank notes.'

The inspector laughed heartily.

'That's a good one.'

'I suppose really he had just the usual things in his pockets?'

'And very few at that. A handkerchief, not marked. Some loose change, a packet of cigarettes and a couple of treasury notes—loose, not in a case. No letters. We'd have had a job to identify him if it hadn't been for the photo. Providential, you might call it.'

'I wonder,' said Frankie.

In view of her private knowledge, she considered providential a singularly inappropriate word. She changed the conversation.

'I went to see Mr Jones, the Vicar's son, yesterday. The one who's been poisoned. What an extraordinary thing that was.'

'Ah!' said the inspector. 'Now that is extraordinary, if you like. Never heard of anything like it happening before. A nice young gentleman without an enemy in the world, or so you'd say. You know, Lady Frances, there are some queer customers going about. All the same, I never heard of a homicidal maniac who acted just this way.'

'Is there any clue at all to who did it?'

Frankie was all wide-eyed inquiry.

'It's so interesting to hear all this,' she added.

The inspector swelled with gratification. He enjoyed this friendly conversation with an Earl's daughter. Nothing stuck up or snobbish about Lady Frances.

'There was a car seen in the vicinity,' said the inspector. 'Dark-blue Talbot saloon. A man on Lock's Corner reported dark-blue Talbot, No. GG 8282, passed going direction St Botolph's.'

'And you think?'

'GG 8282 is the number of the Bishop of Botolph's car.'

Frankie toyed for a minute or two with the idea of a homicidal bishop who offered sacrifices of clergymen's sons, but rejected it with a sigh.

'You don't suspect the Bishop, I suppose?' she said.

'We've found out that the Bishop's car never left the Palace garage that afternoon.'

'So it was a false number.'

'Yes. We've got that to go on all right.'

With expressions of admiration, Frankie took her leave. She made no damping remark, but she thought to herself:

'There must be a large number of dark-blue Talbots in England.'

On her return home she took a directory of Marchbolt from its place on the writing-table in the library and removed it to her own room. She worked over it for some hours.

The result was not satisfactory.

There were four hundred and eighty-two Evanses in Marchbolt.

'Damn!' said Frankie.

She began to make plans for the future.

CHAPTER 10

Preparations for an Accident

A week later Bobby had joined Badger in London. He had received several enigmatical communications from Frankie, most in such an illegible scrawl that he was quite unable to do more than guess at their meaning. However, their general purport seemed to be that Frankie had a plan and that he (Bobby) was to do nothing until he heard from her. This was as well, for Bobby would certainly have had no leisure to do anything, since the unlucky Badger had already succeeded in embroiling himself and his business in every way ingenuity could suggest, and Bobby was kept busy disentangling the extraordinary mess his friend seemed to have got into.

Meanwhile, the young man remained very strictly on his guard. The effect of eight grains of morphia was to render their taker extremely suspicious of food and drink and had also induced him to bring to London a service revolver, the possession of which was extremely irksome to him.

He was just beginning to feel that the whole thing had

been an extravagant nightmare when Frankie's Bentley roared down the Mews and drew up outside the garage. Bobby, in grease-stained overalls, came out to receive it. Frankie was at the wheel and beside her sat a rather gloomy-looking young man.

'Hullo, Bobby,' said Frankie. 'This is George Arbuthnot. He's a doctor, and we shall need him.'

Bobby winced slightly as he and George Arbuthnot made faint recognitions of each other's presence.

'Are you sure we're going to need a doctor?' he asked. 'Aren't you being a bit pessimistic?'

'I didn't mean we should need him in that way,' said Frankie. 'I need him for a scheme that I've got on. Look here, is there anywhere we can go and talk?'

Bobby looked round him.

'Well, there's my bedroom,' he said doubtfully.

'Excellent,' said Frankie.

She got out of the car and she and George Arbuthnot followed Bobby up some outside steps and into a microscopic bedroom.

'I don't know,' said Bobby, looking round dubiously, 'if there's anywhere to sit.'

There was not. The only chair was loaded with, apparently, the whole of Bobby's wardrobe.

'The bed will do,' said Frankie.

She plumped down on it. George Arbuthnot did the same and the bed groaned protestingly.

'I've got everything planned out,' said Frankie. 'To begin with, we want a car. One of yours will do.'

'Do you mean you want to buy one of our cars?'

75

'Yes.'

'That's really very nice of you, Frankie,' said Bobby, with warm appreciation. 'But you needn't. I really do draw the line at sticking my friends.'

'You've got it all wrong,' said Frankie. 'It isn't like that at all. I know what you mean—it's like buying perfectly appalling clothes and hats from one's friends who are just starting in business. A nuisance, but it's got to be done. But this isn't like that at all. I really need a car.'

'What about the Bentley?'

'The Bentley's no good.'

'You're mad,' said Bobby.

'No, I'm not. The Bentley's no good for what I want it for.'

'What's that?'

'Smashing it up.'

Bobby groaned and put a hand to his head.

'I don't seem very well this morning.'

George Arbuthnot spoke for the first time. His voice was deep and melancholy.

'She means,' he said, 'that's she going to have an accident.'

'How does she know?' said Bobby wildly.

Frankie gave an exasperated sigh.

'Somehow or other,' she said, 'we seem to have started wrong. Now just listen quietly, Bobby, and try and take in what I'm going to say. I know your brains are practically negligible, but you ought to be able to understand if you really concentrate.'

She paused, then resumed.

'I am on the trail of Bassington-ffrench.'

'Hear, hear.'

'Bassington-ffrench—our particular Bassington-ffrench—lives at Merroway Court at the village of Staverley in Hampshire. Merroway Court belongs to our Bassington-ffrench's brother, and our Bassington-ffrench lives there with his brother and his wife.'

'Whose wife?'

'The brother's wife, of course. That isn't the point. The point is how are you or I or both of us is going to worm ourselves into the household. I've been down and reconnoitred the ground. Staverley's a mere village. Strangers arriving there to stay would stick out a mile. It would be the sort of thing that simply isn't done. So I've evolved a plan. This is what is going to happen: Lady Frances Derwent, driving her car more recklessly than well, crashes into the wall near the gates of Merroway Court. Complete wreckage of the car, less complete wreckage of Lady Frances, who is carried to the house, suffering from concussion and shock and must emphatically not be moved.'

'Who says so?'

'George. Now you see where George comes in. We can't risk a strange doctor saying there is nothing the matter with me. Or perhaps some officious person might pick up my prostrate form and take it to some local hospital. No, what happens is this: George is passing, also in a car (you'd better sell us a second one), sees the accident, leaps out and takes charge. "I am a doctor. Stand back, everybody." (That is, if there is anybody to stand back). "We must take her into that house—what is it, Merroway Court? That

will do. I must be able to make a thorough examination."
I am carried to the best spare room, the Bassington-ffrenches
either sympathetic or bitterly resisting, but in any case,
George will overbear them. George makes his examination
and emerges with his verdict. Happily, it is not as serious
as he thought. No bones broken, but danger of concussion.
I must on no account be moved for two or three days.
After that, I shall be able to return to London.

'And then George departs and it's up to me to ingratiate
myself with the household.'

'And where do I come in?'

'You don't.'

'But look here—'

'My dear child, do remember that Bassington-ffrench
knows you. He doesn't know me from Adam. And I'm in
a frightfully strong position, because I've got a title. You see
how useful that is. I'm not just a stray young woman gaining
admission to the house for mysterious purposes. I am an
earl's daughter and therefore highly respectable. And George
is a real doctor and everything is quite above suspicion.'

'Oh! I suppose it's all right,' said Bobby unhappily.

'It's a remarkably well-planned scheme, I think,' said
Frankie with pride.

'And I don't do anything at all?' asked Bobby.

He still felt injured—much like a dog who has been
unexpectedly deprived of a bone. This, he felt, was his own
particular crime, and now he was being ousted.

'Of course you do, darling. You grow a moustache.'

'Oh! I grow a moustache, do I?'

'Yes. How long will it take?'

'Two or three weeks, I expect.'

'Heavens! I'd no idea it was such a slow process. Can't you speed it up?'

'No. Why can't I wear a false one?'

'They always look so false and they twist or come off or smell of spirit gum. Wait a minute, though, I believe there is a kind you can get stuck on hair by hair, so to speak, that absolutely defies detection. I expect a theatrical wigmaker would do it for you.'

'He'd probably think I was trying to escape from justice.'

'It doesn't matter what he thinks.'

'Once I've got the moustache, what do I do?'

'Put on a chauffeur's uniform and drive the Bentley down to Staverley.'

'Oh, I see.'

Bobby brightened.

'You see my idea is this,' said Frankie: 'Nobody looks at a chauffeur in the way they look at a *person*. In any case, Bassington-ffrench only saw you for a minute or two and he must have been too rattled wondering if he could change the photograph in time to look at you much. You were just a young golfing ass to him. It isn't like the Caymans who sat opposite you and talked to you and who were deliberately trying to sum you up. I'd bet anything that seeing you in chauffeur's uniform, Bassington-ffrench wouldn't recognize you even without the moustache. He might just possibly think that your face reminded him of somebody—no more than that. And with the moustache it ought to be perfectly safe. Now tell me, what do you think of the plan?'

Bobby turned it over in his mind.

'To tell you the truth, Frankie,' he said generously, 'I think it's pretty good.'

'In that case,' said Frankie briskly. 'Let's go and buy some cars. I say, I think George has broken your bed.'

'It doesn't matter,' said Bobby hospitably. 'It was never a particularly good bed.'

They descended to the garage, where a nervous-looking young man with a curious lack of chin and an agreeable smile greeted them with a vague 'Haw, haw, haw!' His general appearance was slightly marred by the fact that his eyes had a distinct disinclination to look in the same direction.

'Hullo, Badger,' said Bobby. 'You remember Frankie, don't you?'

Badger clearly didn't, but he said, 'Haw, haw, haw!' again in an amiable manner.

'Last time I saw you,' said Frankie, 'you were head downward in the mud and we had to pull you out by the legs.'

'No, not really?' said Badger. 'Why, that m-m-must have been W-w-w-wales.'

'Quite right,' said Frankie. 'It was.'

'I always was a p-p-putrid r-r-r-rider,' said Badger. 'I s-s-s-still am,' he added mournfully.

'Frankie wants to buy a car,' said Bobby.

'Two cars,' said Frankie. 'George has got to have one, too. He's crashed his at the moment.'

'We can hire him one,' said Bobby.

'Well, come and look at what we've got in s-s-stock,' said Badger.

'They look very smart,' said Frankie, dazzled by lurid hues of scarlet and apple-green.

'They *look* all right,' said Bobby darkly.

'That's r-r-remarkably good value in a s-s-second-hand Chrysler,' said Badger.

'No, not that one,' said Bobby. 'Whatever she buys has got to go at least forty miles.'

Badger cast his partner a look of reproach.

'The Standard is pretty much on its last legs,' mused Bobby. 'But I think it would just get you there. The Essex is a bit too good for the job. She'll go at least two hundred before breaking down.'

'All right,' said Frankie. 'I'll have the Standard.'

Badger drew his colleague a little aside.

'W-w-what do you think about p-p-price?' he murmured. 'Don't want to s-s-stick a friend of yours too much. T-t-t-ten pounds?'

'Ten pounds is all right,' said Frankie, entering the discussion. 'I'll pay for it now.'

'Who is she really?' asked Badger in a loud whisper.

Bobby whispered back.

'F-f-f-first time I ever knew anyone with a t-t-t-title who c-c-could pay cash,' said Badger with respect.

Bobby followed the other two out to the Bentley.

'When is this business going to take place?' he demanded.

'The sooner the better,' said Frankie. 'We thought tomorrow afternoon.'

'Look here, can't I be there? I'll put on a beard if you like.'

'Certainly not,' said Frankie. 'A beard would probably

ruin everything by falling off at the wrong moment. But I
don't see why you shouldn't be a motor-cyclist—with a lot
of cap and goggles. What do you think, George?'

George Arbuthnot spoke for the second time:

'All right,' he said, 'the more the merrier.'

His voice was even more melancholy than before.

CHAPTER 11

The Accident Happens

The rendezvous for the great accident party was fixed at a spot about a mile from Staverley village where the road to Staverley branched off from the main road to Andover.

All three arrived there safely, though Frankie's Standard had shown unmistakable signs of decrepitude at every hill.

The time fixed had been one o'clock.

'We don't want to be interrupted when we're staging the thing,' Frankie had said. 'Hardly anything ever goes down this road, I should imagine, but at lunch time we ought to be perfectly safe.'

They proceeded for half a mile on the side road and then Frankie pointed out the place she had selected for the accident to take place.

'It couldn't be better in my opinion,' she said. 'Straight down this hill and then, as you see, the road gives a sudden very sharp turn round that bulging bit of wall. The wall is actually the wall of Merroway Court. If we start the car and let it run down the hill it will crash straight into the wall and something pretty drastic ought to happen to it.'

'I should say so,' Bobby agreed. 'But someone ought to be on the lookout at the corner to be sure someone isn't coming round it in the opposite direction.'

'Quite right,' said Frankie. 'We don't want to involve anybody else in a mess and perhaps maim them for life. George can take his car down there and turn it as though he were coming from the other direction. Then when he waves a handkerchief it will show that all is clear.'

'You're looking very pale, Frankie,' said Bobby anxiously. 'Are you sure you're all right?'

'I'm made up pale,' explained Frankie. 'Ready for the concussion. You don't want me to be carried into the house blooming with health.'

'How wonderful women are,' said Bobby appreciatively. 'You look exactly like a sick monkey.'

'I think you're very rude,' said Frankie. 'Now, then, I shall go and prospect at the gate into Merroway Court. It's just this side of the bulge. There's no lodge, fortunately. When George waves his handkerchief and I wave mine, you start her off.'

'Right,' said Bobby. 'I'll stay on the running board to guide her until the pace gets too hot and then I'll jump off.'

'Don't hurt yourself,' said Frankie.

'I shall be extremely careful not to. It would complicate matters to have a real accident on the spot of the faked one.'

'Well, start off, George,' said Frankie.

George nodded, jumped into the second car and ran slowly down the hill. Bobby and Frankie stood looking after him.

'You'll—look after yourself, won't you, Frankie?' said

Bobby with a sudden gruffness. 'I mean—don't go doing anything foolish.'

'I shall be all right. Most circumspect. By the way, I don't think I'd better write to you direct. I'll write to George or my maid or someone or other to pass on to you.'

'I wonder if George is going to be a success in his profession.'

'Why shouldn't he?'

'Well, he doesn't seem to have acquired a chatty bedside manner yet.'

'I expect that will come,' said Frankie. 'I'd better be going now. I'll let you know when I want you to come down with the Bentley.'

'I'll get busy with the moustache. So long, Frankie.'

'They looked at each other for a moment, and then Frankie nodded and began to walk down the hill.

George had turned the car and then backed it round the bulge.

Frankie disappeared for a moment then reappeared in the road, waving a handkerchief. A second handkerchief waved from the bottom of the road at the turn.

Bobby put the car into third gear, then, standing on the footboard, he released the brake. The car moved grudgingly forward, impeded by being in gear. The slope, however, was sufficiently steep. The engine started. The car gathered way. Bobby steadied the steering wheel. At the last possible moment he jumped off.

The car went on down the hill and crashed into the wall with considerable force. All was well—the accident had taken place successfully.

Bobby saw Frankie run quickly to the scene of the crime and plop down amid the wreckage. George in his car came round the corner and pulled up.

With a sigh Bobby mounted his motor cycle and rode away in the direction of London.

At the scene of the accident things were busy.

'Shall I roll about in the road a bit,' asked Frankie, 'to get myself dusty?'

'You might as well,' said George. 'Here, give me your hat.'

He took it and inflicted a terrific dent on it. Frankie gave a faint anguished cry.

'That's the concussion,' explained George. 'Now, then, lie doggo just where you are. I think I heard a bicycle bell.'

Sure enough, at that moment, a boy of about seventeen came whistling round the corner. He stopped at once, delighted with the pleasurable spectacle that met his eyes.

'Ooer!' he ejaculated, ''as there been an accident?'

'No,' said George sarcastically. 'The young lady ran her car into the wall on purpose.'

Accepting, as he was meant to do, this remark as irony rather than the simple truth which it was, the boy said with relish:

'Looks bad, don't she? Is she dead?'

'Not yet,' said George. 'She must be taken somewhere at once. I'm a doctor. What's this place in here?'

'Merroway Court. Belongs to Mr Bassington-ffrench. He's a JP, he is.'

'She must be carried there at once,' said George authoritatively. 'Here, leave your bicycle and lend me a hand.'

Only too willing, the boy propped his bicycle against the wall and came to assist. Between them George and the boy carried Frankie up the drive to a pleasant old-fashioned-looking manor house.

Their approach had been observed, for an elderly butler came out to meet them.

'There's been an accident,' said George curtly. 'Is there a room I can carry this lady into? She must be attended to at once.'

The butler went back into the hall in a flustered way. George and the boy followed him up closely, still carrying the limp body of Frankie. The butler had gone into a room on the left and from there a woman emerged. She was tall, with red hair, and about thirty years of age. Her eyes were a light clear blue.

She dealt with the situation quickly.

'There is a spare bedroom on the ground floor,' she said. 'Will you bring her in there? Ought I to telephone for a doctor?'

'I am a doctor,' explained George. 'I was passing in my car and saw the accident occur.'

'Oh! how very fortunate. Come this way, will you?'

She showed them the way into a pleasant bedroom with windows giving on the garden.

'Is she badly hurt?' she inquired.

'I can't tell yet.'

Mrs Bassington-ffrench took the hint and retired. The

boy accompanied her and launched out into a description of the accident as though he had been an actual witness of it.

'Run smack into the wall she did. Car's all smashed up. There she was lying on the ground with her hat all dinted in. The gentleman, he was passing in his car—'

He proceeded *ad lib* till got rid of with a half-crown.

Meanwhile Frankie and George were conversing in careful whispers.

'George, darling, this won't blight your career, will it? They won't strike you off the register, or whatever it is, will they?'

'Probably,' said George gloomily. 'That is, if it ever comes out.'

'It won't,' said Frankie. 'Don't worry, George. I shan't let you down.' She added thoughtfully: 'You did it very well. I've never heard you talk so much before.'

George sighed. He looked at his watch.

'I shall give my examination another three minutes,' he said.

'What about the car?'

'I'll arrange with a garage to have that cleared up.'

'Good.'

George continued to study his watch. Finally he said with an air of relief:

'Time.'

'George,' said Frankie, 'you've been an angel. I don't know why you did it.'

'No more do I,' said George. 'Damn fool thing to do.'

He nodded to her.

'Bye bye. Enjoy yourself.'

'I wonder if I shall,' said Frankie.

She was thinking of that cool impersonal voice with the slight American accent.

George went in search of the owner of it, whom he found waiting for him in the drawing-room.

'Well,' he said abruptly. 'I'm glad to say it's not so bad as I feared. Concussion very slight and already passing off. She ought to stay quietly where she is for a day or so, though.' He paused. 'She seems to be a Lady Frances Derwent.'

'Oh, fancy!' said Mrs Bassington-ffrench. 'Then I know some cousins of hers—the Draycotts—quite well.'

'I don't know if it's inconvenient for you to have her here,' said George. 'But if she *could* stay where she is for a day or two . . .' Here George paused.

'Oh, of course. That will be quite all right, Dr—?'

'Arbuthnot. By the way, I'll see to the car business. I shall be passing a garage.'

'Thank you very much, Dr Arbuthnot. How very lucky you happened to be passing. I suppose a doctor ought to see her tomorrow just to see she's getting on all right.'

'Don't think it's necessary,' said George. 'All she needs is quiet.'

'But I should feel happier. And her people ought to know.'

'I'll attend to that,' said George. 'And as to the doctoring business—well, it seems she's a Christian Scientist and won't have doctors at any price. She wasn't too pleased at finding me in attendance.'

'Oh, dear!' said Mrs Bassington-ffrench.

'But she'll be quite all right,' said George reassuringly. 'You can take my word for it.'

'If you really think so, Dr Arbuthnot,' said Mrs Bassington-ffrench rather doubtfully.

'I do,' said George. 'Goodbye. Dear me. I left one of my instruments in the bedroom.'

He came rapidly into the room and up to the bedside.

'Frankie,' he said in a quick whisper. 'You're a Christian Scientist. Don't forget.'

'But why?'

'I had to do it. Only way.'

'All right,' said Frankie. 'I won't forget.'

CHAPTER 12

In the Enemy's Camp

'Well, here I am,' thought Frankie. 'Safely in the enemy's camp. Now, it's up to me.'

There was a tap on the door and Mrs Bassington-ffrench entered.

Frankie raised herself a little on her pillows.

'I'm so frightfully sorry,' she said in a faint voice. 'Causing you all this bother.'

'Nonsense,' said Mrs Bassington-ffrench. Frankie heard anew that cool attractive drawling voice with a slight American accent, and remembered that Lord Marchington had said that one of the Hampshire Bassington-ffrenches had married an American heiress. 'Dr Arbuthnot says you will be quite all right in a day or two if you just keep quiet.'

Frankie felt that she ought at this point to say something about 'error' or 'mortal mind', but was frightened of saying the wrong thing.

'He seems nice,' she said. 'He was very kind.'

'He seemed a most capable young man,' said Mrs

Agatha Christie

Bassington-ffrench. 'It was very fortunate that he just happened to be passing.'

'Yes, wasn't it? Not, of course, that I really needed him.'

'But you mustn't talk,' continued her hostess. 'I'll send my maid along with some things for you and then she can get you properly into bed.'

'It's frightfully kind of you.'

'Not at all.'

Frankie felt a momentary qualm as the other woman withdrew.

'A nice kind creature,' she said to herself. 'And beautifully unsuspecting.'

For the first time she felt that she was playing a mean trick on her hostess. Her mind had been so taken up with the vision of a murderous Bassington-ffrench pushing an unsuspecting victim over a precipice that lesser characters in the drama had not entered her imagination.

'Oh, well,' thought Frankie, 'I've got to go through with it now. But I wish she hadn't been so nice about it.'

She spent a dull afternoon and evening lying in her darkened room. Mrs Bassington-ffrench looked in once or twice to see how she was but did not stay.

The next day, however, Frankie admitted the daylight and expressed a desire for company and her hostess came and sat with her for some time. They discovered many mutual acquaintances and friends and by the end of the day, Frankie felt, with a guilty qualm, that they had become friends.

Mrs Bassington-ffrench referred several times to her husband and to her small boy, Tommy. She seemed a simple woman, deeply attached to her home, and yet, for some reason or other, Frankie fancied that she was not quite happy. There was an anxious expression in her eyes sometimes that did not agree with a mind at peace with itself.

On the third day Frankie got up and was introduced to the master of the house.

He was a big man, heavy jowled, with a kindly but rather abstracted air. He seemed to spend a good deal of his time shut up in his study. Yet Frankie judged him to be very fond of his wife, though interesting himself very little in her concerns.

Tommy, the small boy, was seven, and a healthy, mischievous child. Sylvia Bassington-ffrench obviously adored him.

'It's so nice down here,' said Frankie with a sigh.

She was lying out on a long chair in the garden.

'I don't know whether it's the bang on the head, or what it is, but I just don't feel I want to move. I'd like to lie here for days and days.'

'Well, do,' said Sylvia Bassington-ffrench in her calm, incurious tones. 'No, really, I mean it. Don't hurry back to town. You see,' she went on, 'it's a great pleasure to me to have you here. You're so bright and amusing. It quite cheers me up.'

'So she needs cheering up,' flashed across Frankie's mind.

At the same time she felt ashamed of herself.

'I feel we really have become friends,' continued the other woman.

Frankie felt still more ashamed.

It was a mean thing she was doing—mean—mean—mean. She would give it up! Go back to town—

Her hostess went on:

'It won't be too dull here. Tomorrow my brother-in-law is coming back. You'll like him, I'm sure. Everyone likes Roger.'

'He lives with you?'

'Off and on. He's a restless creature. He calls himself the ne'er-do-weel of the family, and perhaps it's true in a way. He never sticks to a job for long—in fact I don't believe he's ever done any real work in his life. But some people just are like that—especially in old families. And they're usually people with a great charm of manner. Roger is wonderfully sympathetic. I don't know what I should have done without him this spring when Tommy was ill.'

'What was the matter with Tommy?'

'He had a bad fall from the swing. It must have been tied on to a rotten branch and the branch gave way. Roger was very upset because he was swinging the child at the time—you know, giving him high ones, such as children love. We thought at first Tommy's spine was hurt, but it turned out to be a very slight injury and he's quite all right now.'

'He certainly looks it,' said Frankie, smiling, as she heard faint yells and whoops in the distance.

'I know. He seems in perfect condition. It's such a relief. He's had bad luck in accidents. He was nearly drowned last winter.'

'Was he really?' said Frankie thoughtfully.

She no longer meditated returning to town. The feeling of guilt had abated.

Accidents!

Did Roger Bassington-ffrench specialize in accidents, she wondered.

She said:

'If you're sure you mean it, I'd love to stay a little longer. But won't your husband mind my butting in like this?'

'Henry?' Mrs Bassington-ffrench's lips curled in a strange expression. 'No, Henry won't mind. Henry never minds anything—nowadays.'

Frankie looked at her curiously.

'If she knew me better she'd tell me something,' she thought to herself. 'I believe there are lots of odd things going on in this household.'

Henry Bassington-ffrench joined them for tea and Frankie studied him closely. There was certainly something odd about the man. His type was an obvious one—a jovial, sport-loving, simple country gentleman. But such a man ought not to sit twitching nervously, his nerves obviously on edge, now sunk in an abstraction from which it was impossible to rouse him, now giving out bitter and sarcastic replies to anything said to him. Not that he was always like that. Later that evening, at dinner, he showed out in quite a new light. He joked, laughed, told stories, and was, for a man of his abilities, quite brilliant. Too brilliant, Frankie felt. The brilliance was just as unnatural and out of character.

'He has such queer eyes,' she thought. 'They frighten me a little.'

And yet surely she did not suspect *Henry* Bassington-ffrench of anything? It was his brother, not he, who had been in Marchbolt on that fatal day.

As to the brother, Frankie looked forward to seeing him with eager interest. According to her and to Bobby, the man was a murderer. She was going to meet a murderer face to face.

She felt momentarily nervous.

Yet, after all, how could he guess?

How could he, in any way, connect her with a successfully accomplished crime?

'You're making a bogey for yourself out of nothing,' she said to herself.

Roger Bassington-ffrench arrived just before tea on the following afternoon.

Frankie did not meet him till tea time. She was still supposed to 'rest' in the afternoon.

When she came out on to the lawn where tea was laid, Sylvia said smiling:

'Here is our invalid. This is my brother-in-law, Lady Frances Derwent.'

Frankie saw a tall, slender young man of something over thirty with very pleasant eyes. Although she could see what Bobby meant by saying he ought to have a monocle and a toothbrush moustache, she herself was more inclined to notice the intense blue of his eyes. They shook hands.

He said: 'I've been hearing all about the way you tried to break down the park wall.'

'I'll admit,' said Frankie, 'that I'm the world's worst driver. But I was driving an awful old rattle-trap. My own car was laid up and I bought a cheap one second-hand.'

'She was rescued from the ruins by a very good-looking young doctor,' said Sylvia.

'He was rather sweet,' agreed Frankie.

Tommy arrived at this moment and flung himself upon his uncle with squeaks of joy.

'Have you brought me a Hornby train? You said you would. You said you would.'

'Oh, Tommy! You mustn't ask for things,' said Sylvia.

'That's all right, Sylvia. It was a promise. I've got your train all right, old man.' He looked casually at his sister-in-law. 'Isn't Henry coming to tea?'

'I don't think so.' The constrained note was in her voice. 'He isn't feeling awfully well today, I imagine.'

Then she said impulsively:

'Oh, Roger, I'm glad you're back.'

He put his hand on her arm for a minute.

'That's all right, Sylvia, old girl.'

After tea, Roger played trains with his nephew.

Frankie watched them, her mind in a turmoil.

Surely this wasn't the sort of man to push people over cliffs! This charming young man couldn't be a cold-blooded murderer!

But, then—she and Bobby must have been wrong all along. Wrong, that is, about this part of it.

She felt sure now that it wasn't Bassington-ffrench who had pushed Pritchard over the cliff.

Then who was it?

She was still convinced he had been pushed over. Who had done it? And who had put the morphia in Bobby's beer?

With the thought of morphia suddenly the explanation of Henry Bassington-ffrench's peculiar eyes came to her, with their pin-point pupils.

Was Henry Bassington-ffrench *a drug fiend*?

CHAPTER 13

Alan Carstairs

Strangely enough, she received confirmation of this theory no later than the following day, and it came from Roger.

They had been playing a single at tennis against each other and were sitting afterwards sipping iced drinks.

They had been talking about various indifferent subjects and Frankie had become more and more sensible of the charm of someone who had, like Roger Bassington-ffrench, travelled about all over the world. The family ne'er-do-weel, she could not help thinking, contrasted very favourably with his heavy, serious-minded brother.

A pause had fallen while these thoughts were passing through Frankie's mind. It was broken by Roger—speaking this time in an entirely different tone of voice.

'Lady Frances, I'm going to do a rather peculiar thing. I've known you less than twenty-four hours, but I feel instinctively that you're the one person I can ask advice from.'

'Advice?' said Frankie, surprised.

'Yes. I can't make up my mind between two different courses of action.'

He paused. He was leaning forward, swinging a racquet between his knees, a light frown on his forehead. He looked worried and upset.

'It's about my brother, Lady Frances.'

'Yes?'

'He is taking drugs. I am sure of it.'

'What makes you think so?' asked Frankie.

'Everything. His appearance. His extraordinary changes of mood. And have you noticed his eyes? The pupils are like pinpoints.'

'I had noticed that,' admitted Frankie. 'What do you think it is?'

'Morphia or some form of opium.'

'Has it been going on for long?'

'I date the beginning of it from about six months ago. I remember that he complained of sleeplessness a good deal. How he first came to take the stuff, I don't know, but I think it must have begun soon after then.'

'How does he get hold of it?' inquired Frankie practically.

'I think it comes to him by post. Have you noticed that he is particularly nervous and irritable some days at tea time?'

'Yes, I have.'

'I suspect that that is when he has finished up his supply and is waiting for more. Then, after the six o'clock post has come, he goes into his study and emerges for dinner in quite a different mood.'

Frankie nodded. She remembered that unnatural brilliance of conversation sometimes at dinner.

'But where does the supply come from?' she asked.

'Ah, that I don't know. No reputable doctor would give it to him. There are, I suppose, various sources where one could get it in London by paying a big price.'

Frankie nodded thoughtfully.

She was remembering having said to Bobby something about a gang of drug smugglers and his replying that one could not mix up too many crimes. It was queer that so soon in their investigations they should have come upon the traces of such a thing.

It was queerer that it should be the chief suspect who should draw her attention to the fact. It made her more inclined than ever to acquit Roger Bassington-ffrench of the charge of murder.

And yet there was the inexplicable matter of the changed photograph. The evidence against him, she reminded herself, was still exactly what it had been. On the other side was only the personality of the man himself. And everyone always said that murderers were charming people!

She shook off these reflections and turned to her companion.

'Why exactly are you telling me this?' she asked frankly.

'Because I don't know what to do about Sylvia,' he said simply.

'You think she doesn't know?'

'Of course she doesn't know. Ought I to tell her?'

'It's very difficult—'

'It *is* difficult. That's why I thought you might be able

to help me. Sylvia has taken a great fancy to you. She doesn't care much for any of the people round about, but she liked you at once, she tells me. What ought I to do, Lady Frances? By telling her I shall add a great burden to her life.'

'If she knew she might have some influence,' suggested Frankie.

'I doubt it. When it's a case of drug-taking, nobody, even the nearest and dearest, has any influence.'

'That's rather a hopeless point of view, isn't it?'

'It's a fact. There are ways, of course. If Henry would only consent to go in for a cure—there's a place actually near here. Run by a Dr Nicholson.'

'But he'd never consent, would he?'

'He might. You can catch a morphia taker in a mood of extravagant remorse sometimes when they'd do anything to cure themselves. I'm inclined to think that Henry might be got to that frame of mind more easily if he thought Sylvia didn't know—if her knowing was held over him as a kind of threat. If the cure was successful (they'd call it "nerves", of course) she never need know.'

'Would he have to go away for the cure?'

'The place I mean is about three miles from here, the other side of the village. It's run by a Canadian—Dr Nicholson. A very clever man, I believe. And, fortunately, Henry likes him. Hush—here comes Sylvia.'

Mrs Bassington-ffrench joined them, observing:

'Have you been very energetic?'

'Three sets,' said Frankie. 'And I was beaten every time.'

'You play a very good game,' said Roger.

'I'm terribly lazy about tennis,' said Sylvia. 'We must ask the Nicholsons over one day. She's very fond of a game. Why—what is it?' She had caught the glance the other two had exchanged.

'Nothing—only I happened to be talking about the Nicholsons to Lady Frances.'

'You'd better call her Frankie like I do,' said Sylvia. 'Isn't it odd how whenever one talks of any person or thing, somebody else does the same immediately afterwards?'

'They are Canadians, aren't they?' inquired Frankie.

'He is, certainly. I rather fancy she is English, but I'm not sure. She's a very pretty little thing—quite charming with the most lovely big wistful eyes. Somehow or other, I fancy she isn't terribly happy. It must be a depressing life.'

'He runs a kind of sanatorium, doesn't he?'

'Yes—nerve cases and people who take drugs. He's very successful, I believe. He's rather an impressive man.'

'You like him?'

'No,' said Sylvia abruptly, 'I don't.' And rather vehemently, after a moment or two, she added: 'Not at all.'

Later on, she pointed out to Frankie a photograph of a charming large-eyed woman which stood on the piano.

'That's Moira Nicholson. An appealing face, isn't it? A man who came down here with some friends of ours some time ago was quite struck with it. He wanted an introduction to her, I think.'

She laughed.

'I'll ask them to dinner tomorrow night. I'd like to know what you think of him.'

'Him?'

'Yes. As I told you, I dislike him, and yet he's quite an attractive-looking man.'

Something in her tone made Frankie look at her quickly, but Sylvia Bassington-ffrench had turned away and was taking some dead flowers out of a vase.

'I must collect my ideas,' thought Frankie, as she drew a comb through her thick dark hair when dressing for dinner that night. 'And,' she added resolutely, 'it's time I made a few experiments.'

Was, or was not, Roger Bassington-ffrench the villain she and Bobby assumed him to be?

She and Bobby had agreed that whoever had tried to put the latter out of the way must have easy access to morphia. Now in a way this held good for Roger Bassington-ffrench. If his brother received supplies of morphia by post, it would be easy enough for Roger to abstract a packet and use it for his own purposes.

'Mem.,' wrote Frankie on a sheet of paper: '(1) Find out where Roger was on the 16th—day when Bobby was poisoned.'

She thought she saw her way to doing that fairly clearly.

'(2),' she wrote. 'Produce picture of dead man and observe reactions if any. Also note if R.B.F. admits being in Marchbolt then.'

She felt slightly nervous over the second resolution. It

meant coming out into the open. On the other hand, the tragedy had happened in her own part of the world, and to mention it casually would be the most natural thing in the world.

She crumpled up the sheet of paper and burnt it.

She managed to introduce the first point fairly naturally at dinner.

'You know,' she said frankly to Roger. 'I can't help feeling that we've met before. And it wasn't very long ago, either. It wasn't, by any chance, at that party of Lady Shane's at Claridges. On the 16th it was.'

'It couldn't have been on the 16th,' said Sylvia quickly. 'Roger was here then. I remember, because we had a children's party that day and what I should have done without Roger I simply don't know.'

She gave a grateful glance at her brother-in-law and he smiled back at her.

'I don't feel I've ever met you before,' he said thoughtfully to Frankie, and added: 'I'm sure if I had I'd remember it.'

He said it rather nicely.

'One point settled,' thought Frankie. 'Roger Bassington-ffrench was not in Wales on the day that Bobby was poisoned.'

The second point came up fairly easily later. Frankie led the talk to country places, the dullness thereof, and the interest aroused by any local excitement.

'We had a man fall over the cliff last month,' she remarked. 'We were all thrilled to the core. I went to the inquest full of excitement, but it was all rather dull, really.'

'Was that a place called Marchbolt?' asked Sylvia suddenly.

Frankie nodded.

'Derwent Castle is only about seven miles from Marchbolt,' she explained.

'Roger, that must have been your man,' cried Sylvia.

Frankie looked inquiringly at him.

'I was actually in at the death,' said Roger. 'I stayed with the body till the police came.'

'I thought one of the Vicar's sons did that,' said Frankie.

'He had to go off to play the organ or something—so I took over.'

'How perfectly extraordinary,' said Frankie. 'I did hear somebody else had been there, too, but I never heard the name. So it was *you*?'

There was a general atmosphere of 'How curious. Isn't the world small?' Frankie felt she was doing this rather well.

'Perhaps that's where you saw me before—in Marchbolt?' suggested Roger.

'I wasn't there actually at the time of the accident,' said Frankie. 'I came back from London a couple of days afterwards. Were you at the inquest?'

'No. I went back to London the morning after the tragedy.'

'He had some absurd idea of buying a house down there,' said Sylvia.

'Utter nonsense,' said Henry Bassington-ffrench.

'Not at all,' said Roger good-humouredly.

'You know perfectly well, Roger, that as soon as you'd bought it, you'd get a fit of wanderlust and go off abroad again.'

'Oh, I shall settle down some day, Sylvia.'

'When you do you'd better settle down near us,' said Sylvia. 'Not go off to Wales.'

Roger laughed. Then he turned to Frankie.

'Any points of interest about the accident? It didn't turn out to be suicide or anything?'

'Oh, no, it was all painfully above board and some appalling relations came and identified the man. He was on a walking tour, it seems. Very sad, really, because he was awfully good-looking. Did you see his picture in the papers?'

'I think I did,' said Sylvia vaguely. 'But I don't remember.'

'I've got a cutting upstairs from our local paper.'

Frankie was all eagerness. She ran upstairs and came down with the cutting in her hand. She gave it to Sylvia. Roger came and looked over Sylvia's shoulder.

'Don't you think he's good-looking?' she demanded in a rather school-girlish manner.

'He is, rather,' said Sylvia. 'He looks very like that man, Alan Carstairs, don't you think so, Roger? I believe I remembered saying so at the time.'

'He's got quite a look of him here,' agreed Roger. 'But there wasn't much real resemblance, you know.'

'You can't tell from newspaper pictures, can you?' said Sylvia, as she handed the cutting back.

Frankie agreed that you couldn't.

The conversation passed to other matters.

107

Frankie went to bed undecided. Everyone seemed to have reacted with perfect naturalness. Roger's house-hunting stunt had been no secret.

The only thing she had succeeded in getting was a name. The name of Alan Carstairs.

CHAPTER 14

Dr Nicholson

Frankie attacked Sylvia the following morning.

She started by saying carelessly:

'What was that man's name you mentioned last night? Alan Carstairs, was it? I feel sure I've heard that name before.'

'I daresay you have. He's rather a celebrity in his way, I believe. He's a Canadian—a naturalist and big game hunter and explorer. I don't really know him. Some friends of ours, the Rivingtons, brought him down here one day for lunch. A very attractive man—big and bronzed and nice blue eyes.'

'I was sure I'd heard of him.'

'He'd never been over to this country before, I believe. Last year he went on a tour through Africa with that millionaire man, John Savage—the one who thought he had cancer and killed himself in that tragic way. Carstairs has been all over the world. East Africa, South America—simply everywhere, I believe.'

'Sounds a nice adventurous person,' said Frankie.

'Oh, he was. Distinctly attractive.'

'Funny—his being so like the man who fell over the cliff at Marchbolt,' said Frankie.

'I wonder if everyone has a double.'

They compared instances, citing Adolf Beck and referring lightly to the Lyons Mail. Frankie was careful to make no further references to Alan Carstairs. To show too much interest in him would be fatal.

In her own mind, however, she felt she was getting on now. She was quite convinced that Alan Carstairs had been the victim of the cliff tragedy at Marchbolt. He fulfilled all the conditions. He had no intimate friends or relations in this country and his disappearance was unlikely to be noticed for some time. A man who frequently ran off to East Africa and South America was not likely to be missed at once. Moreover, Frankie noted, although Sylvia Bassington-ffrench had commented on the resemblance in the newspaper reproduction, it had not occurred to her for a moment that it actually *was* the man.

That, Frankie thought, was rather an interesting bit of psychology.

We seldom suspect people who are 'news' of being people we have usually seen or met.

Very good, then. Alan Carstairs was the dead man. The next step was to learn more about Alan Carstairs. His connection with the Bassington-ffrenches seemed to have been of the slightest. He had been brought down there quite by chance by friends. What was the name? Rivington. Frankie stored it in her memory for future use.

That certainly was a possible avenue of inquiry. But it would be well to go slowly. Inquiries about Alan Carstairs must be very discreetly made.

'I don't want to be poisoned or knocked on the head,' thought Frankie with a grimace. 'They were ready enough to bump off Bobby for practically nothing at all—'

Her thoughts flew off at a tangent to that tantalizing phrase that had started the whole business.

Evans! Who was Evans? Where did Evans fit in?

'A dope gang,' decided Frankie. Perhaps some relation of Carstairs was victimized, and he was determined to bust it up. Perhaps he came to England for that purpose. Evans may have been one of the gang who had retired and gone to Wales to live. Carstairs had bribed Evans to give the others away and Evans had consented and Carstairs went there to see him, and someone followed him and killed him.

Was that somebody Roger Bassington-ffrench? It seemed very unlikely. The Caymans, now, were far more what Frankie imagined a gang of dope smugglers would be likely to be.

And yet—that photograph. If only there was some explanation of that photograph.

That evening, Dr Nicholson and his wife were expected to dinner. Frankie was finishing dressing when she heard their car drive up to the front door. Her window faced that way and she looked out.

A tall man was just alighting from the driver's seat of a dark-blue Talbot.

Frankie withdrew her head thoughtfully.

Carstairs had been a Canadian. Dr Nicholson was a Canadian. And Dr Nicholson had a dark-blue Talbot.

Absurd to build anything upon that, of course, but wasn't it just faintly suggestive?

Dr Nicholson was a big man with a manner that suggested great reserves of power. His speech was slow, on the whole he said very little, but contrived somehow to make every word sound significant. He wore strong glasses and behind them his very pale-blue eyes glittered reflectively.

His wife was a slender creature of perhaps twenty-seven, pretty, indeed beautiful. She seemed, Frankie, thought, slightly nervous and chattered rather feverishly as though to conceal the fact.

'You had an accident, I hear, Lady Frances,' said Dr Nicholson as he took his seat beside her at the dinner table.

Frankie explained the catastrophe. She wondered why she should feel so nervous doing so. The doctor's manner was simple and interested. Why should she feel as though she were rehearsing a defence to a charge that had never been made? Was there any earthly reason why the doctor should disbelieve in her accident?

'That was too bad,' he said, as she finished, having, perhaps, made a more detailed story of it than seemed strictly necessary. 'But you seem to have made a very good recovery.'

'We won't admit she's cured yet. We're keeping her with us,' said Sylvia.

The doctor's gaze went to Sylvia. Something like a very faint smile came to his lips but passed almost immediately.

'I should keep her with you as long as possible,' he said gravely.

Frankie was sitting between her host and Dr Nicholson. Henry Bassington-ffrench was decidedly moody tonight. His hands twitched, he ate next to nothing and he took no part in the conversation.

Mrs Nicholson, opposite, had a difficult time with him, and turned to Roger with obvious relief. She talked to him in a desultory fashion, but Frankie noticed that her eyes were never long absent from her husband's face.

Dr Nicholson was talking about life in the country.

'Do you know what a culture is, Lady Frances?'

'Do you mean book learning?' asked Frankie, rather puzzled.

'No, no. I was referring to germs. They develop, you know, in specially prepared serum. The country, Lady Frances, is a little like that. There is time and space and infinite leisure—suitable conditions, you see, for development.'

'Do you mean bad things?' asked Frankie, puzzled.

'That depends, Lady Frances, on the kind of germ cultivated.'

Idiotic conversation, thought Frankie, and why should it make me feel creepy, but it does!

She said flippantly:

'I expect I'm developing all sorts of dark qualities.'

He looked at her and said calmly:

'Oh, no, I don't think so, Lady Frances. I think you would always be on the side of law and order.'

Was there a faint emphasis on the word *law*?

Suddenly, across the table, Mrs Nicholson said:

'My husband prides himself on summing up character.'

Dr Nicholson nodded his head gently.

'Quite right, Moira. Little things interest me.' He turned to Frankie again. 'I had heard of your accident, you know. One thing about it intrigued me very much.'

'Yes?' said Frankie, her heart beating suddenly.

'The doctor who was passing—the one who brought you in here.'

'Yes?'

'He must have had a curious character—to turn his car before going to the rescue.'

'I don't understand.'

'Of course not. You were unconscious. But young Reeves, the message boy, came from Staverley on his bicycle and no car passed him, yet he comes round the corner, finds the smash, and the doctor's car pointing the same way he was going—towards London. You see the point? The doctor did not come from the direction of Staverley so he must have come the other way, down the hill. But in that case his car should have been pointing towards Staverley. But it wasn't. Therefore he must have turned it.'

'Unless he had come from Staverley some time before,' said Frankie.

'Then his car would have been standing there as you came down the hill. Was it?'

The pale-blue eyes were looking at her very intently through the thick glasses.

'I don't remember,' said Frankie. 'I don't think so.'

'You sound like a detective, Jasper,' said Mrs Nicholson. 'And all about nothing at all.'

'Little things interest me,' said Nicholson.

He turned to his hostess, and Frankie drew a breath of relief.

Why had he catechized her like that? How had he found out all about the accident? 'Little things interest me,' he had said. Was that all there was to it?

Frankie remembered the dark-blue Talbot saloon, and the fact that Carstairs had been a Canadian. It seemed to her that Dr Nicholson was a sinister man.

She kept out of his way after dinner, attaching herself to the gentle, fragile Mrs Nicholson. She noticed that all the time Mrs Nicholson's eyes still watched her husband. Was it love, Frankie wondered, or fear?

Nicholson devoted himself to Sylvia and at half-past ten he caught his wife's eye and they rose to go.

'Well,' said Roger after they had gone, 'what do you think of our Dr Nicholson? A very forceful personality, hasn't he?'

'I'm like Sylvia,' said Frankie. 'I don't think I like him very much. I like her better.'

'Good-looking, but rather a little idiot,' said Roger. 'She either worships him or is scared to death of him—I don't know which.'

'That's just what I wondered,' agreed Frankie.

'I don't like him,' said Sylvia, 'but I must admit that he's got a lot of—of *force*. I believe he's cured drug takers in the most marvellous way. People whose relations despaired utterly. They've gone there as a last hope and come out absolutely cured.'

'Yes,' cried Henry Bassington-ffrench suddenly. 'And do

115

you know what goes on there? Do you know the awful suffering and mental torment? A man's used to a drug and they cut him off it—cut him off it—till he goes raving mad for the lack of it and beats his head against the wall. That's what he does—your "forceful" doctor tortures people—tortures them—sends them to Hell—drives them mad . . .'

He was shaking violently. Suddenly he turned and left the room.

Sylvia Bassington-ffrench looked startled.

'What is the matter with Henry?' she said wonderingly. 'He seems very upset.'

Frankie and Roger dared not look at each other.

'He's not looked well all the evening,' ventured Frankie.

'No. I noticed that. He's very moody lately. I wish he hadn't given up riding. Oh, by the way, Dr Nicholson invited Tommy over tomorrow, but I don't like him going there very much—not with all those queer nerve cases and dope-takers.'

'I don't suppose the doctor would allow him to come into contact with them,' said Roger. 'He seems very fond of children.'

'Yes, I think it's a disappointment he hasn't got any of his own. Probably to her, too. She looks very sad—and terribly delicate.'

'She's like a sad Madonna,' said Frankie.

'Yes, that describes her very well.'

'If Dr Nicholson is so fond of children I suppose he came to your children's party?' said Frankie carelessly.

'Unfortunately he was away for a day or two just then. I think he had to go to London for some conference.'

'I see.'

They went up to bed. Before she went to sleep, Frankie wrote to Bobby.

CHAPTER 15

A Discovery

Bobby had had an irksome time. His forced inaction was exceedingly trying. He hated staying quietly in London and doing nothing.

He had been rung up on the telephone by George Arbuthnot who, in a few laconic words, told him that all had gone well. A couple of days later, he had a letter from Frankie, delivered to him by her maid, the letter having gone under cover to her at Lord Marchington's town house.

Since then he had heard nothing.

'Letter for you,' called out Badger.

Bobby came forward excitedly but the letter was one addressed in his father's handwriting, and postmarked Marchbolt.

At that moment, however, he caught sight of the neat black-gowned figure of Frankie's maid approaching down the Mews. Five minutes later he was tearing open Frankie's second letter.

Dear Bobby (wrote Frankie), *I think it's about time you came down. I've given them instructions at home that you're to have the Bentley whenever you ask for it. Get a chauffeur's livery—dark-green ours always are. Put it down to father at Harrods. It's best to be correct in details. Concentrate on making a good job of the moustache. It makes a frightful difference to anyone's face.*

Come down here and ask for me. You might bring me an ostensible note from Father. Report that the car is now in working order again. The garage here only holds two cars and as it's got the family Daimler and Roger Bassington-ffrench's two-seater in it, it is fortunately full up, so you will go to Staverley and put up there.

Get what local information you can when there— particularly about a Dr Nicholson who runs a place for dope patients. Several suspicious circumstances about him—he has a dark-blue Talbot saloon, he was away from home on the 16th when your beer was doctored, and he takes altogether too detailed an interest in the circumstances of my accident.

I think I've identified the corpse!!!

Au revoir, my fellow sleuth.

Love from your successfully concussed,

Frankie.

P.S. I shall post this myself.

Bobby's spirits rose with a bound.

Discarding his overalls and breaking the news of his immediate departure to Badger, he was about to hurry off when he remembered that he had not yet opened his father's letter. He did so with a rather qualified enthusiasm since the Vicar's letters were actuated by a spirit of duty rather than pleasure and breathed an atmosphere of Christian forbearance which was highly depressing.

The Vicar gave conscientious news of doings in Marchbolt, describing his own troubles with the organist and commenting on the unchristian spirit of one of his churchwardens. The rebinding of the hymn books was also touched upon. And the Vicar hoped that Bobby was sticking manfully to his job and trying to make good, and remained his ever affectionate father.

There was a postscript:

By the way, someone called who asked for your address in London. I was out at the time and he did not leave his name. Mrs Roberts describes him as a tall, stooping gentleman with pince-nez. He seemed very sorry to miss you and very anxious to see you again.

A tall, stooping man with pince-nez. Bobby ran over in his mind anyone of his acquaintance likely to fit that description but could think of nobody.

Suddenly a quick suspicion darted into his mind. Was this the forerunner of a new attempt upon his life? Were these mysterious enemies, or enemy, trying to track him down?

He sat still and did some serious thinking. They, whoever they were, had only just discovered that he had left the neighbourhood. All unsuspecting, Mrs Roberts had given his new address.

So that already they, whoever they were, might be keeping a watch upon the place. If he went out he would be followed—and just as things were at the moment that would never do.

'Badger,' said Bobby.

'Yes, old lad.'

'Come here.'

The next five minutes were spent in genuine hard work. At the end of ten minutes Badger could repeat his instructions by heart.

When he was word perfect, Bobby got into a two-seater Fiat dating from 1902 and drove dashingly down the Mews. He parked the Fiat in St James's Square and walked straight from there to his club. There he did some telephoning and a couple of hours later certain parcels were delivered to him. Finally, about half-past three, a chauffeur in dark green livery walked to St James's Square and went rapidly up to a large Bentley which had been parked there about half an hour previously. The parking attendant nodded to him—the gentleman who had left the car had remarked, stammering slightly as he did so, that his chauffeur would be fetching it shortly.

Bobby let in the clutch and drew neatly out. The abandoned Fiat still stood demurely awaiting its owner. Bobby, despite the intense discomfort of his upper lip, began to enjoy himself. He headed north, not south, and, before long, the powerful engine was forging ahead on the Great North Road.

It was only an extra precaution that he was taking. He was pretty sure that he was not being followed. Presently he turned off to the left and made his way by circuitous roads to Hampshire.

It was just after tea that the Bentley purred up the drive of Merroway Court, a stiff and correct chauffeur at the wheel.

'Hullo,' said Frankie lightly. 'There's the car.'

She went out to the front door. Sylvia and Roger came with her.

'Is everything all right, Hawkins?'

The chauffeur touched his cap.

'Yes, m'lady. She's been thoroughly overhauled.'

'That's all right, then.'

The chauffeur produced a note.

'From his lordship, m'lady.'

Frankie took it.

'You'll put up at the—what is it—Anglers' Arms in Staverley, Hawkins. I'll telephone in the morning if I want the car.'

'Very good, your ladyship.'

Bobby backed, turned and sped down the drive.

'I'm so sorry we haven't room here,' said Sylvia. 'It's a lovely car.'

'You get some pace out of that,' said Roger.

'I do,' admitted Frankie.

She was satisfied that no faintest quiver of recognition had shown on Roger's face. She would have been surprised if it had. She would not have recognized Bobby herself had she met him casually. The small moustache had a perfectly natural appearance, and that, with the stiff demeanour so uncharacteristic of the natural Bobby, completed the disguise enhanced by the chauffeur's livery.

The voice, too, had been excellent, and quite unlike Bobby's own. Frankie began to think that Bobby was far more talented than she had given him credit for being.

Meanwhile Bobby had successfully taken up his quarters at the Anglers' Arms.

It was up to him to create the part of Edward Hawkins, chauffeur to Lady Frances Derwent.

As to the behaviour of chauffeurs in private life, Bobby was singularly ill-informed, but he imagined that a certain haughtiness would not come amiss. He tried to feel himself a superior being and to act accordingly. The admiring attitude of various young women employed in the Anglers' Arms had a distinctly encouraging effect and he soon found that Frankie and her accident had provided the principal topic of conversation in Staverley ever since it had happened. Bobby unbent towards the landlord, a stout, genial person of the name of Thomas Askew, and permitted information to leak from him.

'Young Reeves, he was there and saw it happen,' declared Mr Askew.

Bobby blessed the natural mendacity of the young. The famous accident was now vouched for by an eye witness.

'Thought his last moment had come, he did,' went on Mr Askew. 'Straight for him down the hill it come—and then took the wall instead. A wonder the young lady wasn't killed.'

'Her ladyship takes some killing,' said Bobby.

'Had many accidents, has she?'

'She's been lucky,' said Bobby. 'But I assure you, Mr Askew, that when her ladyship's taken over the wheel from

123

me as she sometimes does—well, I've made sure my last hour has come.'

Several persons present shook their heads wisely and said they didn't wonder and it's just what they would have thought.

'Very nice little place you have here, Mr Askew,' said Bobby kindly and condescendingly. 'Very nice and snug.'

Mr Askew expressed gratification.

'Merroway Court the only big place in the neighbourhood?'

'Well, there's the Grange, Mr Hawkins. Not that you'd call that a place exactly. There's no family living there. No, it had been empty for years until this American doctor took it.'

'An American doctor?'

'That's it—Nicholson his name is. And if you ask me, Mr Hawkins, there are some very queer goings on there.'

The barmaid at this point remarked that Dr Nicholson gave her the shivers, he did.

'Goings on, Mr Askew?' said Bobby. 'Now, what do you mean by goings on?'

Mr Askew shook his head darkly.

'There's those there that don't want to be there. Put away by their relations. I assure you, Mr Hawkins, the moanings and the shrieks and the groans that go on there you wouldn't believe.'

'Why don't the police interfere?'

'Oh, well, you see, it's supposed to be all right. Nerve cases, and such like. Loonies that aren't so very bad. The gentleman's a doctor and it's all all right, so to speak—'

Here the landlord buried his face in a pint pot and emerged again to shake his head in a very doubtful fashion.

'Ah!' said Bobby in a dark and meaning way. 'If we knew everything that went on in these places . . .'

And he, too, applied himself to a pewter pot.

The barmaid chimed in eagerly.

'That's what I say, Mr Hawkins. What goes on there? Why, one night a poor young creature escaped—in her nightgown she was—and the doctor and a couple of nurses out looking for her. "Oh! don't let them take me back!" That's what she was crying out. Pitiful it was. And about her being rich really and her relations having her put away. But they took her back, they did, and the doctor he explained that she'd got a persecution mania—that's what he called it. Kind of thinking everyone was against her. But I've often wondered—yes, I have. I've often wondered . . .'

'Ah!' said Mr Askew. 'It's easy enough to say—'

Somebody present said that there was no knowing what went on in places. And somebody else said that was right.

Finally the meeting broke up and Bobby announced his intention of going for a stroll before turning in.

The Grange was, he knew, on the other side of the village from Merroway Court, so he turned his footsteps in that direction. What he had heard that evening seemed to him worthy of attention. A lot of it could, of course, be discounted. Villages are usually prejudiced against newcomers, and still more so if the newcomer is of a different nationality. If Nicholson ran a place for curing drug takers, in all probability there would be strange sounds issuing from it—groans and even shrieks might be heard without any sinister reason for them, but all the same, the story of the escaping girl struck Bobby unpleasantly.

Supposing the Grange were really a place where people were kept against their will? A certain amount of genuine cases might be taken as camouflage.

At this point in his meditations Bobby arrived at a high wall with an entrance of wrought-iron gates. He stepped up to the gates and tried one gently. It was locked. Well, after all, why not?

And yet somehow, the touch of that locked gate gave him a faintly sinister feeling. The place was like a prison.

He moved a little farther along the road measuring the wall with his eye. Would it be possible to climb over? The wall was smooth and high and presented no accommodating crannies. He shook his head. Suddenly he came upon a little door. Without much real hope he tried it. To his surprise it yielded. It was not locked.

'Bit of an oversight here,' thought Bobby with a grin.

He slipped through, closing the door softly behind him.

He found himself on a path leading through a shrubbery. He followed the path which twisted a good deal—in fact, it reminded Bobby of the one in *Alice Through the Looking Glass*.

Suddenly, without any warning, the path gave a sharp turn and emerged into an open space close to the house. It was a moonlit night and the space was clearly lit. Bobby had stepped full into the moonlight before he could stop himself.

At the same moment a woman's figure came round the corner of the house. She was treading very softly, glancing from side to side with—or so it seemed to the watching Bobby—the nervous alertness of a hunted animal. Suddenly she stopped dead and stood, swaying as though she would fall.

Bobby rushed forward and caught her. Her lips were white and it seemed to him that never had he seen such an awful fear on any human countenance.

'It's all right,' he said reassuringly in a very low voice. 'It's quite all right.'

The girl, for she was little more, moaned faintly, her eyelids half closed.

'I'm so frightened,' she murmured. 'I'm so terribly frightened.'

'What's the matter?' said Bobby.

The girl only shook her head and repeated faintly:

'I'm so frightened. I'm so horribly frightened.'

Suddenly some sound seemed to come to her ears. She sprang upright, away from Bobby. Then she turned to him.

'Go away,' she said. 'Go away at once.'

'I want to help you,' said Bobby.

'Do you?' She looked at him for a minute or two, a strange searching and moving glance. It was as though she explored his soul.

Then she shook her head.

'No one can help me.'

'I can,' said Bobby. 'I'd do anything. Tell me what it is that frightens you so.'

She shook her head.

'Not now. Oh! quick—they're coming! You can't help me unless you go now. At once—at once.'

127

Bobby yielded to her urgency.

With a whispered: 'I'm at the Anglers' Arms,' he plunged back along the path. The last he saw of her was an urgent gesture bidding him hurry.

Suddenly he heard footsteps on the path in front of him. Someone was coming along the path from the little door. Bobby plunged abruptly into the bushes at the side of the path.

He had not been mistaken. A man was coming along the path. He passed close to Bobby but it was too dark for the young man to see his face.

When he had passed, Bobby resumed his retreat. He felt that he could do nothing more that night.

Anyway, his head was in a whirl.

For he had recognized the girl—recognized her beyond any possible doubt.

She was the original of the photograph which had so mysteriously disappeared.

CHAPTER 16

Bobby Becomes a Solicitor

'Mr Hawkins?'

'Yes,' said Bobby, his voice slightly muffled owing to a large mouthful of bacon and eggs.

'You're wanted on the telephone.'

Bobby took a hasty gulp of coffee, wiped his mouth and rose. The telephone was in a small dark passage. He took up the receiver.

'Hullo,' said Frankie's voice.

'Hullo, Frankie,' said Bobby incautiously.

'This is Lady Frances Derwent speaking,' said the voice coldly. 'Is that Hawkins?'

'Yes, m'lady.'

'I shall want the car at ten o'clock to take me up to London.'

'Very good, your ladyship.'

Bobby replaced the receiver.

'When does one say, "my lady", and when does one say, "your ladyship"?' he cogitated. 'I ought to know, but I

129

don't. It's the sort of thing that will lead a real chauffeur or butler to catch me out.'

At the other end, Frankie hung up the receiver and turned to Roger Bassington-ffrench.

'It's a nuisance,' she observed lightly, 'to have to go up to London today. All owing to Father's fuss.'

'Still,' said Roger, 'you'll be back this evening?'

'Oh, yes!'

'I'd half thought of asking you if you'd give me a lift to town,' said Roger carelessly.

Frankie paused for an infinitesimal second before her answer—given with an apparent readiness.

'Why, of course,' she said.

'But on second thoughts I don't think I will go up today,' went on Roger. 'Henry's looking even odder than usual. Somehow I don't very much like leaving Sylvia alone with him.'

'I know,' said Frankie.

'Are you driving yourself?' asked Roger casually as they moved away from the telephone.

'Yes, but I shall take Hawkins. I've got some shopping to do as well and it's a nuisance if you're driving yourself—you can't leave the car anywhere.'

'Yes, of course.'

He said no more, but when the car came around, Bobby at the wheel very stiff and correct of demeanour, he came out on the doorstep to see her off.

'Goodbye,' said Frankie.

Under the circumstances she did not think of holding out a hand, but Roger took hers and held it a minute.

'You *are* coming back?' he said with curious insistence.
Frankie laughed.

'Of course. I only meant goodbye till this evening.'

'Don't have any more accidents.'

'I'll let Hawkins drive if you like.'

She sprang in beside Bobby, who touched his cap. The
car moved off down the drive, Roger still standing on
the step looking after it.

'Bobby,' said Frankie, 'do you think it possible that Roger
might fall for me?'

'Has he?' inquired Bobby.

'Well, I just wondered.'

'I expect you know the symptoms pretty well,' said Bobby.
But he spoke absently. Frankie shot him a quick glance.

'Has anything—happened?' she asked.

'Yes, it has. Frankie, I've found the original of the photograph!'

'You mean—*the* one—the one you talked so much
about—the one that was in the dead man's pocket?'

'Yes.'

'*Bobby!* I've got a few things to tell you, but nothing to
this. Where did you find her?'

Bobby jerked his head back over his shoulder.

'In Dr Nicholson's nursing home.'

'Tell me.'

Carefully and meticulously Bobby described the events
of the previous night. Frankie listened breathlessly.

'Then *we are* on the right track,' she said. 'And Dr
Nicholson *is* mixed up in all this! Bobby, I'm afraid of that
man.'

'What is he like?'

'Oh! big and forceful—and he watches you. Very intently behind glasses. And you feel he knows all about you.'

'When did you meet him?'

'He came to dinner.'

She described the dinner party and Dr Nicholson's insistent dwelling on the details of her 'accident'.

'I felt he was suspicious,' she ended up.

'It's certainly queer his going into details like that,' said Bobby. 'What do you think is at the bottom of all this business, Frankie?'

'Well, I'm beginning to think that your suggestion of a dope gang, which I was so haughty about at the time, isn't such a bad guess after all.'

'With Dr Nicholson at the head of the gang?'

'Yes. This nursing home business would be a very good cloak for that sort of thing. He'd have a certain supply of drugs on the premises quite legitimately. While pretending to cure drug cases, he might really be supplying them with the stuff.'

'That seems plausible enough,' agreed Bobby.

'I haven't told you yet about Henry Bassington-ffrench.'

Bobby listened attentively to her description of her host's idiosyncrasies.

'His wife doesn't suspect?'

'I'm sure she doesn't.'

'What is she like? Intelligent?'

'I never thought exactly. No, I suppose she isn't very. And yet in some ways she seems quite shrewd. A frank, pleasant woman.'

'And our Bassington-ffrench?'

'There I'm puzzled,' said Frankie slowly. 'Do you think, Bobby, that just possibly we might be all wrong about him?'

'Nonsense,' said Bobby. 'We worked it all out and decided that he must be the villain of the piece.'

'Because of the photograph?'

'Because of the photograph. No one else *could* have changed that photograph for the other.'

'I know,' said Frankie. 'But that one incident is all that we have against him.'

'It's quite enough.'

'I suppose so. And yet—'

'Well?'

'I don't know, but I have a queer sort of feeling that he's innocent—that he's not concerned in the matter at all.'

Bobby looked at her coldly.

'Did you say that he had fallen for you or that you had fallen for him?' he inquired politely.

Frankie flushed.

'Don't be so absurd, Bobby. I just wondered if there couldn't be some innocent explanation, that's all.'

'I don't see that there can be. Especially now that we've actually found the girl in the neighbourhood. That seems to clinch matters. If we only had some inkling as to who the dead man was—'

'Oh, but I have. I told you so in my letter. I'm nearly sure that the murdered man was somebody called Alan Carstairs.'

Once more she plunged into narrative.

'You know,' said Bobby, 'we really are getting on. Now we must try, more or less, to reconstruct the crime. Let's spread out our facts and see what sort of a job we can make of it.'

He paused for a moment and the car slackened speed as though in sympathy. Then he pressed his foot down once more on the accelerator and at the same time spoke.

'First, we'll assume that you are right about Alan Carstairs. He certainly fulfils the conditions. He's the right sort of man, he led a wandering life, he had very few friends and acquaintances in England, and if he disappeared he wasn't likely to be missed or sought after.

'So far, good. Alan Carstairs comes down to Staverley with these people—what did you say their name was—?'

'Rivington. There's a possible channel of inquiry there. In fact, I think we ought to follow it up.'

'We will. Very well, Carstairs comes down to Staverley with the Rivingtons. Now, is there anything in that?'

'You mean did he get them to bring him down here deliberately?'

'That's what I mean. Or was it just a casual chance? Was he brought down here by them and did he then come across the girl by accident just as I did? I presume he knew her before or he wouldn't have had her photograph on him.'

'The alternative being,' said Frankie thoughtfully, 'that he was already on the track of Nicholson and his gang.'

'And used the Rivingtons as a means of getting to this part of the world naturally?'

'That's quite a possible theory,' said Frankie. 'He may have been on the track of this gang.'

'Or simply on the track of the girl.'

'The girl?'

'Yes. She may have been abducted. He may have come over to England to find her.'

'Well, but if he had tracked her down to Staverley, why should he go off to Wales?'

'Obviously, there's a lot we don't know yet,' said Bobby.

'Evans,' said Frankie thoughtfully. 'We don't get any clues as to Evans. The Evans part of it must have to do with Wales.'

They were both silent for a moment or two. Then Frankie woke up to her surroundings.

'My dear, we're actually at Putney Hill. It seems like five minutes. Where are we going and what are we doing?'

'That's for you to say. I don't even know why we've come up to town.'

'The journey to town was only an excuse for getting a talk with you. I couldn't very well risk being seen walking the lanes at Staverley deep in conversation with my chauffeur. I used the pseudo-letter from Father as an excuse for driving up to town and talking to you on the way and even that was nearly wrecked by Bassington-ffrench coming too.'

'That would have torn it severely.'

'Not really. We'd have dropped him wherever he liked and then we'd have gone on to Brook Street and talked there. I think we'd better do that, anyway. Your garage place may be watched.'

Bobby agreed and related the episode of the inquiries made about him at Marchbolt.

'We'll go to the Derwents' town residence,' said Frankie. 'There's no one there but my maid and a couple of caretakers.'

They drove to Brook Street. Frankie rang the bell and was admitted, Bobby remaining outside. Presently Frankie opened the door again and beckoned him in. They went upstairs to the big drawing-room and pulled up some of the blinds and removed the swathing from one of the sofas.

'There's one other thing I forgot to tell you,' said Frankie. 'On the 16th, the day you were poisoned, Bassington-ffrench was at Staverley, but Nicholson was away—supposedly at a conference in London. And his car is a dark-blue Talbot.'

'And he has access to morphia,' said Bobby.

They exchanged significant glances.

'It's not exactly evidence, I suppose,' said Bobby, 'but it fits in nicely.'

Frankie went to a side table and returned with a telephone directory.

'What are you going to do?'

'I'm looking up the name Rivington.'

She turned pages rapidly.

'A. Rivington & Sons, Builders. B. A. C. Rivington, Dental Surgeon. D. Rivington, Shooters Hill, I think not. Miss Florence Rivington. Col. H. Rivington, D.S.O.—that's more like it—Tite Street, Chelsea.'

She continued her search.

'There's M. R. Rivington, Onslow Square. He's possible. And there's a William Rivington at Hampstead. I think Onslow Square and Tite Street are the most likely ones. The Rivingtons, Bobby, have got to be seen without delay.'

'I think you're right. But what are we going to say? Think up a few good lies, Frankie. I'm not much good at that sort of thing.'

Frankie reflected for a minute or two.

'I think,' she said, 'that you'll have to go. Do you feel you could be the junior partner of a solicitors' firm?'

'That seems a most gentlemanly rôle,' said Bobby. 'I was afraid you might think of something much worse than that. All the same, it's not quite in character, is it?'

'How do you mean?'

'Well, solicitors never do make personal visits, do they? Surely they always write letters at six and eightpence a time, or else write and ask someone to keep an appointment at their office.'

'This particular firm of solicitors is unconventional,' said Frankie. 'Wait a minute.'

She left the room and returned with a card.

'*Mr Frederick Spragge*,' she said, handing it to Bobby. 'You are a young member of the firm of Spragge, Spragge, Jenkinson and Spragge, of Bloomsbury Square.'

'Did you invent that firm, Frankie?'

'Certainly not. They're Father's solicitors.'

'And suppose they have me up for impersonation?'

'That's all right. There isn't any young Spragge. The only Spragge is about a hundred, and anyway he eats out of my hand. I'll fix him if things go wrong. He's a great snob—he loves lords and dukes, however little money he makes out of them.'

'What about clothes? Shall I ring up Badger to bring some along?'

Frankie looked doubtful.

'I don't want to insult your clothes, Bobby,' she said. 'Or throw your poverty in your teeth, or anything like that. But will they carry conviction? I think, myself, that we'd better raid Father's wardrobe. His clothes won't fit you too badly.'

A quarter of an hour later, Bobby, attired in a morning coat and striped trousers of exquisitely correct cut and passable fit, stood surveying himself in Lord Marchington's pier glass.

'Your father does himself well in clothes,' he remarked graciously. 'With the might of Savile Row behind me, I feel a great increase of confidence.'

'I suppose you'll have to stick to your moustache,' said Frankie.

'It's sticking to me,' said Bobby. 'It's a work of art that couldn't be repeated in a hurry.'

'You'd better keep it, then. Though it's more legal-looking to be clean-shaven.'

'It's better than a beard,' said Bobby. 'Now, then, Frankie, do you think your father could lend me a hat?'

CHAPTER 17

Mrs Rivington Talks

'Supposing,' said Bobby, pausing on the doorstep, 'that Mr M. R. Rivington of Onslow Square is himself a solicitor? That would be a blow.'

'You'd better try the Tite Street colonel first,' said Frankie. 'He won't know anything about solicitors.'

Accordingly, Bobby took a taxi to Tite Street. Colonel Rivington was out. Mrs Rivington, however, was at home. Bobby delivered over to the smart parlourmaid his card on which he had written: 'From Messrs Spragge, Spragge, Jenkinson & Spragge. Very Urgent.'

The card and Lord Marchington's clothes produced their effect upon the parlourmaid. She did not for an instant suspect that Bobby had come to sell miniatures or tout for insurances. He was shown into a beautifully and expensively furnished drawing-room and presently Mrs Rivington, beautifully and expensively dressed and made up, came into the room.

'I must apologize for troubling you, Mrs Rivington,' said Bobby. 'But the matter was rather urgent and we wished to avoid the delay of letters.'

That any solicitor could ever wish to avoid delay seemed so transparently impossible that Bobby for a moment wondered anxiously whether Mrs Rivington would see through the pretence.

Mrs Rivington, however, was clearly a woman of more looks than brains who accepted things as they were presented to her.

'Oh, do sit down!' she said. 'I got the telephone message just now from your office saying that you were on your way here.'

Bobby mentally applauded Frankie for this last minute flash of brilliance.

He sat down and endeavoured to look legal.

'It is about our client, Mr Alan Carstairs,' he said.

'Oh, yes?'

'He may have mentioned that we were acting for him.'

'Did he now? I believe he did,' said Mrs Rivington, opening very large blue eyes. She was clearly of a suggestible type. 'But of course, I know about you. You acted for Dolly Maltravers, didn't you, when she shot that dreadful dressmaker man? I suppose you know all the details?'

She looked at him with frank curiosity. It seemed to Bobby that Mrs Rivington was going to be easy meat.

'We know a lot that never comes into court,' he said, smiling.

'Oh, I suppose you must.' Mrs Rivington looked at him enviously. 'Tell me, did she really—I mean, was she dressed as that woman said?'

'The story was contradicted in court,' said Bobby solemnly. He slightly dropped the corner of his eyelid.

140

'Oh, I see,' breathed Mrs Rivington, enraptured.

'About Mr Carstairs,' said Bobby, feeling that he had now established friendly relations and could get on with his job. 'He left England very suddenly, as perhaps you know?'

Mrs Rivington shook her head.

'Has he left England? I didn't know. We haven't seen him for some time.'

'Did he tell you how long he expected to be over here?'

'He said he might be here for a week or two or it might be six months or a year.'

'Where was he staying?'

'At the Savoy.'

'And you saw him last—when?'

'Oh, about three weeks or a month ago. I can't remember.'

'You took him down to Staverley one day?'

'Of course! I believe that's the last time we saw him. He rang up to know when he could see us. He'd just arrived in London and Hubert was very put out because we were going up to Scotland the next day, and we were going down to Staverley to lunch and dining out with some dreadful people that we couldn't get rid of, and he wanted to see Carstairs because he liked him so much, and so I said: "My dear, let's take him down to the Bassington-ffrenches with us. They won't mind." And we did. And, of course, they didn't.'

She came breathlessly to a pause.

'Did he tell you his reasons for being in England?' asked Bobby.

'No. Did he have any? Oh yes, I know. We thought it

was something to do with that millionaire man, that friend of his, who had such a tragic death. Some doctor told him he had cancer and he killed himself. A very wicked thing for a doctor to do, don't you think so? And they're often quite wrong. Our doctor said the other day that my little girl had measles and it turned out to be a sort of heat rash. I told Hubert I should change him.'

Ignoring Mrs Rivington's treatment of doctors as though they were library books, Bobby returned to the point.

'Did Mr Carstairs know the Bassington-ffrenches?'

'Oh, no! But I think he liked them. Though he was very queer and moody on the way back. I suppose something that had been said must have upset him. He's a Canadian, you know, and I often think Canadians are so touchy.'

'You don't know what it was that upset him?'

'I haven't the least idea. The silliest things do it sometimes, don't they?'

'Did he take any walks in the neighbourhood?' asked Bobby.

'Oh, no! What a very odd idea!' She stared at him.

Bobby tried again.

'Was there a party? Did he meet any of the neighbours?'

'No, it was just ourselves and them. But it's odd your saying that—'

'Yes,' said Bobby eagerly, as she paused.

'Because he asked a most frightful lot of questions about some people who lived near there.'

'Do you remember the name?'

'No, I don't. It wasn't anyone very interesting—some doctor or other.'

'Dr Nicholson?'

'I believe that was the name. He wanted to know all about him and his wife and when they came there—all sorts of things. It seemed so odd when he didn't know them, and he wasn't a bit a curious man as a rule. But, of course, perhaps he was only making conversation, and couldn't think of anything to say. One does do things like that sometimes.'

Bobby agreed that one did and asked how the subject of the Nicholsons had come up, but that Mrs Rivington was unable to tell him. She had been out with Henry Bassington-ffrench in the garden and had come in to find the others discussing the Nicholsons.

So far, the conversation had proceeded easily, Bobby pumping the lady without any camouflage, but she now displayed a sudden curiosity.

'But what is it you want to know about Mr Carstairs?' she asked.

'I really wanted his address,' explained Bobby. 'As you know, we act for him and we've just had a rather important cable from New York—you know, there's rather a serious fluctuation in the dollar just now—'

Mrs Rivington nodded with desperate intelligence.

'And so,' continued Bobby rapidly, 'we wanted to get into touch with him—to get his instructions—and he hasn't left an address—and, having heard him mention he was a friend of yours, I thought you might possibly have news of him.'

'Oh, I see,' said Mrs Rivington, completely satisfied. 'What a pity. But he's always rather a vague man, I should think.'

'Oh, distinctly so,' said Bobby. 'Well,' he rose, 'I apologize for taking up so much of your time.'

'Oh, not at all,' said Mrs Rivington. 'And it's so interesting to know that Dolly Maltravers really did—as you say she did.'

'I said nothing at all,' said Bobby.

'Yes, but then lawyers are so discreet, aren't they?' said Mrs Rivington with a little gurgle of laughter.

'So that's all right,' thought Bobby, as he walked away down Tite Street. 'I seem to have taken Dolly Whatsername's character away for good, but I daresay she deserves it, and that charming idiot of a woman will never wonder why, if I wanted Carstairs' address, I didn't simply ring up and ask for it!'

Back in Brook Street he and Frankie discussed the matter from every angle.

'It looks as though it were really pure chance that took him to the Bassington-ffrenches,' said Frankie thoughtfully.

'I know. But evidently when he was down there some chance remark directed his attention to the Nicholsons.'

'So that, really, it is Nicholson who is at the heart of the mystery, not the Bassington-ffrenches?'

Bobby looked at her.

'Still intent on whitewashing your hero,' he inquired coldly.

'My dear, I'm only pointing out what it looks like. It's the mention of Nicholson and his nursing home that excited Carstairs. Being taken down to the Bassington-ffrenches was a pure matter of chance. You must admit that.'

'It seems like it.'

144

'Why only "seems"?'

'Well, there is just one other possibility. In some way, Carstairs may have found out that the Rivingtons were going down to lunch with the Bassington-ffrenches. He may have overheard some chance remark in a restaurant—at the Savoy, perhaps. So he rings them up, very urgent to see them, and what he hopes may happen does happen. They're very booked up and they suggest his coming down with them—their friends won't mind and they do so want to see him. That is possible, Frankie.'

'It is *possible*, I suppose. But it seems a very roundabout method of doing things.'

'No more roundabout than your accident,' said Bobby.

'My accident was vigorous direct action,' said Frankie coldly.

Bobby removed Lord Marchington's clothes and replaced them where he had found them. Then he donned his chauffeur's uniform once more and they were soon speeding back to Staverley.

'If Roger has fallen for me,' said Frankie demurely, 'he'll be pleased I've come back so soon. He'll think I can't bear to be away from him for long.'

'I'm not sure that you can bear it, either,' said Bobby. 'I've always heard that really dangerous criminals were singularly attractive.'

'Somehow I can't believe he is a criminal.'

'So you remarked before.'

'Well, I feel like that.'

'You can't get over the photograph.'

'Damn the photograph!' said Frankie.

Bobby drove up the drive in silence. Frankie sprang out and went into the house without a backward glance. Bobby drove away.

The house seemed very silent. Frankie glanced at the clock. It was half-past two.

'They don't expect me back for hours yet,' she thought. 'I wonder where they are?'

She opened the door of the library and went in, stopping suddenly on the threshold.

Dr Nicholson was sitting on the sofa, holding both Sylvia Bassington-ffrench's hands in his.

Sylvia jumped to her feet and came across the room towards Frankie.

'He's been telling me,' she said.

Her voice was stifled. She put both hands to her face as though to hide it from view.

'It's too terrible,' she sobbed, and, brushing past Frankie, she ran out of the room.

Dr Nicholson had risen. Frankie advanced a step or two towards him. His eyes, watchful as ever, met hers.

'Poor lady,' he said suavely. 'It has been a great shock to her.'

The muscles at the corner of his mouth twitched. For a moment or two Frankie fancied that he was amused. And then, quite suddenly, she realized that it was quite a different emotion.

The man was angry. He was holding himself in, hiding his anger behind a suave bland mask, but the emotion was there. It was all he could do to hold that emotion in.

There was a moment's pause.

146

'It was best that Mrs Bassington-ffrench should know the truth,' said the doctor. 'I want her to induce her husband to place himself in my hands.'

'I'm afraid,' said Frankie gently, 'that I interrupted you.' She paused. 'I came back sooner than I meant.'

CHAPTER 18

The Girl of the Photograph

On Bobby's return to the inn he was greeted with the information that someone was waiting to see him.

'It's a lady. You'll find her in Mr Askew's little sitting-room.'

Bobby made his way there slightly puzzled. Unless she had flown there on wings he could not see how Frankie could possibly have got to the Anglers' Arms ahead of him, and that his visitor could be anyone else but Frankie never occurred to him.

He opened the door of the small room which Mr Askew kept as his private sitting-room. Sitting bolt upright in a chair was a slender figure dressed in black—the girl of the photograph.

Bobby was so astonished that for a moment or two he could not speak. Then he noticed that the girl was terribly nervous. Her small hands were trembling and closed and unclosed themselves on the arm of the chair. She seemed too nervous even to speak, but her large eyes held a kind of terrified appeal.

'So it's you?' said Bobby at last. He shut the door behind him and came forward to the table.

Still the girl did not speak—still those large, terrified eyes looked into his. At last words came—a mere hoarse whisper.

'You said—you said—you'd help me. Perhaps I shouldn't have come—'

Here Bobby broke in, finding words and assurance at the same time.

'Shouldn't have come? Nonsense. You did quite right to come. Of course, you should have come. And I'll do anything—anything in the world—to help you. Don't be frightened. You're quite safe now.'

The colour rose a little in the girl's face. She said abruptly:

'Who are you? You're—you're—not a chauffeur. I mean, you may be a chauffeur, but you're not one really.'

Bobby understood her meaning in spite of the confused form of words in which she had cloaked them.

'One does all sorts of jobs nowadays,' he said. 'I used to be in the Navy. As a matter of fact, I'm not exactly a chauffeur—but that doesn't matter now. But, anyway, I assure you you can trust me and—and tell me all about it.'

Her flush had deepened.

'You must think me mad,' she murmured. 'You must think me quite mad.'

'No, no.'

'Yes—coming here like this. But I was so frightened—so terribly frightened—' Her voice died away. Her eyes widened as though they saw some vision of terror.

Bobby seized her hand firmly.

'Look here,' he said, 'it's quite all right. Everything's going to be all right. You're safe now—with—with a friend. Nothing shall happen to you.'

He felt the answering pressure of her fingers.

'When you stepped out into the moonlight the other night,' she said in a low, hurried voice, 'it was—it was like a dream—a dream of deliverance. I didn't know who you were or where you came from, but it gave me hope and I determined to come and find you—and—tell you.'

'That's right,' said Bobby encouragingly. 'Tell me. Tell me everything.'

She drew her hand away suddenly.

'If I do, you'll think I'm mad—that I've gone wrong in my head from being in that place with those others.'

'No, I shan't. I shan't, really.'

'You will. It *sounds* mad.'

'I shall know it isn't. Tell me. Please tell me.'

She drew a little farther away from him, sitting very upright, her eyes staring straight in front of her.

'It's just this,' she said. 'I'm afraid I'm going to be murdered.'

Her voice was dry and hoarse. She was speaking with obvious self-restraint but her hands were trembling.

'Murdered?'

'Yes, that sounds mad, doesn't it? Like—what do they call it?—persecution mania.'

'No,' said Bobby. 'You don't sound mad at all— just frightened. Tell me, who wants to murder you and why?'

She was silent a minute or two, twisting and untwisting her hands. Then she said in a low voice:

'My husband.'

'Your husband?' Thoughts whirled round in Bobby's head. 'Who are you?' he said abruptly.

It was her turn to look surprised.

'Don't you know?'

'I haven't the least idea.'

She said: 'I'm Moira Nicholson. My husband is Dr Nicholson.'

'Then you're not a patient there?'

'A patient? Oh, no!' Her face darkened suddenly. 'I suppose you think I speak like one.'

'No, no, I didn't mean that at all.' He was at pains to reassure her. 'Honestly, I didn't mean it that way. I was only surprised at finding you married—and—all that. Now, go on with what you're telling me—about your husband wanting to murder you.'

'It sounds mad, I know. But it isn't—it isn't! I see it in his eyes when he looks at me. And queer things have happened—accidents.'

'Accidents?' said Bobby sharply.

'Yes. Oh! I know it sounds hysterical and as though I was making it all up—'

'Not a bit,' said Bobby. 'It sounds perfectly reasonable. Go on. About these accidents.'

'They were just accidents. He backed the car not seeing I was there—I just jumped aside in time—and some stuff that was in the wrong bottle—oh, stupid things—and things that people would think quite all right, but they

151

weren't—they were *meant*. I know it. And it's wearing me out—watching for them—being on my guard—trying to save my life.'

She swallowed convulsively.

'Why does your husband want to do away with you?' asked Bobby.

Perhaps he hardly expected a definite answer—but the answer came promptly:

'Because he wants to marry Sylvia Bassington-ffrench.'

'What? But she's married already.'

'I know. But he's arranging for that.'

'How do you mean?'

'I don't know exactly. But I know that he's trying to get Mr Bassington-ffrench brought to the Grange as a patient.'

'And then?'

'I don't know, but I think something would happen.'

She shuddered.

'He's got some hold over Mr Bassington-ffrench. I don't know what it is.'

'Bassington-ffrench takes morphia,' said Bobby.

'Is that it? Jasper gives it to him, I suppose.'

'It comes by post.'

'Perhaps Jasper doesn't do it directly—he's very cunning. Mr Bassington-ffrench mayn't know it comes from Jasper—but I'm sure it does. And then Jasper would have him at the Grange and pretend to cure him—and once he was there—'

She paused and shivered.

'All sorts of things happen at the Grange,' she said.

152

'Queer things. People come there to get better—and they don't get better—they get worse.'

As she spoke, Bobby was aware of a glimpse into a strange, evil atmosphere. He felt something of the terror that had enveloped Moira Nicholson's life so long.

He said abruptly:

'You say your husband wants to marry Mrs Bassington-ffrench?'

Moira nodded.

'He's crazy about her.'

'And she?'

'I don't know,' said Moira slowly. 'I can't make up my mind. On the surface she seems fond of her husband and little boy and content and peaceful. She seems a very simple woman. But sometimes I fancy that she isn't so simple as she seems. I've even wondered sometimes whether she is an entirely different woman from what we all think she is . . . whether, perhaps, she isn't playing a part and playing it very well . . . But, really, I think, that's nonsense—foolish imagination on my part . . . When you've lived at a place like the Grange your mind gets distorted and you do begin imagining things.'

'What about the brother Roger?' asked Bobby.

'I don't know much about him. He's nice, I think, but he's the sort of person who would be very easily deceived. He's quite taken in by Jasper, I know. Jasper is working on him to persuade Mr Bassington-ffrench to come to the Grange. I believe he thinks it's all his own idea.' She leaned forward suddenly and caught Bobby's sleeve. 'Don't let him come to the Grange,' she implored. 'If he does, something awful will happen. I know it will.'

Bobby was silent a minute or two, turning over the amazing story in his mind.

'How long have you been married to Nicholson?' he said at last.

'Just over a year—' She shivered.

'Haven't you ever thought of leaving him?'

'How could I? I've nowhere to go. I've no money. If anyone took me in, what sort of story could I tell? A fantastic tale that my husband wanted to murder me? Who would believe me?'

'Well, I believe you,' said Bobby.

He paused a moment, as though making up his mind to a certain course of action. Then he went on:

'Look here,' he said bluntly. 'I'm going to ask you a question straight out. Did you know a man called Alan Carstairs?'

He saw the colour come up in her cheeks.

'Why do you ask me that?'

'Because it's rather important that I should know. My idea is that you did know Alan Carstairs, that perhaps at some time or other you gave him your photograph.'

She was silent a moment, her eyes downcast. Then she lifted her head and looked him in the face.

'That's quite true,' she said.

'You knew him before you were married?'

'Yes.'

'Has he been down here to see you since you were married?'

She hesitated, then said:

'Yes, once.'

'About a month ago would that be?'

'Yes. I suppose it would be about a month.'

'He knew you were living down here?'

'I don't know how he knew—I hadn't told him. I had never even written to him since my marriage.'

'But he found out and came here to see you. Did your husband know that?'

'No.'

'You think not. But he might have known all the same?'

'I suppose he might, but he never said anything.'

'Did you discuss your husband at all with Carstairs? Did you tell him of your fears as to your safety?'

She shook her head.

'I hadn't begun to suspect then.'

'But you were unhappy?'

'Yes.'

'And you told him so?'

'No. I tried not to show in any way that my marriage hadn't been a success.'

'But he might have guessed it all the same,' said Bobby gently.

'I suppose he might,' she admitted in a low voice.

'Do you think—I don't know how to put it—but do you think that he knew anything about your husband—that he suspected, for instance, that this nursing home place mightn't be quite what it seemed to be?'

Her brows furrowed as she tried to think.

'It's possible,' she said at last. 'He asked one or two rather peculiar questions—but—no. I don't think he can really have known anything about it.'

155

Bobby was silent again for a few minutes. Then he said:

'Would you call your husband a jealous man?'

Rather to his surprise, she answered:

'Yes. Very jealous.'

'Jealous, for instance, of you.'

'You mean even though he doesn't care? But, yes, he would be jealous, just the same. I'm his property, you see. He's a queer man—a very queer man.'

She shivered.

Then she asked suddenly:

'You're not connected with the police in any way, are you?'

'I? Oh, no!'

'I wondered, I mean—'

Bobby looked down at his chauffeur's livery.

'It's rather a long story,' he said.

'You are Lady Frances Derwent's chauffeur, aren't you? So the landlord here said. I met her at dinner the other night.'

'I know.' He paused. 'We've got to get hold of her,' he said. 'And it's a bit difficult for me to do. Do you think you could ring up and ask to speak to her and then get her to come and meet you somewhere outdoors?'

'I suppose I could—' said Moira slowly.

'I know it must seem frightfully odd to you. But it won't when I've explained. We must get hold of Frankie as soon as possible. It's essential.'

Moira rose.

'Very well,' she said.

With her hand on the door-handle she hesitated.

'Alan,' she said, 'Alan Carstairs. Did you say you'd seen him?'

'I have seen him,' said Bobby slowly. 'But not lately.'

And he thought, with a shock:

'Of course—she doesn't know he's dead . . .'

He said:

'Ring up Lady Frances. Then I'll tell you everything.'

CHAPTER 19

A Council of Three

Moira returned a few minutes later.

'I got her,' she said. 'I've asked her to come and meet me at a little summer-house down near the river. She must have thought it very odd, but she said she'd come.'

'Good,' said Bobby. 'Now, just where is this place exactly?'

Moira described it carefully, and the way to get to it.

'That's all right,' said Bobby. 'You go first. I'll follow on.'

They adhered to this programme, Bobby lingering to have a word with Mr Askew.

'Odd thing,' he said casually, 'that lady, Mrs Nicholson, I used to work for an uncle of hers. Canadian gentleman.'

Moira's visit to him might, he felt, give rise to gossip, and the last thing he wanted was for gossip of that kind to get about and possibly find its way to Dr Nicholson's ears.

'So that's it, is it?' said Mr Askew. 'I rather wondered.'

'Yes,' said Bobby. 'She recognized me, and came along

to hear what I was doing now. A nice, pleasant-spoken lady.'

'Very pleasant, indeed. She can't have much of a life living at the Grange.'

'It wouldn't be *my* fancy,' agreed Bobby.

Feeling that he had achieved his object, he strolled out into the village and with an aimless air betook himself in the direction indicated by Moira.

He reached the rendezvous successfully and found her there waiting for him. Frankie had not yet put in an appearance.

Moira's glance was frankly inquiring, and Bobby felt he must attempt the somewhat difficult task of explanation.

'There's an awful lot I've got to tell you,' he said, and stopped awkwardly.

'Yes?'

'To begin with,' said Bobby plunging, 'I'm not really a chauffeur, although I do work in a garage in London. And my name isn't Hawkins—it's Jones—Bobby Jones. I come from Marchbolt in Wales.'

Moira was listening attentively, but clearly the mention of Marchbolt meant nothing to her. Bobby set his teeth and went bravely to the heart of the matter.

'Look here, I'm afraid I'm going to give you rather a shock. This friend of yours—Alan Carstairs—he's, well—you've got to know—he's dead.'

He felt the start she gave and tactfully he averted his eyes from her face. Did she mind very much? Had she been—dash it all—keen on the fellow?

She was silent a moment or two, then she said in a low, thoughtful voice:

'So that's why he never came back? I wondered.'

Bobby ventured to steal a look at her. His spirits rose. She looked sad and thoughtful—but that was all.

'Tell me about it,' she said.

Bobby complied.

'He fell over the cliff at Marchbolt—the place where I live. I and the doctor there happened to be the ones to find him.' He paused and then added: 'He had your photograph in his pocket.'

'Did he?' She gave a sweet, rather sad smile. 'Dear Alan, he was—very faithful.'

There was silence for a moment or two and then she asked:

'When did this happen?'

'About a month ago. October 3rd to be exact.'

'That must have been just after he came down here.'

'Yes. Did he mention that he was going to Wales?'

She shook her head.

'You don't know anyone called Evans, do you?' said Bobby.

'Evans?' Moira frowned, trying to think. 'No, I don't think so. It's a very common name, of course, but I can't remember anybody. What is he?'

'That's just what we don't know. Oh! hullo, here's Frankie.'

Frankie came hurrying along the path. Her face, at the sight of Bobby and Mrs Nicholson sitting chatting together, was a study in conflicting expressions.

'Hullo, Frankie,' said Bobby. 'I'm glad you've come. We've got to have a great pow-wow. To begin with it's Mrs Nicholson who is the original of *the* photograph.'

'Oh!' said Frankie blankly.

She looked at Moira and suddenly laughed.

'My dear,' she said to Bobby, 'now I see why the sight of Mrs Cayman at the inquest was such a shock to you!'

'Exactly,' said Bobby.

What a fool he had been. However could he have imagined for one moment that any space of time could have turned a Moira Nicholson into an Amelia Cayman.

'Lord, what a fool I've been!' he exclaimed.

Moira was looking bewildered.

'There's such an awful lot to tell,' said Bobby, 'and I don't quite know how to put it all.'

He described the Caymans and their identification of the body.

'But I don't understand,' said Moira, bewildered. 'Whose body was it really, her brother's or Alan Carstairs?'

'That's where the dirty work comes in,' explained Bobby.

'And then,' continued Frankie, 'Bobby was poisoned.'

'Eight grains of morphia,' said Bobby reminiscently.

'Don't start on that,' said Frankie. 'You're capable of going on for hours on the subject and it's really very boring to other people. Let me explain.'

She took a long breath.

'You see,' she said, 'those Cayman people came to see Bobby after the inquest to ask him if the brother (supposed) had said anything before he died, and Bobby said, "No." But afterwards he remembered that he had said something about a man called Evans, so he wrote and told them so, and a few days afterwards he got a letter offering him a job in Peru or somewhere and when he wouldn't take it, the next thing was that someone put a lot of morphia—'

'Eight grains,' said Bobby.

'—in his beer. Only, having a most extraordinary inside or something, it didn't kill him. And so then we saw at once that Pritchard—or Carstairs, you know—must have been pushed over the cliff.'

'But why?' asked Moira.

'Don't you see? Why, it seems perfectly clear to us. I expect I haven't told it very well. Anyway, we decided that he had been and that Roger Bassington-ffrench had probably done it.'

'Roger Bassington-ffrench?' Moira spoke in tones of the liveliest amusement.

'We worked it out that way. You see, he was there at the time, and your photograph disappeared, and he seemed to be the only man who could have taken it.'

'I see,' said Moira thoughtfully.

'And then,' continued Frankie, 'I happened to have an accident just here. An amazing coincidence, wasn't it?' She looked hard at Bobby with an admonishing eye. 'So I telephoned to Bobby and suggested that he should come down here pretending to be my chauffeur and we'd look into the matter.'

'So now you see how it was,' said Bobby, accepting Frankie's one discreet departure from the truth. 'And the final climax was when last night I strolled into the grounds of the Grange and ran right into you—the original of the mysterious photograph.'

'You recognized me very quickly,' said Moira, with a faint smile.

'Yes,' said Bobby. 'I would have recognized the original of that photograph anywhere.'

For no particular reason, Moira blushed.

Then an idea seemed to strike her and she looked sharply from one to the other.

'Are you telling me the truth?' she asked. 'Is it really true that you came down here—by accident? Or did you come because—because'—her voice quavered in spite of herself—'you suspected my husband?'

Bobby and Frankie looked at each other. Then Bobby said:

'I give you my word of honour that we'd never even heard of your husband till we came down here.'

'Oh, I see.' She turned to Frankie. 'I'm sorry, Lady Frances, but, you see, I remembered that evening when we came to dinner. Jasper went on and on at you—asking you things about your accident. I couldn't think why. But I think now that perhaps he suspected it wasn't genuine.'

'Well, if you really want to know, it wasn't,' said Frankie. 'Whoof—now I feel better! It was all camouflaged very carefully. But it was nothing to do with your husband. The whole thing was staged because we wanted to—to—what does one call it?—get a line on Roger Bassington-ffrench.'

'Roger?' Moira frowned and smiled perplexedly.

'It seems absurd,' she said frankly.

'All the same, facts are facts,' said Bobby.

'Roger—oh, no.' She shook her head. 'He might be weak—or wild. He might get into debt, or get mixed up in a scandal—but pushing someone over a cliff—no, I simply can't imagine it.'

'Do you know,' said Frankie, 'I can't very well imagine it either.'

'But he must have taken that photograph,' said Bobby stubbornly. 'Listen, Mrs Nicholson, while I go over the facts.'

He did so slowly and carefully. When he had finished, she nodded her head comprehendingly.

'I see what you mean. It seems very queer.' She paused a minute and then said unexpectedly:

'Why don't you ask him?'

CHAPTER 20

Council of Two

For a moment, the bold simplicity of the question quite took their breath away. Both Frankie and Bobby started to speak at once:

'That's impossible—' began Bobby, just as Frankie said: 'That would never do.'

Then they both stopped dead as the possibilities of the idea sank in.

'You see,' said Moira eagerly, 'I do see what you mean. It does seem as though Roger *must* have taken that photograph, but I don't believe for one moment that he pushed Alan over. Why should he? He didn't even know him. They'd only met once—at lunch down here. They'd never come across each other in any way. There's no motive.'

'Then who *did* push him over?' asked Frankie bluntly.

A shadow crossed Moira's face.

'I don't know,' she said constrainedly.

'Look here,' said Bobby. 'Do you mind if I tell Frankie what you told me? About what you're afraid of.'

Moira turned her head away.

'If you like. But it sounds so melodramatic and hysterical. I can't believe it myself this minute.'

And indeed the bald statement, made unemotionally in the open air of the quiet English countryside, did seem curiously lacking in reality.

Moira got up abruptly.

'I really feel I've been terribly silly,' she said, her lip trembling. 'Please don't pay any attention to what I said, Mr Jones. It was just—nerves. Anyway, I must be going now. Goodbye.'

She moved rapidly away. Bobby sprang up to follow her, but Frankie pushed him firmly back.

'Stay there, idiot, leave this to me.'

She went rapidly off after Moira. She returned a few minutes later.

'Well?' queried Bobby anxiously.

'That's all right. I calmed her down. It was a bit hard on her having her private fears blurted out in front of her to a third person. I made her promise we'd have a meeting—all three of us—again soon. Now that you're not hampered by her being there, tell us all about it.'

Bobby did so. Frankie listened attentively. Then she said:

'It fits in with two things. First of all, I came back just now to find Nicholson holding both Sylvia Bassington-ffrench's hands—and didn't he look daggers at me! If looks could kill I feel sure he'd have made me a corpse then and there.'

'What's the second thing?' asked Bobby.

'Oh, just an incident. Sylvia described how Moira's photograph had made a great impression on some stranger who had come to the house. Depend upon it, that was Carstairs. He recognized the photograph, Mrs Bassington-ffrench tells him that it is a portrait of a Mrs Nicholson, and that explains how he came to find out where she was. But you know, Bobby, I don't see yet where Nicholson comes in. Why should he want to do away with Alan Carstairs?'

'You think it was him and not Bassington-ffrench? Rather a coincidence if he and Bassington-ffrench should both be in Marchbolt on the same day.'

'Well, coincidences do happen. But if it was Nicholson, I don't yet see the motive. Was Carstairs on the track of Nicholson as the head of a dope gang? Or is your new lady friend the motive for the murder?'

'It might be both,' suggested Bobby. 'He may know that Carstairs and his wife had an interview, and he may have believed that his wife gave him away somehow.'

'Now, that is a possibility,' said Frankie. 'But the first thing is to make sure about Roger Bassington-ffrench. The only thing we've got against him is the photograph business. If he can clear that up satisfactorily—'

'You're going to tackle him on the subject? Frankie, is that wise? If he is the villain of the piece, as we decided he must be, it means that we're going to show him our hand.'

'Not quite—not the way I shall do it. After all, in every other way he's been perfectly straightforward and above board. We've taken that to be super-cunning—but suppose it just happens to be innocence? *If* he can explain the photograph—and I shall be watching him when he does explain—and if there's the least sign of hesitation of guilt I shall see it—as I say, *if* he can explain the photograph—then he may be a very valuable ally.'

'How do you mean, Frankie?'

'My dear, your little friend may be an emotional scaremonger who likes to exaggerate, but supposing she isn't— that all she says is gospel truth—that her husband wants to get rid of her and marry Sylvia. Don't you realize that, in that case, Henry Bassington-ffrench is in mortal danger, too. At all costs we've got to prevent him being sent to the Grange. And at present Roger Bassington-ffrench is on Nicholson's side.'

'Good for you, Frankie,' said Bobby quietly. 'Go ahead with your plan.'

Frankie got up to go, but before departing she paused for a moment.

'Isn't it odd?' she said. 'We seem, somehow, to have got in between the covers of a book. We're in the middle of someone else's story. It's a frightfully queer feeling.'

'I know what you mean,' said Bobby. 'There is something rather uncanny about it. I should call it a play rather than a book. It's as though we'd walked on to the stage in the middle of the second act and we haven't really got parts in the play at all, but we have to pretend, and what makes it so frightfully hard is that we haven't the faintest idea what the first act was about.'

Frankie nodded eagerly.

'I'm not even so sure it's the second act—I think it's more like the third. Bobby, I'm sure we've got to go back a long way . . . And we've got to be quick because I fancy the play is frightfully near the final curtain.'

'With corpses strewn everywhere,' said Bobby. 'And what brought us into the show was a regular cue—five words—quite meaningless as far as we are concerned.'

'"*Why didn't they ask Evans?*" Isn't it odd, Bobby, that though we've found out a good deal and more and more characters come into the thing, we never get any nearer to the mysterious Evans?'

'I've got an idea about Evans. I've a feeling that Evans doesn't really matter at all—that although he's been the starting point as it were, yet in himself he's probably quite inessential. It will be like that story of Wells where a prince built a marvellous palace or temple round the tomb of his beloved. And when it was finished there was just one little thing that jarred. So he said: "Take it away." And the thing was actually the tomb itself.'

'Sometimes,' said Frankie, 'I don't believe there is an Evans.'

Saying which, she nodded to Bobby and retraced her steps towards the house.

CHAPTER 21

Roger Answers a Question

Fortune favoured her, for she fell in with Roger not far from the house.

'Hullo,' he said. 'You're back early from London.'

'I wasn't in the mood for London,' said Frankie.

'Have you been to the house yet?' he asked. His face grew grave. 'Nicholson, I find, has been telling Sylvia the truth about poor old Henry. Poor girl, she's taken it hard. It seems she had absolutely no suspicion.'

'I know,' said Frankie. 'They were both together in the library when I came in. She was—very upset.'

'Look here, Frankie,' said Roger. 'Henry has absolutely got to be cured. It isn't as though this drug habit had a real hold on him. He hasn't been taking it so very long. And he's got every incentive in the world to make him keen on being cured—Sylvia, Tommy, his home. He's got to be made to see the position clearly. Nicholson is just the man to put the thing through. He was talking to me the other day. He's had some amazing successes— even with people who have been slaves for years to the

170

beastly stuff. If Henry will only consent to go to the Grange—'

Frankie interrupted.

'Look here,' she said. 'There's something I want to ask you. Just a question. I hope you won't think I'm simply frightfully impertinent.'

'What is it?' asked Roger, his attention arrested.

'Do you mind telling me if you took a photograph out of that man's pocket—the one who fell over the cliff at Marchbolt?'

She was studying him closely, watching every detail of his expression. She was satisfied with what she saw.

Slight annoyance, a trace of embarrassment—no flash of guilt or dismay.

'Now, how on earth did you come to guess that?' he said. 'Or did Moira tell you—but, then, she doesn't know?'

'You did, then?'

'I suppose I'll have to admit it.'

'Why?'

Roger seemed embarrassed again.

'Well, look at it as I did. Here I am, mounting guard over a strange dead body. Something is sticking out of his pocket. I look at it. By an amazing coincidence it's the photograph of a woman I know—a married woman—and a woman who I guess is not too happily married. What's going to happen? An inquest. Publicity. Possibly the wretched girl's name in all the papers. I acted on impulse. Took the photo and tore it up. I daresay I acted wrongly, but Moira Nicholson is a nice little soul and I didn't want her to get landed in a mess.'

Frankie drew a deep breath.

'So that was it,' she said. 'If you only knew—'

'Knew what?' said Roger puzzled.

'I don't know that I can tell you just now,' said Frankie. 'I may later. It's all rather complicated. I can quite see why you took the photograph, but was there any objection to your saying you recognized the man? Oughtn't you to have told the police who he was?'

'Recognized him?' said Roger. He looked bewildered. 'How could I recognize him? I didn't know him.'

'But you'd met him down here—only about a week before.'

'My dear girl, are you quite mad?'

'Alan Carstairs—you did meet Alan Carstairs?'

'Ah, yes! Man who came down with the Rivingtons. But the dead man wasn't Alan Carstairs.'

'But he *was*!'

They stared at each other, then Frankie said with a renewal of suspicion:

'Surely you must have recognized him?'

'I never saw his face,' said Roger.

'What?'

'No. There was a handkerchief spread over it.'

Frankie stared at him. Suddenly she remembered that in Bobby's first account of the tragedy he had mentioned putting a handkerchief over the face of the dead man.

'You never thought of looking?' went on Frankie.

'No. Why should I?'

'Of course,' thought Frankie, 'if *I'd* found a photograph of somebody I knew in a dead person's pocket, I should

172

simply have had to look at the person's face. How beautifully incurious men are!

'Poor little thing,' she said. 'I'm so terribly sorry for her.'

'Who do you mean—Moira Nicholson? Why are you so sorry for her?'

'Because she's frightened,' said Frankie slowly.

'She always looks half scared to death. What is she frightened of?'

'Her husband.'

'I don't know that I'd care to be up against Jasper Nicholson myself,' admitted Roger.

'She's sure he's trying to murder her,' said Frankie abruptly.

'Oh, my dear!' He looked at her incredulously.

'Sit down,' said Frankie. 'I'm going to tell you a lot of things. I've got to prove to you that Dr Nicholson is a dangerous criminal.'

'A criminal?'

Roger's tone was frankly incredulous.

'Wait till you've heard the whole story.'

She gave him a clear and careful narrative of all that had occurred since the day Bobby and Dr Thomas had found the body. She only kept back the fact that her accident had not been genuine, but she let it appear that she had lingered at Merroway Court through her intense desire to get to the bottom of the mystery.

She could complain of no lack of interest on the part of her listener. Roger seemed quite fascinated by the story.

'Is this really true?' he demanded. 'All this about the fellow Jones being poisoned and all that?'

'Absolute gospel truth, my dear.'

'Sorry for my incredulity—but the facts do take a bit of swallowing, don't they?'

He was silent a minute, frowning.

'Look here,' he said at last. 'Fantastic as the whole thing sounds, I think you must be right in your first deduction. This man, Alex Pritchard, or Alan Carstairs, must have been murdered. If he wasn't, there seems no point in the attack upon Jones. Whether the key word to the situation is the phrase, "*Why didn't they ask Evans?*" or not doesn't seem to me to matter much since you've no clue to who Evans is or as to what he was to have been asked. Let's put it that the murderer or murderers assumed that Jones was in possession of some knowledge, whether he knew it himself or not, which was dangerous to them. So, accordingly, they tried to eliminate him, and probably would try again if they got on his track. So far that seems sense—but I don't see by what process of reasoning you fix on Nicholson as the criminal.'

'He's such a sinister man, and he's got a dark-blue Talbot and he was away from here on the day that Bobby was poisoned.'

'That's all pretty thin as evidence.'

'There are all the things Mrs Nicholson told Bobby.'

She recited them, and once again they sounded melo-dramatic and unsubstantial repeated aloud against the background of the peaceful English landscape.

Roger shrugged his shoulders.

'She thinks he supplies Henry with the drug—but that's pure conjecture, she's not a particle of evidence that he

174

does so. She thinks he wants to get Henry to the Grange as a patient—well, that's a very natural wish for a doctor to have. A doctor wants as many patients as he can get. She thinks he's in love with Sylvia. Well, as to that, of course, I can't say.'

'If she thinks so, she's probably right,' interrupted Frankie. 'A woman would know all right about her own husband.'

'Well, granting that that's the case, it doesn't necessarily mean that the man's a dangerous criminal. Lots of respectable citizens fall in love with other people's wives.'

'There's her belief that he wants to murder her,' urged Frankie.

Roger looked at her quizzically.

'You take that seriously?'

'She believes it, anyhow.'

Roger nodded and lit a cigarette.

'The question is, how much attention to pay that belief of hers,' he said. 'It's a creepy sort of place, the Grange, full of queer customers. Living there would be inclined to upset a woman's balance, especially if she were of the timid nervous type.'

'Then you don't think it's true?'

'I don't say that. She probably believes quite honestly that he is trying to kill her—but is there any foundation in fact for that belief? There doesn't seem to be.'

Frankie remembered with curious clearness Moira saying, 'It's just nerves.' And somehow the mere fact that she had said that seemed to Frankie to point to the fact that it was not nerves, but she found it difficult to know how to explain her point of view to Roger.

175

Meanwhile the young man was going on:

'Mind you, if you could show that Nicholson had been in Marchbolt on the day of the cliff tragedy that would be very different, or if we could find any definite motive linking him with Carstairs, but it seems to me you're ignoring the real suspects.'

'What real suspects?'

'The—what did you call them—Haymans?'

'Caymans.'

'That's it. Now, they are undoubtedly in it up to the hilt. First, there's the false identification of the body. Then there's their insistence on the point of whether the poor fellow said anything before he died. And I think it's logical to assume, as you did, that the Buenos Aires offer came from, or was arranged for, by them.'

'It's a bit annoying,' said Frankie, 'to have the most strenuous efforts made to get you out of the way because you know something—and not to know yourself what the something you know is. Bother—what a mess one gets into with words.'

'Yes,' said Roger grimly, 'that was a mistake on their part. A mistake that it's going to take them all their time to remedy.'

'Oh!' cried Frankie. 'I've just thought of something. Up to now, you see, I've been assuming that the photograph of Mrs Cayman was substituted for the one of Moira Nicholson.'

'I can assure you,' said Roger gravely, 'that I have never treasured the likeness of a Mrs Cayman against my heart. She sounds a most repulsive creature.'

176

'Well, she was handsome in a way,' admitted Frankie. 'A sort of bold, coarse, vampish way. But the point is this: Carstairs must have had her photograph on him as well as Mrs Nicholson's.'

Roger nodded.

'And you think—' he suggested.

'I think one was love and the other was business! Carstairs was carrying about the Caymans' photograph for a reason. He wanted it identified by somebody, perhaps. Now, listen—what happens? Someone, the male Cayman perhaps, is following him and, seeing a good opportunity, steals up behind him in the mist and gives him a shove. Carstairs goes over the cliff with a startled cry. Male Cayman makes off as fast as he can; he doesn't know who may be about. We'll say that he doesn't know that Alan Carstairs is carrying about that photograph. What happens next? The photograph is published—'

'Consternation in the Cayman ménage,' said Roger helpfully.

'Exactly. What is to be done? The bold thing—grasp the nettle. Who knows Carstairs as Carstairs? Hardly anyone in this country. Down goes Mrs Cayman, weeping crocodile tears and recognizing body as that of a convenient brother. They also do a little hocus pocus of posting parcels to bolster up the walking-tour theory.'

'You know, Frankie. I think that's positively brilliant,' said Roger with admiration.

'I think it's pretty good myself,' said Frankie. 'And you're quite right. We ought to get busy on the track of the Caymans. I can't think why we haven't done so before.'

This was not quite true, since Frankie knew quite well the reason—namely that they had been on the track of Roger himself. However, she felt it would be tactless, just at this stage, to reveal the fact.

'What are we going to do about Mrs Nicholson?' she asked abruptly.

'What do you mean—do about her?'

'Well, the poor thing is terrified to death. I do think you're callous about her, Roger.'

'I'm not, really, but people who can't help themselves always irritate me.'

'Oh! but do be fair. What can she do? She's no money and nowhere to go.'

Roger said unexpectedly:

'If you were in her place, Frankie, you'd find something to do.'

'Oh!' Frankie was rather taken aback.

'Yes, you would. If you really thought somebody was trying to murder you, you wouldn't just stay there tamely waiting to be murdered. You'd run away and make a living somehow, or you'd murder the other person first! You'd do *something*.'

Frankie tried to think what she would do.

'I'd certainly do something,' she said thoughtfully.

'The truth of the matter is that you've got guts and she hasn't,' said Roger with decision.

Frankie felt complimented. Moira Nicholson was not really the type of woman she admired and she had also felt just slightly ruffled by Bobby's absorption in her. 'Bobby,' she thought to herself, 'likes them helpless.' And

178

she remembered the curious fascination that the photograph had had for him from the start of the affair.

'Oh, well,' thought Frankie, 'at any rate, Roger's different.'

Roger, it was clear, did not like them helpless. Moira, on the other hand, clearly did not think very much of Roger. She had called him weak and had scouted the possibility of his having the guts to murder anyone. He was weak, perhaps—but undeniably he had charm. She had felt it from the first moment of arriving at Merroway Court.

Roger said quietly:

'If you liked, Frankie, you could make anything you chose of a man . . .'

Frankie felt a sudden little thrill—and at the same time an acute embarrassment. She changed the subject hastily.

'About your brother,' she said. 'Do you still think he should go to the Grange?'

CHAPTER 22

Another Victim

'No,' said Roger. 'I don't. After all, there are heaps of other places where he can be treated. The really important thing is to get Henry to agree.'

'Do you think that will be difficult?' asked Frankie.

'I'm afraid it may be. You heard him the other night. On the other hand, if we just catch him in the repentant mood, that's very different. Hullo—here comes Sylvia.'

Mrs Bassington-ffrench emerged from the house and looked about her, then seeing Roger and Frankie, she walked across the grass towards them.

They could see that she was looking terribly worried and strained.

'Roger,' she began, 'I've been looking for you everywhere.' Then, as Frankie made a movement to leave them—'No, my dear, don't go. Of what use are concealments? In any case, I think you know all there is to know. You've suspected this business for some time, haven't you?'

Frankie nodded.

'While I've been blind—blind—' said Sylvia bitterly. 'Both

180

of you saw what I never even suspected. I only wondered why Henry had changed so to all of us. It made me very unhappy, but I never suspected the reason.'

She paused, then went on again with a slight change of tone.

'As soon as Dr Nicholson had told me the truth, I went straight to Henry. I've only just left him now.' She paused, swallowing a sob.

'Roger—it's going to be all right. He's agreed. He will go to the Grange and put himself in Dr Nicholson's hands tomorrow.'

'Oh! no—' The exclamation came from Roger and Frankie simultaneously. Sylvia looked at them—astonished.

Roger spoke awkwardly.

'Do you know, Sylvia, I've been thinking it over, and I don't believe the Grange would be a good plan, after all.'

'You think he can fight it by himself?' asked Sylvia doubtfully.

'No, I don't. But there are other places—places not—so—well, not so near at hand. I'm convinced that staying in this district would be a mistake.'

'I'm sure of it,' said Frankie, coming to his rescue.

'Oh! I don't agree,' said Sylvia. 'I couldn't bear him to go away somewhere. And Dr Nicholson has been so kind and understanding. I shall feel happy about Henry being under his charge.'

'I thought you didn't like Nicholson, Sylvia,' said Roger.

'I've changed my mind.' She spoke simply. 'Nobody could have been nicer or kinder than he was this afternoon. My silly prejudice against him has quite vanished.'

There was a moment's silence. The position was awkward. Neither Roger nor Sylvia knew quite what to say next.

'Poor Henry,' said Sylvia. 'He broke down. He was terribly upset at my knowing. He agreed that he must fight this awful craving for my sake and Tommy's, but he said I hadn't a conception of what it meant. I suppose I haven't, though Dr Nicholson explained very fully. It becomes a kind of obsession—people aren't responsible for their actions—so he said. Oh, Roger, it seems so awful. But Dr Nicholson was really kind. I trust him.'

'All the same, I think it would be better—' began Roger. Sylvia turned on him.

'I don't understand you, Roger. Why have you changed your mind? Half an hour ago you were all for Henry's going to the Grange.'

'Well—I've—I've had time to think the matter over since—'

Again Sylvia interrupted.

'Anyway, I've made up my mind. Henry shall go to the Grange and nowhere else.'

They confronted her in silence, then Roger said:

'Do you know, I think I will ring up Nicholson. He will be home now. I'd like—just to have a talk with him about matters.'

Without waiting for her reply he turned away and went rapidly into the house. The two women stood looking after him.

'I cannot understand Roger,' said Sylvia impatiently. 'About a quarter of an hour ago he was positively urging me to arrange for Henry to go to the Grange.'

Her tone held a distinct note of anger.

'All the same,' said Frankie, 'I agree with him. I'm sure I've read somewhere that people ought always to go for a cure somewhere far away from their homes.'

'I think that's just nonsense,' said Sylvia.

Frankie felt in a dilemma. Sylvia's unexpected obstinacy was making things difficult, and also she seemed suddenly to have become as violently pro-Nicholson as she formerly had been against him. It was very hard to know what arguments to use. Frankie considered telling the whole story to Sylvia—but would Sylvia believe it? Even Roger had not been very impressed by the theory of Dr Nicholson's guilt. Sylvia, with her new-found partisanship where the doctor was concerned, would probably be even less so. She might even go and repeat the whole thing to him. It was certainly difficult.

An aeroplane passed low overhead in the gathering dusk, filling the air with its loud beat of engines. Both Sylvia and Frankie stared up at it, glad of the respite it afforded, since neither of them quite knew what to say next. It gave Frankie time to collect her thoughts, and Sylvia time to recover from her fit of sudden anger.

As the aeroplane disappeared over the trees and its roar receded into the distance, Sylvia turned abruptly to Frankie.

'It's been so awful—' she said brokenly. 'And you all seem to want to send Henry far away from me.'

'No, no,' said Frankie. 'It wasn't that at all.'

She cast about for a minute.

'It was only that I thought he ought to have the best treatment. And I do think that Dr Nicholson is rather—well, rather a quack.'

'I don't believe it,' said Sylvia. 'I think he's a very clever man and just the kind of man Henry needs.'

She looked defiantly at Frankie. Frankie marvelled at the hold Dr Nicholson had acquired over her in such a short time. All her former distrust of the man seemed to have vanished completely.

At a loss what to say or do next, Frankie relapsed into silence. Presently Roger came out again from the house. He seemed slightly breathless.

'Nicholson isn't in yet,' he said. 'I left a message.'

'I don't see why you want to see Dr Nicholson so urgently,' said Sylvia. 'You suggested this plan, and it's all arranged and Henry has consented.'

'I think I've got some say in the matter, Sylvia,' said Roger gently. 'After all, I'm Henry's brother.'

'You suggested the plan yourself,' said Sylvia obstinately.

'Yes, but I've heard a few things about Nicholson since.'

'What things? Oh! I don't believe you.'

She bit her lip, turned away and plunged into the house. Roger looked at Frankie.

'This is a bit awkward,' he said.

'Very awkward, indeed.'

'Once Sylvia has made her mind up she can be obstinate as the devil.'

'What are we going to do?'

They sat down again on the garden seat and went into the matter carefully. Roger agreed with Frankie that to tell the whole story to Sylvia would be a mistake. The best plan, in his opinion, would be to tackle the doctor.

'But what are you going to say exactly?'

'I don't know that I shall say much—but I shall hint a good deal. At any rate, I agree with you about one thing—Henry mustn't go to the Grange. Even if we come right out into the open, we've got to stop that.'

'We give the whole show away if we do,' Frankie reminded him.

'I know. That's why we've got to try everything else first. Curse Sylvia, why must she turn obstinate just at this minute?'

'It shows the power of the man,' Frankie said.

'Yes. You know, it inclines me to believe that, evidence or no evidence, you may be right about him after all—what's that?'

They both sprang up.

'It sounded like a shot,' said Frankie. 'From the house.'

They looked at each other, then raced towards the building. They went in by the french window of the drawing-room and passed through into the hall. Sylvia Bassington-ffrench was standing there, her face white as paper.

'Did you hear?' she said. 'It was a shot—from Henry's study.'

She swayed and Roger put an arm round her to steady her. Frankie went to the study door and turned the handle.

'It's locked,' she said.

'The window,' said Roger.

He deposited Sylvia, who was in a half-fainting condition, on a convenient settee and raced out again through the drawing-room, Frankie on his heels. They went round the house till they came to the study window. It was closed, but they put their faces close to the glass and peered in.

185

The sun was setting and there was not much light—but they could see plainly enough.

Henry Bassington-ffrench was lying sprawled out across his desk. There was a bullet wound plainly visible in the temple and a revolver lay on the floor, where it had dropped from his hand.

'He's shot himself,' said Frankie. 'How ghastly! . . .'

'Stand back a little,' said Roger. 'I'm going to break the window.'

He wrapped his hand in his coat and struck the pane of glass a heavy blow that shattered it. Roger picked out the pieces carefully, then he and Frankie stepped into the room. As they did so, Mrs Bassington-ffrench and Dr Nicholson came hurrying along the terrace.

'Here's the doctor,' said Sylvia. 'He's just come. Has—has anything happened to Henry?'

Then she saw the sprawling figure and uttered a cry.

Roger stepped quickly out again through the window and Dr Nicholson thrust Sylvia into his arms.

'Take her away,' he said briefly. 'Look after her. Give her some brandy if she'll take it. Don't let her see more than you can help.'

He himself stepped through the window and joined Frankie. He shook his head slowly.

'This is a tragic business,' he said. 'Poor fellow. So he felt he couldn't face the music. Too bad. Too bad.'

He bent over the body then straightened himself up again.

'Nothing to be done. Death must have been instant-aneous. I wonder if he wrote something first. They usually do.'

Frankie advanced till she stood beside them. A piece of

paper with a few scrawled words on it, evidently freshly written, lay at Bassington-ffrench's elbow. Their purport was clear enough.

I feel this is the best way out, (Henry Bassington-ffrench had written). *This fatal habit has taken too great a hold on me for me to fight it now. Want to do the best I can for Sylvia—Sylvia and Tommy. God bless you both, my dears. Forgive me . . .*

Frankie felt a lump rise in her throat.

'We mustn't touch anything,' said Dr Nicholson. 'There will have to be an inquest, of course. We must ring up the police.'

In obedience to his gesture, Frankie went towards the door. Then she stopped.

'The key's not in the lock,' she said.

'No? Perhaps it's in his pocket.'

He knelt down, investigating delicately. From the dead man's coat pocket he drew out a key.

He tried it in the lock and it fitted. Together they passed out into the hall. Dr Nicholson went straight to the telephone.

Frankie, her knees shaking under her, felt suddenly sick.

CHAPTER 23

Moira Disappears

Frankie rang up Bobby about an hour later.

'Is that Hawkins? Hullo, Bobby—have you heard what has happened? You have? Quick, we must meet somewhere. Early tomorrow morning would be best, I think. I'll stroll out before breakfast. Say eight o'clock—the same place we met today.'

She rang off as Bobby uttered his third respectful 'Yes, your ladyship', for the benefit of any curious ears.

Bobby arrived at the rendezvous first, but Frankie did not keep him waiting long. She looked pale and upset.

'Hullo, Bobby, isn't it awful? I haven't been able to sleep all night.'

'I haven't heard any details,' said Bobby. 'Just that Mr Bassington-ffrench had shot himself. That's right, I suppose?'

'Yes. Sylvia had been talking to him—persuading him to agree to a course of treatment and he said he would. Afterwards, I suppose, his courage must have failed him. He went into his study, locked the door, wrote a few words

188

on a sheet of paper—and—and shot himself. Bobby, it's too ghastly. It's—it's grim.'

'I know,' said Bobby quietly.

They were both silent for a little.

'I shall have to leave today, of course,' said Frankie presently.

'Yes, I suppose you will. How is she—Mrs Bassington-ffrench, I mean?'

'She's collapsed, poor soul. I haven't seen her since we—we found the body. The shock to her must have been awful.'

Bobby nodded.

'You'd better bring the car round about eleven,' continued Frankie.

Bobby did not answer. Frankie looked at him impatiently.

'What's the matter with you, Bobby? You look as though you were miles away.'

'Sorry. As a matter of fact—'

'Yes?'

'Well, I was just wondering. I suppose—well, I suppose it's all right?'

'What do you mean—all right?'

'I mean it's quite certain that he *did* commit suicide?'

'Oh!' said Frankie. 'I see.' She thought a minute. 'Yes,' she said, 'it was suicide all right.'

'You're quite sure? You see, Frankie, we have Moira's word for it that Nicholson wanted two people out of the way. Well, *here's one of them gone.*'

Frankie thought again, but once more she shook her head.

'It must be suicide,' she said. 'I was in the garden with Roger when we heard the shot. We both ran straight in

189

through the drawing-room to the hall. The study door was locked on the inside. We went round to the window. That was fastened also and Roger had to smash it. It wasn't till then that Nicholson appeared upon the scene.'

Bobby reflected upon this information.

'It looks all right,' he agreed. 'But Nicholson seems to have appeared on the scene very suddenly.'

'He'd left a stick behind earlier in the afternoon and had come back for it.'

Bobby was frowning with the process of thought.

'Listen, Frankie. Suppose that actually Nicholson shot Bassington-ffrench—'

'Having induced him first to write a suicide's letter of farewell?'

'I should think that would be the easiest thing in the world to fake. Any alteration in handwriting would be put down to agitation.'

'Yes, that's true. Go on with your theory.'

'Nicholson shoots Bassington-ffrench, leaves the farewell letter, and nips out locking the door—to appear again a few minutes later as though he had just arrived.'

Frankie shook her head regretfully.

'It's a good idea—but it won't work. To begin with, the key was in Henry Bassington-ffrench's pocket—'

'Who found it there?'

'Well, as a matter of fact, Nicholson did.'

'There you are. What's easier for him than to pretend to find it there?'

'I was watching him—remember. I'm sure the key was in the pocket.'

'That's what one says when one watches a conjurer. You *see* the rabbit being put into the hat! If Nicholson is a high-class criminal, a simple little bit of sleight of hand like that would be child's play to him.'

'Well, you may be right about that, but honestly, Bobby, the whole thing's impossible. Sylvia Bassington-ffrench was actually in the house when the shot was fired. The moment she heard it she ran out into the hall. If Nicholson had fired the shot and come out through the study door she would have been bound to see him. Besides, she told us that he actually came up the drive to the front door. She saw him coming as we ran round the house and went to meet him and brought him round to the study window. No, Bobby, I hate to say it, but the man has an alibi.'

'On principle, I distrust people who have alibis,' said Bobby.

'So do I. But I don't see how you can get round this one.'

'No. Sylvia Bassington-ffrench's word ought to be good enough.'

'Yes, indeed.'

'Well,' said Bobby with a sigh. 'I suppose we'll have to leave it at suicide. Poor devil. What's the next angle of attack, Frankie?'

'The Caymans,' said Frankie. 'I can't think how we've been so remiss as not to have looked them up before. You've kept the address Cayman wrote from, haven't you?'

'Yes. It's the same they gave at the inquest. 17 St Leonard's Gardens, Paddington.'

'Don't you agree that we've rather neglected that channel of inquiry?'

191

'Absolutely. All the same, you know, Frankie, I've got a very shrewd idea that you'll find the birds flown. I should imagine that the Caymans weren't exactly born yesterday.'

'Even if they have gone off, I may find out something about them.'

'Why—*I*?'

'Because, once again, I don't think you'd better appear in the matter. It's like coming down here when we thought Roger was the bad man of the show. You are known to them and I am not.'

'And how do you propose to make their acquaintance?' asked Bobby.

'I shall be something political,' said Frankie. 'Canvassing for the Conservative Party. I shall arrive with leaflets.'

'Good enough,' said Bobby. 'But, as I said before, I think you'll find the birds flown. Now there's another thing that requires to be thought of—Moira.'

'Goodness,' said Frankie, 'I'd forgotten all about her.'

'So I noticed,' said Bobby with a trace of coldness in his manner.

'You're right,' said Frankie thoughtfully. 'Something must be done about her.'

Bobby nodded. The strange haunting face came up before his eyes. There was something tragic about it. He had always felt that from the first moment when he had taken the photograph from Alan Carstairs' pocket.

'If you'd seen her that night when I first went to the Grange!' he said. 'She was crazy with fear—and I tell you, Frankie, *she's right*. It's not nerves or imagination, or

192

anything like that. If Nicholson wants to marry Sylvia Bassington-ffrench, two obstacles have got to go. One's gone. I've a feeling that Moira's life is hanging by a hair and that any delay may be fatal.'

Frankie was sobered by the earnestness of his words.

'My dear, you're right,' she said. 'We must act quickly. What shall we do?'

'We must persuade her to leave the Grange—at once.'

Frankie nodded.

'I tell you what,' she said. 'She'd better go down to Wales—to the Castle. Heaven knows, she ought to be safe enough there.'

'If you can fix that, Frankie, nothing could be better.'

'Well, it's simple enough. Father never notices who goes or comes. He'll like Moira—nearly any man would—she's so feminine. It's extraordinary how men like helpless women.'

'I don't think Moira is particularly helpless,' said Bobby.

'Nonsense. She's like a little bird that sits and waits to be eaten by a snake without doing anything about it.'

'What could she do?'

'Heaps of things,' said Frankie vigorously.

'Well, I don't see it. She's got no money, no friends—'

'My dear, don't drone on as though you were recommending a case to the Girls' Friendly Society.'

'Sorry,' said Bobby.

There was an offended pause.

'Well,' said Frankie, recovering her temper. 'As you were. I think we'd better get on to this business as soon as possible.'

'So do I,' said Bobby. 'Really, Frankie, it's awfully decent of you to—'

'That's all right,' said Frankie, interrupting him. 'I don't mind befriending the girl so long as you don't drivel on about her as though she had no hands or feet or tongue or brains.'

'I simply don't know what you mean,' said Bobby.

'Well, we needn't talk about it,' said Frankie. 'Now, my idea is that whatever we're going to do we'd better do it quickly. Is that a quotation?'

'It's a paraphrase of one. Go on, Lady Macbeth.'

'You know, I've always thought,' said Frankie, suddenly digressing wildly from the matter in hand, 'that Lady Macbeth incited Macbeth to do all those murders simply and solely because she was so frightfully bored with life—and incidentally with Macbeth. I'm sure he was one of those meek, inoffensive men who drive their wives distracted with boredom. But, having once committed a murder for the first time in his life, he felt the hell of a fine fellow and began to develop egomania as a compensation for his former inferiority complex.'

'You ought to write a book on the subject, Frankie.'

'I can't spell. Now, where were we? Oh, yes, rescue of Moira. You'd better bring the car round at half-past ten. I'll drive over to the Grange, ask for Moira and, if Nicholson's there when I see her, I'll remind her of her promise to come and stay with me and carry her off then and there.'

'Excellent, Frankie. I'm glad we're not going to waste any time. I've a horror of another accident happening.'

'Half-past ten, then,' said Frankie.

By the time she got back to Merroway Court, it was half-past nine. Breakfast had just been brought in and Roger was pouring himself out some coffee. He looked ill and worn.

'Good morning,' said Frankie. 'I slept awfully badly. In the end I got up about seven and went for a walk.'

'I'm frightfully sorry you should have been let in for all this worry,' said Roger.

'How's Sylvia?'

'They gave her an opiate last night. She's still asleep, I believe. Poor girl, I'm most terribly sorry for her. She was simply devoted to Henry.'

'I know.'

Frankie paused and then explained her plans for departure.

'I suppose you'll have to go,' said Roger resentfully. 'The inquest's on Friday. I'll let you know if you're wanted for it. It all depends on the coroner.'

He swallowed a cup of coffee and a piece of toast and then went off to attend to the many things requiring his attention. Frankie felt very sorry for him. The amount of gossip and curiosity created by a suicide in a family she could imagine only too well. Tommy appeared and she devoted herself to amusing the child.

Bobby brought the car round at half-past ten; Frankie's luggage was brought down. She said goodbye to Tommy and left a note for Sylvia. The Bentley drove away.

They covered the distance to the Grange in a very short time. Frankie had never been there before and the big iron gates and the overgrown shrubbery depressed her spirits.

'It's a creepy place,' she observed. 'I don't wonder Moira gets the horrors here.'

They drove up to the front door and Bobby got down and rang the bell. It was not answered for some minutes. Finally a woman in nurse's kit opened it.

'Mrs Nicholson?' said Bobby.

The woman hesitated, then withdrew into the hall and opened the door wider. Frankie jumped out of the car and passed into the house. The door closed behind her. It had a nasty echoing clang as it shut. Frankie noticed that it had heavy bolts and bars across it. Quite irrationally she felt afraid—as though she was here, in this sinister house, a prisoner.

'Nonsense,' she told herself. 'Bobby's outside in the car. I've come here openly. Nothing can happen to me.' And, shaking off the ridiculous feeling, she followed the nurse upstairs and along a passage. The nurse threw open a door and Frankie passed into a small sitting-room daintily furnished with cheerful chintzes and flowers in the vases. Her spirits rose. Murmuring something, the nurse withdrew.

About five minutes passed and the door opened and Dr Nicholson came in.

Frankie was quite unable to control a slight nervous start, but she masked it by a welcoming smile and shook hands.

'Good morning,' she said.

'Good morning, Lady Frances. You have not come to bring me bad news of Mrs Bassington-ffrench, I hope?'

'She was still asleep when I left,' said Frankie.

'Poor lady. Her own doctor is, of course, looking after her.'

'Oh! yes.' She paused, then said: 'I'm sure you're busy. I mustn't take up your time, Dr Nicholson. I really called to see your wife.'

'To see Moira? That was very kind of you.'

Was it only fancy, or did the pale-blue eyes behind the strong glasses harden ever so slightly?

'Yes,' he repeated. 'That was very kind.'

'If she isn't up yet,' said Frankie, smiling pleasantly, 'I'll sit down and wait.'

'Oh! she's up,' said Dr Nicholson.

'Good,' said Frankie. 'I want to persuade her to come to me for a visit. She's practically promised to.' She smiled again.

'Why, now, that's really very kind of you, Lady Frances— very kind, indeed. I'm sure Moira would have enjoyed that very much.'

'Would have?' asked Frankie sharply.

Dr Nicholson smiled, showing his fine set of even white teeth.

'Unfortunately, my wife went away this morning.'

'Went away?' said Frankie blankly. 'Where?'

'Oh! just for a little change. You know what women are, Lady Frances. This is rather a gloomy place for a young woman. Occasionally Moira feels she must have a little excitement and then off she goes.'

'You don't know where she has gone?' said Frankie.

'London, I imagine. Shops and theatres. You know the sort of thing.'

Frankie felt that his smile was the most disagreeable thing she had ever come across.

'I am going up to London today,' she said lightly. 'Will you give me her address?'

'She usually stays at the Savoy,' said Dr Nicholson. 'But in any case I shall probably hear from her in a day or so. She's not a very good correspondent, I'm afraid, and I believe in perfect liberty between husband and wife. But I think the Savoy is the most likely place for you to find her.'

He held the door open and Frankie found herself shaking hands with him and being ushered to the front door. The nurse was standing there to let her out. The last thing Frankie heard was Dr Nicholson's voice, suave and, perhaps, just a trifle ironical.

'So very kind of you to think of asking my wife to stay, Lady Frances.'

CHAPTER 24

On the Track of the Caymans

Bobby had some ado to preserve his impassive chauffeur's demeanour as Frankie came out alone.

She said: 'Back to Staverley, Hawkins,' for the benefit of the nurse.

The car swept down the drive and out through the gates. Then, when they came to an empty bit of road, Bobby pulled up and looked inquiringly at his companion.

'What about it?' he asked.

Rather pale, Frankie replied:

'Bobby, I don't like it. Apparently, she's gone away.'

'Gone *away*? This morning?'

'Or last night.'

'Without a word to us?'

'Bobby, I just don't believe it. The man was lying—I'm sure of it.'

Bobby had gone very pale. He murmured:

'Too late! Idiots that we've been! We should never have let her go back there yesterday.'

199

'You don't think she's—dead, do you?' whispered Frankie in a shaky voice.

'No,' said Bobby in a violent voice, as though to reassure himself.

They were both silent for a minute or two, then Bobby stated his deductions in a calmer tone.

'She must be still alive, because of the disposing of the body and all that. Her death would have to seem natural and accidental. No, she's either been spirited away somewhere against her will, or else—and this is what I believe—she's still there.'

'At the Grange?'

'At the Grange.'

'Well,' said Frankie, 'what are we going to do?'

Bobby thought for a minute.

'I don't think you can do anything,' he said at last. 'You'd better go back to London. You suggested trying to trace the Caymans. Go on with that.'

'Oh, Bobby!'

'My dear, you can't be of any use down here. You're known—very well known by now. You've announced that you're going—what can you do? You can't stay on at Merroway. You can't come and stay at the Anglers' Arms. You'd set every tongue in the neighbourhood wagging. No, you must go. Nicholson may suspect, but he can't be *sure* that you know anything. You go back to town and I'll stay.'

'At the Anglers' Arms?'

'No, I think your chauffeur will now disappear. I shall take up my headquarters at Ambledever—that's ten miles away—and if Moira's still in that beastly house I shall find her.'

Frankie demurred a little.

'Bobby, you will be careful?'

'I shall be cunning as the serpent.'

With rather a heavy heart Frankie gave in. What Bobby said was certainly sensible enough. She herself could do no further good down here. Bobby drove her up to town and Frankie, letting herself into the Brook Street house, felt suddenly forlorn.

She was not one, however, to let the grass grow under her feet. At three o'clock that afternoon, a fashionably but soberly dressed young woman with pince-nez and an earnest frown might have been seen approaching St Leonard's Gardens, a sheaf of pamphlets and papers in her hand.

St Leonard's Gardens, Paddington, was a distinctly gloomy collection of houses, most of them in a somewhat dilapidated condition. The place had a general air of having seen 'better days' a long time ago.

Frankie walked along, looking up at the numbers. Suddenly she came to a halt with a grimace of vexation.

No. 17 had a board up announcing that it was to be sold or let unfurnished.

Frankie immediately removed the pince-nez and the earnest air.

It seemed that the political canvasser would not be required.

The names of several house agents were given. Frankie selected two and wrote them down. Then, having determined on her plan of campaign, she proceeded to put it into action.

The first agents were Messrs. Gordon & Porter of Praed Street.

'Good afternoon,' said Frankie. 'I wonder if you can give me the address of a Mr Cayman? He was until recently at 17 St Leonard's Gardens.'

'That's right,' said the young man to whom Frankie had addressed herself. 'Only there a short time, though, wasn't he? We act for the owners, you see. Mr Cayman took it on a quarterly tenancy as he might have to take up a post abroad any moment. I believe he's actually done so.'

'Then you haven't got his address?'

'I'm afraid not. He settled up with us and that was all.'

'But he must have had some address originally when he took the house.'

'A hotel—I think it was the G.W.R., Paddington Station, you know.'

'References,' suggested Frankie.

'He paid the quarter's rent in advance and a deposit to cover the electric light and gas.'

'Oh!' said Frankie, feeling despairing.

She saw the young man looking rather curiously at her. House agents are adepts at summing up the 'class' of clients. He obviously found Frankie's interest in the Caymans rather unexpected.

'He owes me a good deal of money,' said Frankie mendaciously.

The young man's face immediately assumed a shocked expression.

Thoroughly sympathetic with beauty in distress, he hunted up files of correspondence and did all he could, but no trace of Mr Cayman's present or late abode could be found.

Frankie thanked him and departed. She took a taxi to the next firm of house agents. She wasted no time in repeating the process. The first agents were the ones who had let Cayman the house. These people would be merely concerned to let it again on behalf of the owner. Frankie asked for an order to view.

This time, to counteract the expression of surprise that she saw appear on the clerk's face, she explained that she wanted a cheap property to open as a hostel for girls. The surprised expression disappeared, and Frankie emerged with the key of 17 Leonard's Gardens, the keys of two more 'properties' which she had no wish to see, and an order to view yet a fourth.

It was a bit of luck, Frankie thought, that the clerk had not wished to accompany her, but perhaps they only did that when it was a question of a furnished tenancy.

The musty smell of a closed-up house assailed Frankie's nostrils as she unlocked and pushed open the front door of No. 17.

It was an unappetising house, cheaply decorated, and with blistered, dirty paint. Frankie went over it methodically from garret to basement. The house had not been cleaned up on departure. There were bits of string, old newspapers and some odd nails and tools. But of personal matter, Frankie could not find so much as the scrap of a torn-up letter.

Agatha Christie

The only thing that struck her as having a possible significance was an ABC railway guide which lay open on one of the window seats. There was nothing to indicate that any of the names of the open page were of special significance, but Frankie copied the lot down in a little note-book as a poor substitute for all she had hoped to find.

As far as tracing the Caymans was concerned, she had drawn a blank.

She consoled herself with the reflection that this was only to be expected. If Mr and Mrs Cayman were associated with the wrong side of the law they would take particularly good care that no one should be able to trace them. It was at least a kind of negative confirmatory evidence.

Still Frankie felt definitely disappointed as she handed back the keys to the house agents and uttered mendacious statements as to communicating with them in a few days.

She walked down towards the Park feeling rather depressed and wondered what on earth she was going to do next. These fruitless meditations were interrupted by a sharp and violent squall of rain. No taxi was in sight and Frankie hurriedly preserved a favourite hat by hurrying into the tube which was close at hand. She took a ticket to Piccadilly Circus and bought a couple of papers at the bookstall.

When she had entered the train—almost empty at this time of day—she resolutely banished thoughts of the vexing problem and, opening her paper, strove to concentrate her attention on its contents.

She read desultory snippets here and there.

Number of road deaths. Mysterious disappearance of a schoolgirl. Lady Peterhampton's party at Claridge's. Sir John Milkington's convalescence after his accident yachting—the *Astradora*—the famous yacht which had belonged to the late Mr John Savage, the millionaire. Was she an unlucky boat? The man who had designed her had met with a tragic death—Mr Savage had committed suicide— Sir John Milkington had just escaped death by a miracle.

Frankie lowered the paper, frowning in an effort of remembrance.

Twice before, the name of Mr John Savage had been mentioned—once by Sylvia Bassington-ffrench when she was speaking of Alan Carstairs, and once by Bobby when he was repeating the conversation he had had with Mrs Rivington.

Alan Carstairs had been a friend of John Savage's. Mrs Rivington had had a vague idea that Carstairs' presence in England had something to do with the death of Savage. Savage had—what was it?—he had committed suicide because he thought he had cancer.

Supposing—supposing Alan Carstairs had not been satisfied with the account of his friend's death. Supposing he had come over to inquire into the whole thing? Supposing that here, in the circumstances surrounding Savage's death—was the first act of the drama that she and Bobby were acting in.

'It's possible,' thought Frankie. 'Yes, it's possible.'

She thought deeply, wondering how best to attack this new phase of the matter. She had no idea as to who had been John Savage's friends or intimates.

Then an idea struck her—his will. If there had been something suspicious about the way he met his death, his will would give a possible clue.

Somewhere in London, Frankie knew, was a place where you went and read wills if you paid a shilling. But she couldn't remember where it was.

The train drew up at a station and Frankie saw that it was the British Museum. She had overshot Oxford Circus, where she meant to have changed, by two stations.

She jumped up and left the train. As she emerged into the street an idea came to her. Five minutes' walk brought her to the office of Messrs Spragge, Spragge, Jenkinson & Spragge.

Frankie was received with deference and was at once ushered into the private fastness of Mr Spragge, the senior member of the firm.

Mr Spragge was exceedingly genial. He had a rich mellow persuasive voice which his aristocratic clients had found extremely soothing when they had come to him to be extricated from some mess. It was rumoured that Mr Spragge knew more discreditable secrets about noble families than any other man in London.

'This is a pleasure indeed, Lady Frances,' said Mr Spragge. 'Do sit down. Now are you sure that chair is quite comfortable? Yes, yes. The weather is very delightful just now, is it not? A St Martin's summer. And how is Lord Marchington? Well, I trust?'

Frankie answered these and other inquiries in a suitable manner.

Then Mr Spragge removed his pince-nez from his

nose and became more definitely the legal guide and adviser.

'And now, Lady Frances,' he said. 'What is it gives me the pleasure of seeing you in my—hm—dingy office this afternoon?'

'Blackmail?' said his eyebrows. 'Indiscreet letters? An entanglement with an undesirable young man? Sued by your dressmaker?'

But the eyebrows asked these questions in a very discreet manner as befitted a solicitor of Mr Spragge's experience and income.

'I want to look at a will,' said Frankie. 'And I don't know where you go and what you do. But there is somewhere you can pay a shilling, isn't there?'

'Somerset House,' said Mr Spragge. 'But what will is it? I think I can possibly tell you anything you want to know about—er—wills in your family. I may say that I believe our firm has had the honour of drawing them up for many years past.'

'It isn't a family will,' said Frankie.

'No?' said Mr Spragge.

And so strong was his almost hypnotic power of drawing confidences out of his clients that Frankie, who had not meant to do so, succumbed to the manner and told him.

'I wanted to see the will of Mr Savage—John Savage.'

'In-deed?' A very real astonishment showed in Mr Spragge's voice. He had not expected this. 'Now that is very extraordinary—very extraordinary indeed.'

There was something so unusual in his voice that Frankie looked at him in surprise.

'Really,' said Mr Spragge. 'Really, I do not know what to do. Perhaps, Lady Frances, you can give me your reasons for wanting to see that will?'

'No,' said Frankie slowly. 'I'm afraid I can't.'

It struck her that Mr Spragge was, for some reason, behaving quite unlike his usual benign omniscient self. He looked actually worried.

'I really believe,' said Mr Spragge, 'that I ought to warn you.'

'Warn me?' said Frankie.

'Yes. The indications are vague, very vague—but clearly there is something afoot. I would not, for the world, have you involved in any questionable business.'

As far as that went, Frankie could have told him that she was already involved up to the neck in a business of which he would have decidedly disapproved. But she merely stared at him inquiringly.

'The whole thing is rather an extraordinary coincidence,' Mr Spragge was going on. 'Something is clearly afoot—clearly. But what it is I am not at present at liberty to say.'

Frankie continued to look inquiring.

'A piece of information has just come to my knowledge,' continued Mr Spragge. His chest swelled with indignation. 'I have been impersonated, Lady Frances. Deliberately impersonated. What do you say to that?'

But for just one panic-stricken minute Frankie could say nothing at all.

CHAPTER 25

Mr Spragge Talks

At last she stammered:

'How did you find out?'

It was not at all what she meant to say. She could, in fact, have bitten out her tongue for stupidity a moment later, but the words had been said, and Mr Spragge would have been no lawyer had he failed to perceive that they contained an admission.

'So you know something of this business, Lady Frances?'

'Yes,' said Frankie.

She paused, drew a deep breath and said:

'The whole thing is really my doing, Mr Spragge.'

'I am amazed,' said Mr Spragge.

There was a struggle in his voice, the outraged lawyer was at war with the fatherly family solicitor.

'How did this come about?' he asked.

'It was just a joke,' said Frankie weakly. 'We—we wanted something to do.'

'And who,' demanded Mr Spragge, 'had the idea of passing himself off as Me?'

Frankie looked at him, her wits working once more, made a rapid decision.

'It was the young Duke of No—' She broke off: 'I really mustn't mention names. It isn't fair.'

But she knew that the tide had turned in her favour. It was doubtful if Mr Spragge could have forgiven a mere vicar's son such audacity, but his weakness for noble names led him to look softly on the impertinences of a duke. His benign manner returned.

'Oh! you Bright Young People—You Bright Young People,' he murmured, wagging a forefinger. 'What trouble you land yourselves in. You would be surprised, Lady Frances, at the amount of legal complications that may ensue from an apparently harmless practical joke determined upon on the spur of the moment. Just high spirits—but sometimes extremely difficult to settle out of court.'

'I think you're too marvellous, Mr Spragge,' said Frankie earnestly. 'I do, really. Not one person in a thousand would have taken it as you have done. I feel really terribly ashamed.'

'No, no, Lady Frances,' said Mr Spragge paternally.

'Oh, but I do. I suppose it was the Rivington woman—what exactly did she tell you?'

'I think I have the letter here. I opened it only half an hour ago.'

Frankie held out a hand and Mr Spragge put the letter into it with the air of one saying: 'There, see for yourself what your foolishness has led you into.'

Dear Mr Spragge (Mrs Rivington had written), *It's really too stupid of me, but I've just remembered something that might have helped you the day you called on me. Alan Carstairs mentioned that he was going to a place called Chipping Somerton. I don't know whether this will be any help to you.*

I was so interested in what you told me about the Maltravers case. With kind regards,

Yours sincerely,

Edith Rivington.

'You can see that the matter might have been very grave,' said Mr Spragge severely, but with a severity tempered by benevolence. 'I took it that some extremely questionable business was afoot. Whether connected with the Maltravers case or with my client, Mr Carstairs—'

Frankie interrupted him.

'Was Alan Carstairs a client of yours?' she inquired excitedly.

'He was. He consulted me when he was last in England a month ago. You know Mr Carstairs, Lady Frances?'

'I think I may say I do,' said Frankie.

'A most attractive personality,' said Mr Spragge. 'He brought quite a breath of the—er—wide open spaces into my office.'

'He came to consult you about Mr Savage's will, didn't he?' said Frankie.

'Ah!' said Mr Spragge. 'So it was you who advised him to come to me? He couldn't remember just who it was. I'm sorry I couldn't do more for him.'

'Just what did you advise him to do?' asked Frankie. 'Or would it be unprofessional to tell me?'

'Not in this case,' said Mr Spragge, smiling. 'My opinion was that there was nothing to be done—nothing, that is, unless Mr Savage's relatives were prepared to spend a lot of money on fighting the case—which I gather they were not prepared, or indeed in a position, to do. I never advise bringing a case into court unless there is every hope of success. The law, Lady Frances, is an uncertain animal. It has twists and turns that surprise the non-legal mind. Settle out of court has always been my motto.'

'The whole thing was very curious,' said Frankie thoughtfully.

She had a little of the sensation of walking barefoot over a floor covered with tin tacks. At any minute she might step on one—and the game would be up.

'Such cases are less uncommon than you might think,' said Mr Spragge.

'Cases of suicide?' inquired Frankie.

'No, no, I meant cases of undue influence. Mr Savage was a hard-headed business man, and yet he was clearly as wax in this woman's hands. I've no doubt she knew her business thoroughly.'

'I wish you'd tell me the whole story properly,' said Frankie boldly. 'Mr Carstairs was—well, was so heated, that I never seemed to get the thing clearly.'

'The case was extremely simple,' said Mr Spragge. 'I can run over the facts to you—they are accessible to everyone— so there is no objection to my doing so.'

'Then tell me all about it,' said Frankie.

'Mr Savage happened to be travelling back from the United States to England in November of last year. He was, as you know, an extremely wealthy man with no near relations. On this voyage he made the acquaintance of a certain lady—a—er—Mrs Templeton. Nothing much is known about Mrs Templeton except that she was a very good-looking woman and had a husband somewhere conveniently in the background.'

'The Caymans,' thought Frankie.

'These ocean trips are dangerous,' went on Mr Spragge, smiling and shaking his head. 'Mr Savage was clearly very much attracted. He accepted the lady's invitation to come down and stay at her little cottage at Chipping Somerton. Exactly how often he went there I have not been able to ascertain, but there is no doubt that he came more and more under this Mrs Templeton's influence.

'Then came the tragedy. Mr Savage had for some time been uneasy about his state of health. He feared that he might be suffering from a certain disease—'

'Cancer?' said Frankie.

'Well, yes, as a matter of fact, cancer. The subject became quite an obsession with him. He was staying with the Templetons at the time. They persuaded him to go up to London and consult a specialist. He did so. Now here, Lady Frances, I preserve an open mind. That specialist—a very distinguished man who has been at the top of his profession for many years—swore at the inquest that Mr Savage was not suffering from cancer and that he had told him so, but that Mr Savage was so obsessed by his own belief that he could not accept the truth when he was told it. Now, strictly without prejudice, Lady Frances, and knowing the medical profession, I think things may have gone a little differently. If Mr Savage's symptoms puzzled the doctor he may have spoken seriously, pulled a long face, spoken of certain expensive treatments and while reassuring him as to cancer yet have conveyed the impression that something was seriously wrong. Mr Savage, having heard that doctors usually conceal from a patient the fact that he *is* suffering from that disease, would interpret this according to his own lights. The doctor's reassuring words were *not* true—he *had* got the disease he thought he had.

'Anyway, Mr Savage came back to Chipping Somerton in a state of great mental distress. He saw ahead of him a painful and lingering death. I understand some members of his family had died of cancer and he determined not to go through what he had seen them suffer. He sent for a solicitor—a very reputable member of an eminently respectable firm—and the latter drew up a will there and then which Mr Savage signed and which he then delivered over to the solicitor for safe keeping. On that same evening Mr Savage took a large overdose of chloral, leaving a letter behind in which he explained that he preferred a quick and painless death to a long and painful one.

'By his will Mr Savage left the sum of seven hundred thousand pounds free of legacy duty to Mrs Templeton and the remainder to certain specified charities.'

Mr Spragge leaned back in his chair. He was now enjoying himself.

'The jury brought in the usual sympathetic verdict of Suicide while of Unsound Mind, but I do not think that

214

we can argue from that that he was necessarily of unsound mind when he made the will. I do not think that any jury would take it so. The will was made in the presence of a solicitor in whose opinion the deceased was undoubtedly sane and in possession of his senses. Nor do I think we can prove undue influence. Mr Savage did not disinherit anyone near and dear to him—his only relatives were distant cousins whom he seldom saw. They actually lived in Australia, I believe.'

Mr Spragge paused.

'Mr Carstairs' contention was that such a will was completely uncharacteristic of Mr Savage. Mr Savage had no liking for organized charities and had always held very strong opinions as to money passing by blood relationship. However, Mr Carstairs had no documentary proof of these assertions and, as I pointed out to him, men change their opinions. In contesting such a will, there would be the charitable organizations to deal with as well as Mrs Templeton. Also, the will had been admitted to probate.'

'There was no fuss made at the time?' asked Frankie.

'As I say, Mr Savage's relatives were not living in this country and they knew very little about the matter. It was Mr Carstairs who took the matter up. He returned from a trip into the interior of Africa, gradually learnt the details of this business and came over to this country to see if something could be done about it. I was forced to tell him that in my view there was nothing to be done. Possession is nine points of the law, and Mrs Templeton was in possession. Moreover, she had left the country and gone, I believe, to the South of France to live. She refused to enter into any communication on the matter. I suggested getting counsel's opinion but Mr Carstairs decided that it was not necessary and took my view that there was nothing to be done—or, alternatively, that whatever might have been done at the time, and in my opinion that was exceedingly doubtful, it was now too late to do it.'

'I see,' said Frankie. 'And nobody knows anything about this Mrs Templeton?'

Mr Spragge shook his head and pursed his lips.

'A man like Mr Savage, with his knowledge of life, ought to have been less easily taken in—but—' Mr Spragge shook his head sadly as a vision of innumerable clients who ought to have known better and who had come to him to have their cases settled out of court passed across his mind.

Frankie rose.

'Men are extraordinary creatures,' she said.

She held out a hand.

'Goodbye, Mr Spragge,' she said. 'You've been wonderful—simply wonderful. I feel too ashamed.'

'You Bright Young People must be more careful,' said Mr Spragge, shaking his head at her.

'You've been an angel,' said Frankie.

She squeezed his hand fervently and departed.

Mr Spragge sat down again before his table.

He was thinking.

'The young Duke of—'

There were only two dukes who could be so described. Which was it?

He picked up a *Peerage*.

CHAPTER 26

Nocturnal Adventure

The inexplicable absence of Moira worried Bobby more than he cared to admit. He told himself repeatedly that it was absurd to jump to conclusions—that it was fantastic to imagine that Moira had been done away with in a house full of possible witnesses—that there was probably some perfectly simple explanation and that at the worst she could only be a prisoner in the Grange.

That she had left Staverley of her own free will Bobby did not for one minute believe. He was convinced that she would never have gone off like that without sending him a word of explanation. Besides, she had stated emphatically that she had nowhere to go.

No, the sinister Dr Nicholson was at the bottom of this. Somehow or other he must have become aware of Moira's activities and this was his counter move. Somewhere within the sinister walls of the Grange Moira was a prisoner, unable to communicate with the outside world.

But she might not remain a prisoner long. Bobby believed implicitly every word Moira had uttered. Her fears were

217

neither the result of a vivid imagination nor yet of nerves. They were simple stark truth.

Nicholson meant to get rid of his wife. Several times his plans had miscarried. Now, by communicating her fears to others, she had forced his hand. He must act quickly or not at all. Would he have the nerve to act?

Bobby believed he would. He must know that, even if these strangers had listened to his wife's fears, they had no evidence. Also, he would believe that he had only Frankie to deal with. It was possible that he had suspected her from the first—his pertinent questioning as to her 'accident' seemed to point to that—but as Lady Frances' chauffeur, Bobby did not believe that he himself was suspected of being anything other than he appeared to be.

Yes, Nicholson would act. Moira's body would probably be found in some district far from Staverley. It might, perhaps, be washed up by the sea. Or it might be found at the foot of a cliff. The thing would appear to be, Bobby was almost sure, an 'accident'. Nicholson specialized in accidents.

Nevertheless, Bobby believed that the planning and carrying out of such an accident would need time—not much time, but a certain amount. Nicholson's hand was being forced—he had to act quicker than he had anticipated. It seemed reasonable to suppose that twenty-four hours at least must elapse before he could put any plan into operation.

Before that interval had elapsed, Bobby meant to have found Moira if she were in the Grange.

After he had left Frankie in Brook Street, he started to

put his plans into operation. He judged it wise to give the Mews a wide berth. For all he knew, a watch might be being kept on it. As Hawkins, he believed himself to be still unsuspected. Now Hawkins in turn was about to disappear.

That evening, a young man with a moustache, dressed in a cheap dark-blue suit, arrived at the bustling little town of Ambledever. The young man put up at an hotel near the station, registering as George Parker. Having deposited his suitcase there he strolled out and entered into negotiations for hiring a motor-cycle.

At ten o'clock that evening a motor-cyclist in cap and goggles passed through the village of Staverley, and came to a halt at a deserted part of the road not far from the Grange.

Hastily shoving the bicycle behind some convenient bushes, Bobby looked up and down the road. It was quite deserted.

Then he sauntered along the wall till he came to the little door. As before, it was unlocked. With another look up and down the road to make sure he was not observed, Bobby slipped quietly inside. He put his hand into the pocket of his coat where a bulge showed the presence of his service revolver. The feel of it was reassuring.

Inside the grounds of the Grange everything seemed quiet.

Bobby grinned to himself as he recalled bloodcurdling stories where the villain of the piece kept a cheetah or some exciting beast of prey about the place to deal with intruders.

Dr Nicholson seemed content with mere bolts and bars and even there he seemed to be somewhat remiss. Bobby felt certain that that little door should not have been left open. As the villain of the piece, Dr Nicholson seemed regrettably careless.

'No tame pythons,' thought Bobby. 'No cheetahs, no electrically-charged wires—the man is shamefully behind the times.'

He made these reflections more to cheer himself up than for any other reason. Every time he thought of Moira a queer constriction seemed to tighten around his heart.

Her face rose in the air before him—the trembling lips—the wide, terrified eyes. It was just about here he had first seen her in the flesh. A little thrill ran through him as he remembered how he had put his arm round her to steady her . . .

Moira—where was she now? What had that sinister doctor done with her? If only she were still alive . . .

'She must be,' said Bobby grimly between set lips. 'I'm not going to think anything else.'

He made a careful reconnaissance round the house. Some of the upstairs windows had lights in them and there was one lighted window on the ground floor.

Towards this window Bobby crept. The curtains were drawn across it, but there was a slight chink between them. Bobby put a knee on the window-sill and hoisted himself noiselessly up. He peered through the slits.

He could see a man's arm and shoulder moving along

as though writing. Presently the man shifted his position and his profile came into view. It was Dr Nicholson.

It was a curious position. Quite unconscious that he was being watched, the doctor wrote steadily on. A queer sort of fascination stole over Bobby. The man was so near him that, but for the intervening glass, he could have stretched out his arm and touched him.

For the first time, Bobby felt, he was really seeing the man. It was a forceful profile, the big, bold nose, the jutting chin, the crisp, well-shaven line of the jaw. The ears, Bobby noted, were small and laid flat to the head and the lobe of the ear was actually joined to the cheek. He had an idea that ears like these were said to have some special significance.

The doctor wrote on—calm and unhurried. Now pausing for a moment or two as though to think of the right word—then setting to once more. His pen moved over the paper, precisely and evenly. Once he took off his pince-nez, polished them and put them on again.

At last with a sigh Bobby let himself slide noiselessly to the ground. From the look of it, Nicholson would be writing for some time to come. Now was the moment to gain admission to the house.

If Bobby could force an entrance by an upstairs window while the doctor was writing in his study he could explore the building at his leisure later in the night.

He made a circuit of the house again and singled out a window on the first floor. The sash was open at the top but there was no light in the room, so that it was probably

221

unoccupied at the moment. Moreover, a very convenient tree seemed to promise an easy means of access.

In another minute, Bobby was swarming up the tree. All went well and he was just stretching out his hand to take a grip of the window ledge when an ominous crack came from the branch he was on and the next minute the bough, a rotten one, had snapped and Bobby was pitchforked head first into a clump of hydrangea bushes below, which fortunately broke his fall.

The window of Nicholson's study was farther along on the same side of the house. Bobby heard an exclamation in the doctor's voice and the window was flung up. Bobby, recovering from the first shock of his fall, sprang up, disentangled himself from the hydrangeas and bolted across the dark patch of shadow into the pathway leading to the little door. He went a short way along it, then dived into the bushes.

He heard the sound of voices and saw lights moving near the trampled and broken hydrangeas. Bobby kept still and held his breath. They might come along the path. If so, finding the door open, they would probably conclude that anyone had escaped that way and would not prosecute the search further.

However, the minutes passed and nobody came. Presently Bobby heard Nicholson's voice raised in a question. He did not hear the words but he heard an answer given in a hoarse, rather uneducated voice.

'All present and correct, sir. I've been the rounds.'

The sounds gradually died down, the lights disappeared. Everyone seemed to have returned to the house.

Very cautiously, Bobby came out of his hiding place. He emerged on to the path, listening. All was still. He took a step or two towards the house.

And then out of the darkness something struck him on the back of the neck. He fell forward . . . into darkness.

CHAPTER 27

'My Brother was Murdered'

On Friday morning the green Bentley drew up outside the Station Hotel at Ambledever.

Frankie had wired Bobby under the name they had agreed upon—George Parker—that she would be required to give evidence at the inquest on Henry Bassington-ffrench and would call in at Ambledever on the way down from London.

She had expected a wire in reply appointing some rendezvous, but nothing had come, so she had come to the hotel.

'Mr Parker, miss?' said the boots. 'I don't think there's any gentleman of that name stopping here, but I'll see.'

He returned a few minutes later.

'Came here Wednesday evening, miss. Left his bag and said he mightn't be in till late. His bag's still here but he hasn't been back to fetch it.'

Frankie felt suddenly rather sick. She clutched at a table for support. The man was looking at her sympathetically.

'Feeling bad, miss?' he inquired.

Frankie shook her head.

224

'It's all right,' she managed to say. 'He didn't leave any message?'

The man went away again and returned, shaking his head.

'There's a telegram come for him,' he said. 'That's all.'

He looked at her curiously.

'Anything I can do, miss?' he asked.

Frankie shook her head.

At the moment she only wanted to get away. She must have time to think what to do next.

'It's all right,' she said and, getting into the Bentley, she drove away.

The man nodded his head wisely as he looked after her.

'He's done a bunk, he has,' he said to himself. 'Disappointed her. Given her the slip. A fine rakish piece of goods she is. Wonder what he was like?'

He asked the young lady in the reception office, but the young lady couldn't remember.

'A couple of nobs,' said the boots wisely. 'Going to get married on the quiet—and he's hooked it.'

Meanwhile, Frankie was driving in the direction of Staverley, her mind a maze of conflicting emotions.

Why had Bobby not returned to the Station Hotel? There could only be two reasons: either he was on the trail—and that trail had taken him away somewhere, or else—or else something had gone wrong. The Bentley swerved dangerously. Frankie recovered control just in time.

She was being an idiot—imagining things. Of course, Bobby was all right. He was on the trail—that was all—on the trail.

225

But why, asked another voice, hadn't he sent her a word of reassurance?

That was more difficult to explain, but there were explanations. Difficult circumstances—no time or opportunity—Bobby would know that she, Frankie, wouldn't get the wind up about him. Everything was all right—bound to be.

The inquest passed like a dream. Roger was there and Sylvia—looking quite beautiful in her widow's weeds. She made an impressive figure and a moving one. Frankie found herself admiring her as though she were admiring a performance at a theatre.

The proceedings were very tactfully conducted. The Bassington-ffrenches were popular locally and everything was done to spare the feelings of the widow and the brother of the dead man.

Frankie and Roger gave their evidence—Dr Nicholson gave his—the dead man's farewell letter was produced. The thing seemed over in no time and the verdict given—'Suicide while of Unsound Mind'.

The 'sympathetic' verdict, as Mr Spragge had called it.

The two events connected themselves in Frankie's mind.

Two suicides while of Unsound Mind. Was there—could there be a connection between them?

That this suicide was genuine enough she knew, for she had been on the scene. Bobby's theory of murder had had to be dismissed as untenable. Dr Nicholson's alibi was cast iron—vouched for by the widow herself.

Frankie and Dr Nicholson remained behind after the

other people departed, the coroner having shaken hands with Sylvia and uttered a few words of sympathy.

'I think there are some letters for you, Frankie dear,' said Sylvia. 'You won't mind if I leave you now and go and lie down. It's all been so awful.'

She shivered and left the room. Nicholson went with her, murmuring something about a sedative.

Frankie turned to Roger.

'Roger, Bobby's disappeared.'

'Disappeared?'

'Yes!'

'Where and how?'

Frankie explained in a few rapid words.

'And he's not been seen since?' said Roger.

'No. What do you think?'

'I don't like the sound of it,' said Roger slowly.

Frankie's heart sank.

'You don't think—?'

'Oh! it may be all right, but—sh, here comes Nicholson.'

The doctor entered the room with his noiseless tread. He was rubbing his hands together and smiling.

'That went off very well,' he said. 'Very well, indeed. Dr Davidson was most tactful and considerate. We may consider ourselves very lucky to have had him as our local coroner.'

'I suppose so,' said Frankie mechanically.

'It makes a lot of difference, Lady Frances. The conduct of an inquest is entirely in the hands of the coroner. He has wide powers. He can make things easy or difficult as he pleases. In this case everything went off perfectly.'

'A good stage performance, in fact,' said Frankie in a hard voice.

Nicholson looked at her in surprise.

'I know what Lady Frances is feeling,' said Roger. 'I feel the same. My brother was murdered, Dr Nicholson.'

He was standing behind the other and did not see, as Frankie did, the startled expression that sprang into the doctor's eyes.

'I mean what I say,' said Roger, interrupting Nicholson as he was about to reply. 'The law may not regard it as such, but murder it was. The criminal brutes who induced my brother to become a slave to that drug murdered him just as truly as if they had struck him down.'

He had moved a little and his angry eyes now looked straight into the doctor's.

'I mean to get even with them,' he said; and the words sounded like a threat.

Dr Nicholson's pale-blue eyes fell before his. He shook his head sadly.

'I cannot say I disagree with you,' he said. 'I know more about drug-taking than you do, Mr Bassington-ffrench. To induce a man to take drugs is indeed a most terrible crime.'

Ideas were whirling through Frankie's head—one idea in particular.

'It can't be,' she was saying to herself. 'That would be too monstrous. And yet—his whole alibi depends on her word. But in that case—'

She roused herself to find Nicholson speaking to her.

'You came down by car, Lady Frances? No accident this time?'

228

Frankie felt she simply hated that smile.

'No,' she said. 'I think it's a pity to go in too much for accidents—don't you?'

She wondered if she had imagined it, or whether his eyelids really flickered for a moment.

'Perhaps your chauffeur drove you this time?'

'My chauffeur,' said Frankie, 'has disappeared.'

She looked straight at Nicholson.

'Indeed?'

'He was last seen heading for the Grange,' went on Frankie.

Nicholson raised his eyebrows.

'Really? Have I—some attraction in the kitchen?' His voice sounded amused. 'I can hardly believe it.'

'At any rate that is where he was last seen,' said Frankie.

'You sound quite dramatic,' said Nicholson. 'Possibly you are paying too much attention to local gossip. Local gossip is very unreliable. I have heard the wildest stories.' He paused. His voice altered slightly in tone. 'I have even had a story brought to my ears that my wife and your chauffeur had been seen talking together down by the river.' Another pause. 'He was, I believe, a very superior young man, Lady Frances.'

'Is that it?' thought Frankie. 'Is he going to pretend that his wife has run off with my chauffeur? Is that his little game?'

Aloud she said:

'Hawkins is quite above the average chauffeur.'

'So it seems,' said Nicholson.

He turned to Roger.

'I must be going. Believe me, all my sympathies are with you and Mrs Bassington-ffrench.'

Roger went out into the hall with him. Frankie followed. On the hall table were a couple of letters addressed to her. One was a bill. The other—

Her heart gave a leap.

The other was in Bobby's handwriting.

Nicholson and Roger were on the doorstep.

She tore it open.

Dear Frankie (wrote Bobby), *I'm on the trail at last. Follow me as soon as possible to Chipping Somerton. You'd better come by train and not by car. The Bentley is too noticeable. The trains aren't too good but you can get there all right. You're to come to a house called Tudor Cottage. I'll explain to you just exactly how to find it. Don't ask the way.* (Here followed some minute directions.) *Have you got that clear? Don't tell* anyone. (This was heavily underlined.) No one at all.

    Yours ever,
    Bobby.

Frankie crushed the letter excitedly in the palm of her hand.

So it was all right.

Nothing dreadful had overtaken Bobby.

He was on the trail—and by a coincidence on the same trail as herself. She had been to Somerset House to look up the will of John Savage. Rose Emily Templeton was given as the wife of Edgar Templeton of Tudor Cottage, Chipping Somerton. And that again had fitted in with the open ABC in the St Leonard's Gardens house. Chipping Somerton had been one of the stations on the open page. The Caymans had gone to Chipping Somerton.

Everything was falling into place. They were nearing the end of the chase.

Roger Bassington-ffrench turned and came towards her.

'Anything interesting in your letter?' he inquired casually.

For a moment Frankie hesitated. Surely Bobby had not meant Roger when he adjured her to tell nobody?

Then she remembered the heavy underlining—remembered, too, her own recent monstrous idea. If *that* were true, Roger might betray them both in all innocence. She dared not hint to him her own suspicions . . .

So she made up her mind and spoke.

'No,' she said. 'Nothing at all.'

She was to repent her decision bitterly before twenty-four hours had passed.

More than once in the course of the next few hours did she bitterly regret Bobby's dictum that the car was not to be used. Chipping Somerton was no very great distance as the crow flies but it involved changing three times, with a long dreary wait at a country station each time, and to one of Frankie's impatient temperament, this slow method of procedure was extremely hard to endure with fortitude.

Still, she felt bound to admit that there was something in what Bobby had said. The Bentley *was* a noticeable car.

Her excuses for leaving it at Merroway had been of the flimsiest order, but she had been unable to think of anything brilliant on the spur of the moment.

It was getting dark when Frankie's train, an extremely

deliberate and thoughtful train, drew into the little station of Chipping Somerton. To Frankie it seemed more like midnight. The train seemed to her to have been ambling on for hours and hours.

It was just beginning to rain, too, which was additionally trying.

Frankie buttoned up her coat to her neck, took a last look at Bobby's letter by the light of the station lamp, got the directions clearly in her head and set off.

The instructions were quite easy to follow. Frankie saw the lights of the village ahead and turned off to the left up a lane which led steeply uphill. At the top of the lane she took the right-hand fork and presently saw the little cluster of houses that formed the village lying below her and a belt of pine trees ahead. Finally, she came to a neat wooden gate and, striking a match, saw Tudor Cottage written on it.

There was no one about. Frankie slipped up the latch and passed inside. She could make out the outlines of the house behind a belt of pine trees. She took up her post within the trees where she could get a clear view of the house. Then, heart beating a little faster, she gave the best imitation she could of the hoot of an owl. A few minutes passed and nothing happened. She repeated the call.

The door of the cottage opened and she saw a figure in chauffeur's dress peer cautiously out. Bobby! He made a beckoning gesture then withdrew inside, leaving the door ajar.

Frankie came out from the trees and up to the door. There was no light in any window. Everything was perfectly dark and silent.

Frankie stepped gingerly over the threshold into a dark hall. She stopped, peering about her.

'Bobby?' she whispered.

It was her nose that gave her warning. Where had she known that smell before—that heavy, sweet odour?

Just as her brain gave the answer 'Chloroform', strong arms seized her from behind. She opened her mouth to scream and a wet pad was clapped over it. The sweet, cloying smell filled her nostrils.

She fought desperately, twisting and turning, kicking. But it was of no avail. Despite the fight she put up, she felt herself succumbing. There was a drumming in her ears, she felt herself choking. And then she knew no more . . .

CHAPTER 28

At the Eleventh Hour

When Frankie came to herself, the immediate reactions were depressing. There is nothing romantic about the after effects of chloroform. She was lying on an extremely hard wooden floor and her hands and feet were tied. She managed to roll herself over and her head nearly collided violently with a battered coal-box. Various distressing events then occurred.

A few minutes later, Frankie was able, if not to sit up, at least to take notice.

Close at hand she heard a faint groan. She peered about her. As far as she could make out, she seemed to be in a kind of attic. The only light came from a skylight in the roof, and at this moment there was very little of that. In a few minutes it would be quite dark. There were a few broken pictures lying against the wall, a dilapidated iron bed and some broken chairs, and the coal-scuttle before mentioned.

The groan seemed to have come from the corner.

Frankie's bonds were not very tight. They permitted

motion of a somewhat crablike type. She wormed her way across the dusty floor.

'Bobby!' she ejaculated.

Bobby it was, also tied hand and foot. In addition, he had a piece of cloth bound round his mouth.

This he had almost succeeded in working loose. Frankie came to his assistance. In spite of being bound together, her hands were still of some use and a final vigorous pull with her teeth finally did the job.

Rather stiffly, Bobby managed to ejaculate:

'Frankie!'

'I'm glad we're together,' said Frankie. 'But it does look as though we'd been had for mugs.'

'I suppose,' said Bobby gloomily, 'it's what they call a "fair cop".'

'How did they get you?' demanded Frankie. 'Was it after you wrote that letter to me?'

'What letter? I never wrote any letter.'

'Oh! I see,' said Frankie, her eyes opening. 'What an idiot I have been! And all that stuff in it about not telling a soul.'

'Look here, Frankie, I'll tell you what happened to me and then you carry on the good work and tell me what happened to you.'

He described his adventures at the Grange and their sinister sequel.

'I came to in this beastly hole,' he said. 'There was some food and drink on a tray. I was frightfully hungry and I had some. I think it must have been doped for I fell asleep almost immediately. What day is it?'

'Friday.'

'And I was knocked out on Wednesday evening. Dash it all, I've been pretty well unconscious all the time. Now tell me what happened to you.'

Frankie recounted her adventures, beginning with the story she had heard from Mr Spragge and carrying on until she thought she recognized Bobby's figure in the doorway.

'And then they chloroformed me,' she finished. 'And oh, Bobby, I've just been sick in a coal-bucket!'

'I call that very resourceful of you, Frankie,' said Bobby approvingly. 'With your hands tied and everything? The thing is: what are we going to do now? We've had it our own way for a long time, but now the tables are turned.'

'If only I'd told Roger about your letter,' lamented Frankie. 'I did think of it and wavered—and then I decided to do exactly what you said and tell nobody at all.'

'With the result that no one knows where we are,' said Bobby gravely. 'Frankie, my dear, I'm afraid I've landed you in a mess.'

'We got a bit too sure of ourselves,' said Frankie sombrely.

'The only thing I can't make out is why they didn't knock us both on the head straight away,' mused Bobby. 'I don't think Nicholson would stick at a little trifle like that.'

'He's got a plan,' said Frankie with a slight shiver.

'Well, we'd better have one, too. We've got to get out of this, Frankie. How are we going to do it?'

'We can shout,' said Frankie.

'Ye-es,' said Bobby. 'Somebody might be passing and hear. But from the fact that Nicholson didn't gag you I should say that the chances in that direction are pretty poor. Your hands are more loosely tied than mine. Let's see if I can get them undone with my teeth.'

The next five minutes were spent in a struggle that did credit to Bobby's dentist.

'Extraordinary how easy these things sound in books,' he panted. 'I don't believe I'm making the slightest impression.'

'You are,' said Frankie. 'It's loosening. Look out! There's somebody coming.'

She rolled away from him. A step could be heard mounting a stair, a heavy, ponderous tread. A gleam of light appeared under the door. Then there was the sound of a key being turned in the lock. The door swung slowly open.

'And how are my two little birds?' said the voice of Dr Nicholson.

He carried a candle in one hand and, though he was wearing a hat pulled down over his eyes and a heavy overcoat with the collar turned up, his voice would have betrayed him anywhere. His eyes glittered palely behind the strong glasses.

He shook his head at them playfully.

'Unworthy of you, my dear young lady,' he said, 'to fall into the trap so easily.'

Neither Bobby nor Frankie made any reply. The honours of the situation so obviously lay with Nicholson that it was difficult to know what to say.

Nicholson put the candle down on a chair.

'At any rate,' he said, 'let me see if you are comfortable.'

He examined Bobby's fastenings, nodded his head approvingly and passed on to Frankie. There he shook his head.

'As they truly used to say to me in my youth,' he remarked, 'fingers were made before forks—and teeth were used before fingers. Your young friend's teeth, I see, have been active.'

A heavy, broken-backed oak chair was standing in a corner.

Nicholson picked up Frankie, deposited her on the chair and tied her securely to it.

'Not too uncomfortable, I trust?' he said. 'Well, it isn't for long.'

Frankie found her tongue.

'What are you going to do with us?' she demanded.

Nicholson walked to the door and picked up his candle.

'You taunted me, Lady Frances, with being too fond of accidents. Perhaps I am. At any rate, I am going to risk one more accident.'

'What do you mean?' said Bobby.

'Shall I tell you? Yes, I think I will. Lady Frances Derwent, driving her car, her chauffeur beside her, mistakes a turning and takes a disused road leading to a quarry. The car crashes over the edge. Lady Frances and her chauffeur are killed.'

There was a slight pause, then Bobby said:

'But we mightn't be. Plans go awry sometimes. One of yours did down in Wales.'

'Your tolerance of morphia was certainly very remarkable—and from our point of view—regrettable,' said

Nicholson. 'But you need have no anxiety on my behalf this time. You and Lady Frances will be quite dead when your bodies are discovered.'

Bobby shivered in spite of himself. There had been a queer note in Nicholson's voice—it was the tone of an artist contemplating a masterpiece.

'He enjoys this,' thought Bobby. 'Really enjoys it.'

He was not going to give Nicholson further cause for enjoyment than he could help. He said in a casual tone of voice:

'You're making a mistake—especially where Lady Frances is concerned.'

'Yes,' said Frankie. 'In that very clever letter you forged you told me to tell nobody. Well, I made just one exception. I told Roger Bassington-ffrench. He knows all about you. If anything happens to us, he will know who is responsible for it. You'd better let us go and clear out of the country as fast as you can.'

Nicholson was silent for a moment. Then he said:

'A good bluff—but I call it.'

He turned to the door.

'What about your wife, you swine?' cried Bobby. 'Have you murdered her, too?'

'Moira is still alive,' said Nicholson. 'How much longer she will remain so, I do not really know. It depends on circumstances.'

He made them a mocking little bow.

'*Au revoir*,' he said. 'It will take me a couple of hours to complete my arrangements. You may enjoy talking the matter over. I shall not gag you unless it becomes necessary.

You understand? Any calls for help and I return and deal with the matter.'

He went out and closed and locked the door behind him.

'It isn't true,' said Bobby. 'It can't be true. These things don't happen.'

But he could not help feeling that they were going to happen—and to him and Frankie.

'In books there's always an eleventh-hour rescue,' said Frankie, trying to speak hopefully.

But she was not feeling very hopeful. In fact, her morale was decidedly low.

'The whole thing's so impossible,' said Bobby as though pleading with someone. 'So fantastic. Nicholson himself was absolutely unreal. I wish an eleventh-hour rescue was possible, but I can't see who's going to rescue us.'

'If only I'd told Roger,' wailed Frankie.

'Perhaps in spite of everything, Nicholson believes you have,' suggested Bobby.

'No,' said Frankie. 'The suggestion didn't go down at all. The man's too damned clever.'

'He's been too clever for us,' said Bobby gloomily. 'Frankie, do you know what annoys me most about this business?'

'No. What?'

'That even now, when we're going to be hurled into the next world, we still don't know who Evans is.'

'Let's ask him,' said Frankie. 'You know—a last minute boon. He can't refuse to tell us. I agree with you that I simply can't die without having my curiosity satisfied.'

There was a silence, then Bobby said:

'Do you think we ought to yell for help—a sort of last chance? It's about the only chance we've got.'

'Not yet,' said Frankie. 'In the first place, I don't believe anyone would hear—he'd never risk it otherwise—and in the second place, I feel I just can't bear waiting here to be killed without being able to speak or be spoken to. Let's leave shouting till the last possible moment. It's—it's so comforting having you to talk to.' Her voice wavered a little over the last words.

'I've got you into an awful mess, Frankie.'

'Oh! that's all right. You couldn't have kept me out. I wanted to come in. Bobby, do you think he'll really pull it off? Us, I mean.'

'I'm terribly afraid he will. He's so damnably efficient.'

'Bobby, do you believe now that it was he who killed Henry Bassington-ffrench?'

'If it were possible—'

'It is possible—granted one thing: *that Sylvia Bassington-ffrench is in it, too.*'

'Frankie!'

'I know. I was just as horrified when the idea occurred to me. But it fits. Why was Sylvia so dense about the morphia—why did she resist so obstinately when we wanted her to send her husband somewhere else instead of the Grange? And then she was in the house when the shot was fired—'

'She might have done it herself.'

'Oh! no, surely.'

'Yes, she might. And then have given the key of the study to Nicholson to put in Henry's pocket.'

'It's all crazy,' said Frankie in a hopeless voice. 'Like looking through a distorting mirror. All the people who seemed most all right are really all wrong—all the nice, everyday people. There ought to be some way of telling criminals—eyebrows or ears or something.'

'My God!' cried Bobby.

'What is it?'

'Frankie, that wasn't Nicholson who came here just now.'

'Have you gone quite mad? Who was it then?'

'I don't know—but it wasn't Nicholson. All along I felt there was something wrong, but couldn't spot it, and your saying ears has given me the clue. When I was watching Nicholson the other evening through the window I especially noticed his ears—the lobes are joined to the face. But this man tonight—his ears weren't like that.'

'But what does it mean?' Frankie asked hopelessly.

'This is a very clever actor impersonating Nicholson.'

'But why—and who could it be?'

'Bassington-ffrench,' breathed Bobby. '*Roger Bassington-ffrench!* We spotted the right man at the beginning and then, like idiots, we went astray after red herrings.'

'Bassington-ffrench,' whispered Frankie. 'Bobby, you're right. It must be him. He was the only person there when I taunted Nicholson about accidents.'

'Then it really is all up,' said Bobby. 'I've still had a kind of sneaking hope that possibly Roger Bassington-ffrench might nose out our trail by some miracle but now the last hope's gone. Moira's a prisoner, you and I are tied hand and foot. Nobody else has the least idea where we are. The game's up, Frankie.'

As he finished speaking there was a sound overhead. The next minute, with a terrific crash, a heavy body fell through the skylight.

It was too dark to see anything.

'What the devil—' began Bobby.

From amidst a pile of broken glass, a voice spoke.

'B-b-b-bobby,' it said.

'Well, I'm damned!' said Bobby. 'It's Badger!'

CHAPTER 29

Badger's Story

There was not a minute to be lost. Already sounds could be heard on the floor below.

'Quick, Badger, you fool!' said Bobby. 'Pull one of my boots off! Don't argue or ask questions! Haul it off somehow. Chuck it down in the middle there and crawl under that bed! *Quick*, I tell you!'

Steps were ascending the stairs. The key turned.

Nicholson—the pseudo Nicholson—stood in the doorway, candle in hand.

He saw Bobby and Frankie as he had left them, but in the middle of the floor was a pile of broken glass and in the middle of the broken glass was a boot!

Nicholson stared in amazement from the boot to Bobby. Bobby's left foot was bootless.

'Very clever, my young friend,' he said dryly. 'Extremely acrobatic.'

He came over to Bobby, examined the ropes that bound him and tied a couple of extra knots. He looked at him curiously.

'I wish I knew how you managed to throw that boot through the skylight. It seems almost incredible. A touch of the Houdini about you, my friend.'

He looked at them both, up at the broken skylight, then shrugging his shoulders, he left the room.

'Quick, Badger.'

Badger crawled out from under the bed. He had a pocket knife and with its aid he soon cut the other two free.

'That's better,' said Bobby, stretching himself. 'Whew! I'm stiff! Well, Frankie, what about our friend Nicholson?'

'You're right,' said Frankie. 'It's Roger Bassington-ffrench. Now that I *know* he's Roger playing the part of Nicholson I can *see* it. But it's a pretty good performance all the same.'

'Entirely voice and pince-nez,' said Bobby.

'I was at Oxford with a B-b-b-bassington-ffrench,' said Badger. 'M-m-m-marvellous actor. B-b-b-bad hat, though. B-b-b-bad business about forging his p-p-pater's n-n-n-name to a cheque. Old m-m-man hushed it up.'

In the minds of both Bobby and Frankie was the same thought. Badger, whom they had judged it wiser not to take into their confidence, could all along have given them valuable information!

'Forgery,' said Frankie thoughtfully. 'That letter from you, Bobby, was remarkably well done. I wonder how he knew your handwriting?'

'If he's in with the Caymans he probably saw my letter about the Evans business.'

The voice of Badger rose plaintively.

'W-w-w-what are we going to do next?' he inquired.

245

'We're going to take up a comfortable position behind this door,' said Bobby. 'And when our friend returns, which I imagine won't be for a little while yet, you and I are going to spring on him from behind and give him the surprise of his life. How about it, Badger? Are you game?'

'Oh! absolutely.'

'As for you, Frankie, when you hear his step you'd better get back on to your chair. He'll see you as soon as he opens the door and will come in without any suspicion.'

'All right,' said Frankie. 'And once you and Badger have got him down I'll join in and bite his ankles or something.'

'That's the true womanly spirit,' said Bobby approvingly. 'Now, let's all sit close together on the floor here and hear all about things. I want to know what miracle brought Badger through that skylight.'

'Well, you s-s-see,' said Badger, 'after you w-w-went off, I got into a bit of a m-m-mess.'

He paused. Gradually the story was extracted: a tale of liabilities, creditors and bailiffs—a typical Badger catastrophe. Bobby had gone off leaving no address, only saying that he was driving the Bentley down to Staverley. So to Staverley came Badger.

'I thought p-p-perhaps you m-m-might be able to let have a f-f-fiver,' he explained.

Bobby's heart smote him. To aid Badger in his enterprise he had come to London and had promptly deserted his post to go off sleuthing with Frankie. And even now the faithful Badger uttered no word of reproach.

Badger had no wish to endanger Bobby's mysterious enterprises, but he was of the opinion that a car like the green Bentley would not be difficult to find in a place the size of Staverley.

As a matter of fact, he came across the car before he got to Staverley, for it was standing outside a pub—empty.

'S-s-so I thought,' went on Badger, 'that I'd give you a little s-s-s-surprise, don't you know? There were some r-r-rugs and things in the b-b-back and nobody about. I g-g-got in and p-p-p-pulled them over me. I thought I'd give you the s-s-surprise of your life.'

What actually happened was that a chauffeur in green livery had emerged from the pub and that Badger, peering from his place of concealment, was thunderstruck to perceive that this chauffeur was not Bobby. He had an idea that the face was in some way familiar to him but couldn't place the man. The stranger got into the car and drove off.

Badger was in a predicament. He did not know what to do next. Explanations and apologies were difficult, and in any case it is not easy to explain to someone who is driving a car at sixty miles an hour. Badger decided to lie low and sneak out of the car when it stopped.

The car finally reached its destination—Tudor Cottage. The chauffeur drove it into the garage and left it there, but, on going out, he shut the garage doors. Badger was a prisoner. There was a small window at one side of the garage and through this about half an hour later Badger had observed Frankie's approach, her whistle and her admission into the house.

The whole business puzzled Badger greatly. He began to suspect that something was wrong. At any rate, he determined to have a look round for himself and see what it was all about.

With the help of some tools lying about in the garage he succeeded in picking the lock of the garage door and set out on a tour of inspection. The windows on the ground floor were all shuttered, but he thought that by getting on to the roof he might manage to have a look into some of the upper windows. The roof presented no difficulties. There was a convenient pipe running up the garage and from the garage roof to the roof of the cottage was an easy climb. In the course of his prowling, Badger had come upon the skylight. Nature and Badger's weight had done the rest.

Bobby drew a long breath as the narrative came to an end.

'All the same,' he said reverently, 'you are a miracle—a singularly beautiful miracle! But for you, Badger, my lad, Frankie and I would have been little corpses in about an hour's time.'

He gave Badger a condensed account of the activities of himself and Frankie. Towards the end he broke off.

'Someone's coming. Get to your post, Frankie. Now, then, this is where our play-acting Bassington-ffrench gets the surprise of his life.'

Frankie arranged herself in a depressed attitude on the broken chair. Badger and Bobby stood ready behind the door.

The steps came up the stairs, a line of candle-light showed underneath the door. The key was put in the lock and turned, the door swung open. The light of the candle disclosed Frankie drooping dejectedly on her chair. Their gaoler stepped through the doorway.

Then, joyously, Badger and Bobby sprang.

The proceedings were short and decisive. Taken utterly by surprise, the man was knocked down, the candle flew wide and was retrieved by Frankie, and a few seconds later the three friends stood looking down with malicious pleasure at a figure securely bound with the same ropes as had previously secured two of them.

'Good evening, Mr Bassington-ffrench,' said Bobby—and if the exultation in his voice was a little crude, who shall blame him? 'It's a nice night for the funeral.'

CHAPTER 30

Escape

The man on the floor stared up at them. His pince-nez had flown off and so had his hat. There could be no further attempt at disguise. Slight traces of make-up were visible about the eyebrows, but otherwise the face was the pleasant, slightly vacuous face of Roger Bassington-ffrench.

He spoke in his own agreeable tenor voice, its note that of pleasant soliloquy.

'Very interesting,' he said. 'I really knew quite well that no man tied up as you were *could* have thrown a boot through that skylight. But because the boot was there among the broken glass I took it for cause and effect and assumed that, though it was impossible, the impossible had been achieved. An interesting light on the limitations of the brain.'

As nobody spoke, he went on still in the same reflective voice:

'So, after all, you've won the round. Most unexpected and extremely regrettable. I thought I'd got you all fooled nicely.'

'So you had,' said Frankie. 'You forged that letter from Bobby, I suppose?'

'I have a talent that way,' said Roger modestly.

'And Bobby?'

Lying on his back, smiling agreeably, Roger seemed to take a positive pleasure in enlightening them.

'I knew he'd go to the Grange. I only had to wait about in the bushes near the path. I was just behind him there when he retreated after rather clumsily falling off a tree. I let the hubbub die down and then got him neatly on the back of the neck with a sandbag. All I had to do was to carry him out to where my car was waiting, shove him in the dickey and drive him here. I was at home again before morning.'

'And Moira?' demanded Bobby. 'Did you entice her away somehow?'

Roger chuckled. The question seemed to amuse him.

'Forgery is a very useful art, my dear Jones,' he said.

'You swine,' said Bobby.

Frankie intervened. She was still full of curiosity, and their prisoner seemed in an obliging mood.

'Why did you pretend to be Dr Nicholson?' she asked.

'Why did I, now?' Roger seemed to be asking the question of himself. 'Partly, I think, the fun of seeing whether I could spoof you both. You were so very sure that poor old Nicholson was in it up to the neck.' He laughed and Frankie blushed. 'Just because he cross-questioned you a bit about the details of your accident—in his pompous way. It was an irritating fad of his—accuracy in details.'

'And really,' said Frankie slowly, 'he was quite innocent?'

'As a child unborn,' said Roger. 'But he did *me* a good turn. He drew my attention to that accident of yours. That and another incident made me realize that you mightn't be quite the innocent young thing you seemed to be. And then I was standing by you when you telephoned one morning and heard your chauffeur's voice say "Frankie". I've got pretty good hearing. I suggested coming up to town with you and you agreed—but you were very relieved when I changed my mind. After that—' He stopped and, as far as he was able, shrugged his bound shoulders. 'It was rather fun seeing you all get worked up about Nicholson. He's a harmless old ass, but he does look exactly like a scientific super-criminal on the films. I thought I might as well keep the deception up. After all, you never know. The best-laid plans go wrong, as my present predicament shows.'

'There's one thing you *must* tell me,' said Frankie. 'I've been driven nearly mad with curiosity. Who is Evans?'

'Oh!' said Bassington-ffrench. 'So you don't know that?'

He laughed—and laughed again.

'That's rather amusing,' he said. 'It shows what a fool one can be.'

'Meaning us?' asked Frankie.

'No,' said Roger. 'In this case, meaning me. Do you know, if you don't know who Evans is, I don't think I shall tell you. I'll keep that to myself as my own little secret.'

The position was a curious one. They had turned the

tables on Bassington-ffrench and yet, in some peculiar way, he had robbed them of their triumph. Lying on the floor, bound and a prisoner, it was he who dominated the situation.

'And what are your plans now, may I ask?' he inquired.

Nobody had as yet evolved any plans. Bobby rather doubtfully murmured something about police.

'Much the best thing to do,' said Roger cheerfully. 'Ring them up and hand me over to them. The charge will be abduction, I suppose. I can't very well deny that.' He looked at Frankie. 'I shall plead a guilty passion.'

Frankie reddened.

'What about murder?' she asked.

'My dear, you haven't any evidence. Positively none. Think it over and you'll see you haven't.'

'Badger,' said Bobby, 'you'd better stay here and keep an eye on him. I'll go down and ring the police.'

'You'd better be careful,' said Frankie. 'We don't know how many of them there may be in the house.'

'No one but me,' said Roger. 'I was carrying this through single-handed.'

'I'm not prepared to take your word for that,' said Bobby gruffly.

He bent over and tested the knots.

'He's all right,' he said. 'Safe as houses. We'd better all go down together. We can lock the door.'

'Terribly distrustful, aren't you, my dear chap,' said Roger. 'There's a pistol in my pocket if you'd like it. It may make you feel happier and it's certainly no good to me in my present position.'

Ignoring the other's mocking tone, Bobby bent down and extracted the weapon.

'Kind of you to mention it,' he said. 'If you want to know it does make me feel happier.'

'Good,' said Roger. 'It's loaded.'

Bobby took the candle and they filed out of the attic, leaving Roger lying on the floor. Bobby locked the door and put the key in his pocket. He held the pistol in his hand.

'I'll go first,' he said. 'We've got to be quite sure and not make a mess of things now.'

'He's a qu-qu-queer chap, isn't he?' said Badger with a jerk of his head backwards in the direction of the room they had left.

'He's a damned good loser,' said Frankie.

Even now she was not quite free from the charm of that very remarkable young man, Roger Bassington-ffrench.

A rather rickety flight of steps led down to the main landing. Everything was quiet. Bobby looked over the banisters. The telephone was in the hall below.

'We'd better look into these rooms first,' he said. 'We don't want to be taken in the rear.'

Badger flung open each door in turn. Of the four bedrooms, three were empty. In the fourth a slender figure was lying on the bed.

'It's Moira,' cried Frankie.

The others crowded in. Moira was lying like one dead, except that her breast moved up and down ever so slightly.

'Is she asleep?' asked Bobby.

'She's drugged, I think,' said Frankie.

She looked round. A hypodermic syringe lay on a little enamel tray on a table near the window. There was also a little spirit lamp and a type of morphia hypodermic needle.

'She'll be all right, I think,' she said. 'But we ought to get a doctor.'

'Let's go down and telephone,' said Bobby.

They adjourned to the hall below. Frankie had a half fear that the telephone wires might be cut, but her fears proved quite unfounded. They got through to the police station quite easily, but found a good deal of difficulty in explaining matters. The local police station was highly disposed to regard the summons as a practical joke.

However, they were convinced at last, and Bobby replaced the receiver with a sigh. He had explained that they also wanted a doctor and the police constable promised to bring one along.

Ten minutes later a car arrived with an inspector and a constable and an elderly man who had his profession stamped all over him.

Bobby and Frankie received them and, after explaining matters once more in a somewhat perfunctory fashion, led the way to the attic. Bobby unlocked the door—then stood dumbfounded in the doorway. In the middle of the floor was a heap of severed ropes. Underneath the broken skylight a chair had been placed on the bed, which had been dragged out till it was under the skylight.

Of Roger Bassington-ffrench there was no sign.

Bobby, Badger and Frankie were dumbfounded.

'Talk of Houdini,' said Bobby. 'He must have out-Houdinied Houdini. How the devil did he cut these cords?'

'He must have had a knife in his pocket,' said Frankie.

'Even then, how could he get at it? Both hands were bound together behind his back.'

The inspector coughed. All his former doubts had returned. He was more strongly disposed than ever to regard the whole thing as a hoax.

Frankie and Bobby found themselves telling a long story which sounded more impossible every minute.

The doctor was their salvation.

On being taken to the room where Moira was lying, he declared at once that she had been drugged with morphia or some preparation of opium. He did not consider her condition serious and thought she would awake naturally in four or five hours' time.

He suggested taking her off then and there to a good nursing home in the neighbourhood.

To this Bobby and Frankie agreed, not seeing what else could be done. Having given their own names and addresses to the inspector, who appeared to disbelieve utterly in Frankie's, they themselves were allowed to leave Tudor Cottage and with the assistance of the inspector succeeded in gaining admission to the Seven Stars in the village.

Here, still feeling that they were regarded as criminals, they were only too thankful to go to their rooms—a double one for Bobby and Badger, and a very minute single one for Frankie.

A few minutes after they had all retired, a knock came on Bobby's door.

It was Frankie.

'I've thought of something,' she said. 'If that fool of a police inspector persists in thinking that we made all this up, at any rate I've got evidence that I was chloroformed.'

'Have you? Where?'

'In the coal-bucket,' said Frankie with decision.

CHAPTER 31

Frankie Asks a Question

Exhausted by all her adventures, Frankie slept late the next morning. It was half-past ten when she came down to the small coffee room to find Bobby waiting for her.

'Hullo, Frankie, here you are at last.'

'Don't be so horribly vigorous, my dear.' Frankie subsided into a chair.

'What will you have? They've got haddock and eggs and bacon and cold ham.'

'I shall have some toast and weak tea,' said Frankie, quelling him. 'What is the matter with you?'

'It must be the sandbagging,' said Bobby. 'It's probably broken up adhesions in the brain. I feel absolutely full of pep and vim and bright ideas and a longing to dash out and do things.'

'Well, why not dash?' said Frankie languidly.

'I have dashed. I've been with Inspector Hammond for the last half-hour. We'll have to let it go as a practical joke, Frankie, for the moment.'

'Oh, but, Bobby—'

'I said *for the moment*. We've got to get to the bottom of this, Frankie. We're on the right spot and all we've got to do is to get down to it. We don't want Roger Bassington-ffrench for abduction. We want him for murder.'

'And we'll get him,' said Frankie, with a revival of spirit.

'That's more like it,' said Bobby approvingly. 'Drink some more tea.'

'How's Moira?'

'Pretty bad. She came round in the most awful state of nerves. Scared stiff apparently. She's gone up to London— to a nursing home place in Queen's Gate. She says she'll feel safe there. She was terrified here.'

'She never did have much nerve,' said Frankie.

'Well, anyone might be scared stiff with a queer, cold-blooded murderer like Roger Bassington-ffrench loose in the neighbourhood.'

'He doesn't want to murder *her*. We're the ones he's after.'

'He's probably too busy taking care of himself to worry about us for the moment,' said Bobby. 'Now, Frankie, we've got to get down to it. The start of the whole thing must be John Savage's death and will. There's something wrong about it. Either that will was forged or Savage was murdered or something.'

'It's quite likely the will was forged if Bassington-ffrench was concerned,' said Frankie thoughtfully. 'Forgery seems to be his speciality.'

'It may have been forgery *and* murder. We've got to find out.'

Frankie nodded.

'I've got the notes I made after looking at the will. The

witnesses were Rose Chudleigh, cook, and Albert Mere, gardener. They ought to be quite easy to find. Then there are the lawyers who drew it up—Elford and Leigh—a very respectable firm as Mr Spragge said.'

'Right, we'll start from there. I think you'd better take the lawyers. You'll get more out of them than I would. I'll hunt up Rose Chudleigh and Albert Mere.'

'What about Badger?'

'Badger never gets up till lunch time—you needn't worry about him.'

'We must get his affairs straightened out for him sometime,' said Frankie. 'After all, he did save my life.'

'They'll soon get tangled again,' said Bobby. 'Oh! by the way, what do you think of this?'

He held out a dirty piece of cardboard for her inspection. It was a photograph.

'Mr Cayman,' said Frankie immediately. 'Where did you get it?'

'Last night. It had slipped down behind the telephone.'

'Then it seems pretty clear who Mr and Mrs Templeton were. Wait a minute.'

A waitress had just approached, bearing toast. Frankie displayed the photograph.

'Do you know who that is?' she asked.

The waitress regarded the photograph, her head a little on one side.

'Now, I've seen the gentleman—but I can't quite call to mind. Oh! yes, it's the gentleman who had Tudor Cottage— Mr Templeton. They've gone away now—somewhere abroad, I believe.'

'What sort of man was he?' asked Frankie.

'I really couldn't say. They didn't come down here very often—just weekends now and then. Nobody saw much of him. Mrs Templeton was a very nice lady. But they hadn't had Tudor Cottage very long—only about six months—when a very rich gentleman died and left Mrs Templeton all his money and they went to live abroad. They never sold Tudor Cottage, though. I think they sometimes lend it to people for weekends. But I don't suppose with all that money they'll ever come back here and live in it themselves.'

'They had a cook called Rose Chudleigh, didn't they?' asked Frankie.

But the girl seemed uninterested in cooks. Being left a fortune by a rich gentleman was what really stirred her imagination. In answer to Frankie's question she replied that she couldn't say, she was sure, and withdrew carrying an empty toast-rack.

'That's all plain sailing,' said Frankie. 'The Caymans have given up coming here, but they keep the place on for the convenience of the gang.'

They agreed to divide the labour as Bobby had suggested. Frankie went off in the Bentley, having smartened herself up by a few local purchases, and Bobby went off in quest of Albert Mere, the gardener.

They met at lunch time.

'Well?' demanded Bobby.

Frankie shook her head.

'Forgery's out of the question.' She spoke in a dispirited voice. 'I spent a long time with Mr Elford—he's

261

rather an old dear. He'd got wind of some of our doings last night and was wild to hear a few details. I don't suppose they get much excitement down here. Anyway, I soon got him eating out of my hand. Then I discussed the Savage case—pretended I'd met some of the Savage relations and that they'd hinted at forgery. At that my old dear bristled up—absolutely out of the question! It wasn't a question of letters or anything like that. He saw Mr Savage himself and Mr Savage insisted on the will being drawn up then and there. Mr Elford wanted to go away and do it properly—you know how they do—sheets and sheets all about nothing—'

'I don't know,' said Bobby. 'I've never made any wills.'

'I have—two. The second was this morning. I had to have some excuse for seeing a lawyer.'

'Who did you leave your money to?'

'You.'

'That was a bit thoughtless, wasn't it? If Roger Bassington-ffrench succeeded in bumping you off I should probably be hanged for it!'

'I never thought of that,' said Frankie. 'Well, as I was saying, Mr Savage was so nervous and wrought up that Mr Elford wrote out the will then and there and the servant and the gardener came and witnessed it, and Mr Elford took it away with him for safe keeping.'

'That does seem to knock out forgery,' agreed Bobby.

'I know. You can't have forgery when you've actually seen the man sign his name. As to the other business—murder, it's going to be hard to find out anything about that now. The doctor who was called in has died since.

The man we saw last night is a new man—he's only been here about two months.'

'We seem to have rather an unfortunate number of deaths,' said Bobby.

'Why, who else is dead?'

'Albert Mere.'

'Do you think they've *all* been put out of the way?'

'That seems rather wholesale. We might give Albert Mere the benefit of the doubt—he was seventy-two, poor old man.'

'All right,' said Frankie. 'I'll allow you Natural Causes in his case. Any luck with Rose Chudleigh?'

'Yes. After she left the Templetons she went to the north of England to a place, but she's come back and married a man down here whom it seems she's been walking out with for the last seventeen years. Unfortunately she's a bit of a nitwit. She doesn't seem to remember anything about anyone. Perhaps you could do something with her.'

'I'll have a go,' said Frankie. 'I'm rather good with nitwits. Where's Badger, by the way?'

'Good Lord! I've forgotten all about him,' said Bobby. He got up and left the room, returning a few minutes later.

'He was still asleep,' he explained. 'He's getting up now. A chambermaid seems to have called him four times but it didn't make any impression.'

'Well, we'd better go and see the nitwit,' said Frankie, rising. 'And then I *must* buy a toothbrush and a night-gown and a sponge and a few other necessities of civilized existence. I was so close to Nature last night that I didn't think about any of them. I just stripped off my outer covering and fell upon the bed.'

'I know,' said Bobby. 'So did I.'

'Let's go and talk to Rose Chudleigh,' said Frankie.

Rose Chudleigh, now Mrs Pratt, lived in a small cottage that seemed to be overflowing with china dogs and furniture. Mrs Pratt herself was a bovine-looking woman of ample proportions, with fish-like eyes and every indication of adenoids.

'You see, I've come back,' said Bobby breezily.

Mrs Pratt breathed hard and looked at them both incuriously.

'We were so interested to hear that you had lived with Mrs Templeton,' explained Frankie.

'Yes, ma'am,' said Mrs Pratt.

'She's living abroad now, I believe,' continued Frankie, trying to give an impression of being an intimate of the family.

'I've heard so,' agreed Mrs Pratt.

'You were with her some time, weren't you?' asked Frankie.

'Were I which, ma'am?'

'With Mrs Templeton some time,' said Frankie, speaking slowly and clearly.

'I wouldn't say that, ma'am. Only two months.'

'Oh! I thought you'd been with her longer than that.'

'That was Gladys, ma'am. The house-parlourmaid. She was there six months.'

'There were two of you?'

'That's right. House-parlourmaid she was and I was cook.'

'You were there when Mr Savage died, weren't you?'

'I beg your pardon, ma'am.'

'You were there when Mr Savage died?'

'Mr Templeton didn't die—at least I haven't heard so. He went abroad.'

'Not Mr Templeton—Mr Savage,' said Bobby.

Mrs Pratt looked at him vacantly.

'The gentleman who left her all the money,' said Frankie.

A gleam of something like intelligence passed across Mrs Pratt's face.

'Oh! yes, ma'am, the gentleman there was the inquest on.'

'That's right,' said Frankie, delighted with her success. 'He used to come and stay quite often, didn't he?'

'I couldn't say as to that, ma'am. I'd only just come, you see. Gladys would know.'

'But you had to witness his will, didn't you?'

Mrs Pratt looked blank.

'You went and saw him sign a paper and you had to sign it, too.'

Again the gleam of intelligence.

'Yes, ma'am. Me and Albert. I'd never done such a thing before and I didn't like it. I said to Gladys I don't like signing a paper and that's a fact, and Gladys, she said it must be all right because Mr Elford was there and he was a very nice gentleman as well as being a lawyer.'

'What happened exactly?' asked Bobby.

'I beg your pardon, sir?'

'Who called you to sign your name?' asked Frankie.

'The mistress, sir. She came into the kitchen and said would I go outside and call Albert and would we both come up to the best bedroom (which she'd moved out of for Mr—the gentleman—the night before) and there was the gentleman sitting up in bed—he'd come back from London and gone straight to bed—and a very ill-looking gentleman he was. I hadn't seen him before. But he looked something ghastly, and Mr Elford was there, too, and he spoke very nice and said there was nothing to be afraid of and I was to sign my name where the gentleman had signed his, and I did and put "cook" after it and the address and Albert did the same and I went down to Gladys all of a tremble and said I'd never seen a gentleman look so like death, and Gladys said he'd looked all right the night before, and that it must have been something in London that had upset him. He'd gone up to London very early before anyone was up. And then I said about not liking to write my name to anything, and Gladys said it was all right because Mr Elford was there.'

'And Mr Savage—the gentleman died—when?'

'Next morning as ever was, ma'am. He shut himself up in his room that night and wouldn't let anyone go near him, and when Gladys called him in the morning he was all stiff and dead and a letter propped up by his bedside. "To the Coroner," it said. Oh! it gave Gladys a regular turn. And then there was an inquest and everything. About two months later Mrs Templeton told me she was going abroad to live. But she got me a very good place up north with big wages and she gave me a nice present and everything. A very nice lady, Mrs Templeton.'

Mrs Pratt was by now thoroughly enjoying her own loquacity.

Frankie rose.

'Well,' she said. 'It's been very nice to hear all this.' She slipped a note out of her purse. 'You must let me leave you a—er—little present. I've taken up so much of your time.'

'Well, thank you kindly, I'm sure, ma'am. Good day to you and your good gentleman.'

Frankie blushed and retreated rather rapidly. Bobby followed her after a few minutes. He looked preoccupied.

'Well,' he said. 'We seem to have got at all she knows.'

'Yes,' said Frankie. 'And it hangs together. There seems no doubt that Savage *did* make that will, and I suppose his fear of cancer was genuine enough. They couldn't very well bribe a Harley Street doctor. I suppose they just took advantage of his having made that will to do away with him quickly before he changed his mind. But how we or anyone else can prove they did make away with him I can't see.'

'I know. We may suspect that Mrs T gave him "something to make him sleep", but we can't prove it. Bassington-ffrench may have forged the letter to the coroner, but that again we can't prove by now. I expect the letter is destroyed long ago after being put in as evidence at the inquest.'

'So we come back to the old problem—what on earth are Bassington-ffrench and Co. so afraid of our discovering?'

'Nothing strikes you as odd particularly?'

'No, I don't think so—at least only one thing. Why did

Mrs Templeton send out for the gardener to come and witness the will when the house-parlourmaid was in the house. Why didn't they ask the parlourmaid?'

'It's odd your saying that, Frankie,' said Bobby.

His voice sounded so queer that Frankie looked at him in surprise.

'Why?'

'Because I stayed behind to ask Mrs Pratt for Gladys's name and address.'

'Well?'

'*The parlourmaid's name was Evans!*'

CHAPTER 32

Evans

Frankie gasped.

Bobby's voice rose excitedly.

'You see, you've asked the same question that Carstairs asked. *Why didn't they ask the parlourmaid? Why didn't they ask Evans?*'

'Oh! Bobby, we're getting there at last!'

'The same thing must have struck Carstairs. He was nosing round, just as we were, looking for something fishy—and this point struck him just as it struck us. And, moreover, I believe he came to Wales for that reason. Gladys Evans is a Welsh name—Evans was probably a Welsh girl. He was following her to Marchbolt. And someone was following him—and so, he never got to her.'

'Why *didn't* they ask Evans?' said Frankie. 'There *must* be a reason. It's such a silly little point—and yet it's important. With a couple of maids in the house, why send out for a gardener?'

'Perhaps because both Chudleigh and Albert Mere were chumps, whereas Evans was rather a sharp girl.'

'It can't be only that. Mr Elford was there and he's quite shrewd. Oh! Bobby, the whole situation is there—I know it is. If we could just get at the reason. Evans. Why Chudleigh and Mere and not Evans?'

Suddenly she stopped and put both hands over her eyes.

'It's coming,' she said. 'Just a sort of flicker. It'll come in a minute.'

She stayed dead still for a minute or two, then removed her hands and looked at her companion with an odd flicker in her eyes.

'Bobby,' she said, 'if you're staying in a house with two servants which do you tip?'

'The house-parlourmaid, of course,' said Bobby, surprised. 'One never tips a cook. One never sees her, for one thing.'

'No, and she never sees you. At least she might catch a glimpse of you if you were there some time. But a house-parlourmaid waits on you at dinner and calls you and hands you coffee.'

'What are you getting at, Frankie?'

'They couldn't have Evans witnessing that will—*because Evans would have known that it wasn't Mr Savage who was making it.*'

'Good Lord, Frankie, what do you mean? Who was it then?'

'Bassington-ffrench, of course! Don't you see, he impersonated Savage? I bet it was Bassington-ffrench who went to that doctor and made all that fuss about having cancer. Then the lawyer is sent for—a stranger who doesn't know Mr Savage but who will be able to swear that he saw Mr

270

Savage sign that will and it's witnessed by two people, one of whom hadn't seen him before and the other an old man who was probably pretty blind and who probably had never seen Savage either. Now do you see?'

'But where was the real Savage all that time?'

'Oh! he arrived all right and then I suspect they drugged him and put him in the attic, perhaps, and kept him there for twelve hours while Bassington-ffrench did his impersonation stunt. Then he was put back in his bed and given chloral and Evans finds him dead in the morning.'

'My God, I believe you've hit it, Frankie. But can we prove it?'

'Yes—no—I don't know. Supposing Rose Chudleigh—Pratt, I mean—was shown a photograph of the real Savage? Would she be able to say, "that wasn't the man who signed the will"?'

'I doubt it,' said Bobby. 'She is such a nitwit.'

'Chosen for that purpose, I expect. But there's another thing. An expert ought to be able to detect that the signature is a forgery.'

'They didn't before.'

'Because nobody ever raised the question. There didn't seem any possible moment when the will *could* have been forged. But now it's different.'

'One thing we must do,' said Bobby. 'Find Evans. She may be able to tell us a lot. She was with the Templetons for six months, remember.'

Frankie groaned.

'That's going to make it even more difficult.'

'How about the post office?' suggested Bobby.

They were just passing it. In appearance it was more of a general store than a post office.

Frankie darted inside and opened the campaign. There was no one else in the shop except the postmistress—a young woman with an inquisitive nose.

Frankie bought a two-shilling book of stamps, commented on the weather and then said:

'But I expect you always have better weather here than we do in my part of the world. I live in Wales—Marchbolt. You wouldn't believe the rain we have.'

The young woman with the nose said that they had a good deal of rain themselves and last Bank Holiday it had rained something cruel.

Frankie said:

'There's someone in Marchbolt who comes from this part of the world. I wonder if you know her. Her name was Evans—Gladys Evans.'

The young woman was quite unsuspicious.

'Why, of course,' she said. 'She was in service here. At Tudor Cottage. But she didn't come from these parts. She came from Wales and she went back there and married— Roberts her name is now.'

'That's right,' said Frankie. 'You can't give me her address, I suppose? I borrowed a raincoat from her and forgot to give it back. If I had her address I'd post it to her.'

'Well now,' the other replied, 'I believe I can. I get a p.c. from her now and again. She and her husband have gone into service together. Wait a minute now.'

She went away and rummaged in a corner. Presently she returned with a piece of paper in her hand.

'Here you are,' she said, pushing it across the counter.

Bobby and Frankie read it together. It was the last thing in the world they expected.

'*Mrs Roberts,*
The Vicarage,
Marchbolt,
Wales.'

CHAPTER 33

Sensation in the Orient Café

How Bobby and Frankie got out of the post office without disgracing themselves neither of them ever knew.

Outside, with one accord, they looked at each other and shook with laugher.

'At the Vicarage—all the time!' gasped Bobby.

'And I look through four hundred and eighty Evans,' lamented Frankie.

'*Now* I see why Bassington-ffrench was so amused when he realized we didn't know in the least who Evans was!'

'And of course it was dangerous from their point of view. You and Evans were actually under the same roof.'

'Come on,' said Bobby. 'Marchbolt's the next place.'

'Like where the rainbow ends,' said Frankie. 'Back to the dear old home.'

'Dash it all,' said Bobby, 'we must do something about Badger. Have you any money, Frankie?'

Frankie opened her bag and took out a handful of notes.

'Give these to him and tell him to make some arrangement with his creditors and that Father will buy the garage and put him in as manager.'

'All right,' said Bobby. 'The great thing is to get off quickly.'

'Why this frightful haste?'

'I don't know—but I've a feeling something might happen.'

'How awful. Let's go ever so quickly.'

'I'll settle Badger. You go and start the car.'

'I shall never buy that toothbrush,' said Frankie.

Five minutes saw them speeding out of Chipping Somerton. Bobby had no occasion to complain of lack of speed.

Nevertheless, Frankie suddenly said:

'Look here, Bobby, this isn't quick enough.'

Bobby glanced at the speedometer needle, which was, at the moment, registering eighty, and remarked dryly:

'I don't see what more we can do.'

'We can take an air taxi,' said Frankie. 'We're only about seven miles from Medeshot Aerodrome.'

'My dear girl!' said Bobby.

'If we do that we'll be home in a couple of hours.'

'Good,' said Bobby. 'Let's take an air taxi.'

The whole proceedings were beginning to take on the fantastic character of a dream. Why this wild hurry to get to Marchbolt? Bobby didn't know. He suspected that Frankie didn't know either. It was just a feeling.

At Medeshot Frankie asked for Mr Donald King and

an untidy-looking young man was produced who appeared languidly surprised at the sight of her.

'Hullo, Frankie,' he said. 'I haven't seen you for an age. What do you want?'

'I want an air taxi,' said Frankie. 'You do that sort of thing, don't you?'

'Oh! yes. Where do you want to go?'

'I want to get home quickly,' said Frankie.

Mr Donald King raised his eyebrows.

'Is that all?' he asked.

'Not quite,' said Frankie. 'But it's the main idea.'

'Oh! well, we can soon fix you up.'

'I'll give you a cheque,' said Frankie.

Five minutes later they were off.

'Frankie,' said Bobby. 'Why are we doing this?'

'I haven't the faintest idea,' said Frankie. 'But I feel we must. Don't you?'

'Curiously enough, I do. But I don't know why. After all our Mrs Roberts won't fly away on a broomstick.'

'She might. Remember, we don't know what Bassington-ffrench is up to.'

'That's true,' said Bobby thoughtfully.

It was growing late when they reached their destination. The plane landed them in the Park and five minutes later Bobby and Frankie were driving into Marchbolt in Lord Marchington's Chrysler.

They pulled up outside the Vicarage gate, the Vicarage drive not lending itself to the turning of expensive cars.

Then jumping out they ran up the drive.

'I shall wake up soon,' thought Bobby. 'What are we doing and why?'

A slender figure was standing on the doorstep. Frankie and Bobby recognized her at the same minute.

'Moira!' cried Frankie.

Moira turned. She was swaying slightly.

'Oh! I'm so glad to see you. I don't know what to do.'

'But what on earth brings you here?'

'The same thing that has brought you, I expect.'

'You have found out who Evans is?' asked Bobby.

Moira nodded.

'Yes, it's a long story—'

'Come inside,' said Bobby.

But Moira shrank back.

'No, no,' she said hurriedly. 'Let's go somewhere and talk. There's something I must tell you—before we go into the house. Isn't there a café or some place like that in the town? Somewhere where we could go?'

'All right,' said Bobby, moving unwillingly away from the door. 'But why—'

Moira stamped her foot.

'You'll see when I tell you. Oh! do come. There's not a minute to lose.'

They yielded to her urgency. About half-way down the main street was the Orient Café—a somewhat grand name not borne out by the interior decoration. The three of them filed in. It was a slack moment—half-past six.

They sat down at a small table in the corner and Bobby ordered three coffees.

'Now then?' he said.

'Wait till she's brought the coffee,' said Moira.

The waitress returned and listlessly deposited three cups of tepid coffee in front of them.

'Now then,' said Bobby.

'I hardly know where to begin,' said Moira. 'It was in the train going to London. Really, the most amazing co-incidence. I went along the corridor and—'

She broke off. Her seat faced the door and she leant forward, staring.

'He must have followed me,' she said.

'Who?' cried Frankie and Bobby together.

'Bassington-ffrench,' whispered Moira.

'You've seen him?'

'He's outside. I saw him with a woman with red hair.'

'Mrs Cayman,' cried Frankie.

She and Bobby jumped and ran to the door. A protest came from Moira but neither of them heeded it. They looked up and down the street but Bassington-ffrench was nowhere in sight.

Moira joined them.

'Has he gone?' she asked, her voice trembling. 'Oh! do be careful. He's dangerous—horribly dangerous.'

'He can't do anything so long as we're all together,' said Bobby.

'Brace up, Moira,' said Frankie. 'Don't be such a rabbit.'

'Well, we can't do anything for the moment,' said Bobby, leading the way back to the table. 'Go on with what you were telling us, Moira.'

He picked up his cup of coffee. Frankie lost her

balance and fell against him and the coffee poured over the table.

'Sorry,' said Frankie.

She stretched over the adjoining table which was laid for possible diners. There was a cruet on it with two glass stoppered bottles containing oil and vinegar.

The oddity of Frankie's proceedings riveted Bobby's attention. She took the vinegar bottle, emptied out the vinegar into the slop bowl and began to pour coffee into it from her cup.

'Have you gone batty, Frankie?' asked Bobby. 'What the devil are you doing?'

'Taking a sample of this coffee for George Arbuthnot to analyse,' said Frankie.

She turned to Moira.

'*The game's up, Moira!* The whole thing came to me in a flash as we stood at the door just now! When I jogged Bobby's elbow and made him spill his coffee I saw your face. You put something in our cups when you sent us running to the door to look for Bassington-ffrench. The game's up, *Mrs Nicholson or Templeton or whatever you like to call yourself.*'

'Templeton?' cried Bobby.

'Look at her face,' cried Frankie. 'If she denies it ask her to come to the Vicarage and see if Mrs Roberts doesn't identify her.'

Bobby did look at her. He saw that face, that haunting, wistful face transformed by a demoniac rage. That beautiful mouth opened and a stream of foul and hideous curses poured out.

She fumbled in her handbag.

Bobby was still dazed but he acted in the nick of time. It was his hand that struck the pistol up.

The bullet passed over Frankie's head and buried itself in the wall of the Orient Café.

For the first time in its history one of the waitresses hurried.

With a wild scream she shot out into the street calling: 'Help! Murder! Police!'

CHAPTER 34

Letter from South America

It was some weeks later.

Frankie had just received a letter. It bore the stamp of one of the less well-known South American republics.

After reading it through, she passed it to Bobby.

It ran as follows:

Dear Frankie, Really, I congratulate you! You and your young naval friend have shattered the plans of a lifetime. I had everything so nicely arranged.

Would you really like to hear all about it? My lady friend has given me away so thoroughly (spite, I'm afraid—women are invariably spiteful!) that my most damaging admissions won't do me any further harm. Besides, I am starting life again. Roger Bassington-ffrench is dead.

I fancy I've always been what they call a 'wrong 'un'. Even at Oxford I had a little lapse. Stupid, because it was bound to be found out. The Pater didn't let me down. But he sent me to the Colonies.

I fell in with Moira and her lot fairly soon. She was the real thing. She was an accomplished criminal by the time she was fifteen. When I met her things were getting a bit too hot for her. The American police were on her trail.

She and I liked each other. We decided to make a match of it but we'd a few plans to carry through first.

To begin with, she married Nicholson. By doing so she removed herself to another world and the police lost sight of her. Nicholson was just coming over to England to start a place for nerve patients. He was looking for a suitable house to buy cheap. Moira got him on to the Grange.

She was still working in with her gang in the dope business. Without knowing it, Nicholson was very useful to her.

I had always had two ambitions. I wanted to be the owner of Merroway and I wanted to command an immense amount of money. A Bassington-ffrench played a great part in the reign of Charles II. Since then the family has dwindled down to mediocrity. I felt capable of playing a great part again. But I had to have money.

Moira made several trips across to Canada to 'see her people'. Nicholson adored her and believed anything she told him. Most men did. Owing to the complications of the drug business she travelled under various names. She was travelling as Mrs Templeton when she met Savage. She knew all about Savage and his enormous wealth and she went all out for him. He was attracted, but he wasn't attracted enough to lose his common sense.

However, we concocted a plan. You know pretty well the story of that. The man you know as Cayman acted the part of the unfeeling husband. Savage was induced to come down and stay at Tudor Cottage more than once. The third time he came our plans were laid. I needn't go into all that—you know it. The whole thing went with a bang. Moira cleared the money and went off ostensibly abroad—in reality back to Staverley and the Grange.

In the meantime, I was perfecting my own plans. Henry and young Tommy had to be got out of the way. I had bad luck over Tommy. A couple of perfectly good accidents went wrong. I wasn't going to fool about with accidents in Henry's case. He had a good deal of rheumatic pain after an accident in the hunting field. I introduced him to morphia. He took it in all good faith. Henry was a simple soul. He soon became an addict. Our plan was that he should go to the Grange for treatment and should there either 'commit suicide' or get hold of an overdose of morphia. Moira would do the business. I shouldn't be connected with it in any way.

And then that fool Carstairs began to be active. It seems that Savage had written him a line on board ship mentioning Mrs Templeton and even enclosing a snapshot of her. Carstairs went on a shooting trip soon afterwards. When he came back from the wilds and heard the news of Savage's death and will, he was frankly incredulous. The story didn't ring true to him. He was certain that Savage wasn't worried about his death and he didn't believe he had any special fear of cancer. Also the wording of the will sounded to him highly uncharacteristic. Savage was a hard-headed business man and while he might be quite ready to have an affair with a pretty woman, Carstairs didn't believe he would leave a vast sum of money to her and the rest to charity. The charity touch was my idea. It sounded so respectable and unfishy.

Carstairs came over here, determined to look into the business. He began to poke about.

And straightaway we had a piece of bad luck. Some friends brought him down to lunch and he saw a picture of Moira on the piano, and recognized it as the woman of the snapshot that Savage had sent him. He went down to Chipping Somerton and started to poke about there.

Moira and I began to get the wind up—I sometimes think unnecessarily. But Carstairs was a shrewd chap.

I went down to Chipping Somerton after him. He failed to trace the cook—Rose Chudleigh. She'd gone to the north, but he tracked down Evans, found out her married name and started off for Marchbolt.

Things were getting serious. If Evans identified Mrs Templeton and Mrs Nicholson as one and the same person matters were going to become difficult. Also, she'd been in the house some time and we weren't sure quite how much she might know.

I decided that Carstairs had got to be suppressed. He was making a serious nuisance of himself. Chance came to my aid. I was close behind him when the mist came up. I crept up nearer and a sudden push did the job.

But I was still in a dilemma. I didn't know what incriminating matter he might have on him. However,

*your young naval friend played into my hands very
nicely. I was left alone with the body for a short time—
quite enough for my purpose. He had a photograph of
Moira—he'd got it from the photographers—presumably
for identification. I removed that and any letters or
identifying matter. Then I planted the photograph of one
of the gang.*

*All went well. The pseudo sister and brother-in-law
came down and identified him. All seemed to have gone
off satisfactorily. And then your friend Bobby upset
things. It seemed that Carstairs had recovered
consciousness before he died and that he had been saying
things. He'd mentioned Evans—and Evans was actually
in service at the Vicarage.*

*I admit we were getting rattled by now. We lost our
heads a bit. Moira insisted that he must be put out of
the way. We tried one plan which failed. Then Moira said
she'd see to it. She went down to Marchbolt in the car.
She seized a chance very neatly—slipped some morphia
into his beer when he was asleep. But the young devil
didn't succumb. That was pure bad luck.*

*As I told you, it was Nicholson's cross-questioning
that made me wonder if you were just what you seemed.
But imagine the shock that Moira had when she was
creeping out to meet me one evening and came face to
face with Bobby! She recognized him at once—she'd had
a good look when he was asleep that day. No wonder
she was so scared she nearly passed out. Then she
realized that it wasn't her he suspected and she rallied
and played up.*

She came to the inn and told him a few tall stories. He swallowed them like a lamb. She pretended that Alan Carstairs was an old lover and she piled it on thick about her fear of Nicholson. Also she did her best to disabuse you of your suspicions concerning me. I did the same to you and disparaged her as a weak, helpless creature—Moira, who had the nerve to put any number of people out of the way without turning a hair!

The position was serious. We'd got the money. We were getting on well with the Henry plan. I was in no hurry for Tommy. I could afford to wait a bit. Nicholson could easily be got out of the way when the time came. But you and Bobby were a menace. You'd got your suspicions fixed on the Grange.

It may interest you to know that Henry didn't commit suicide. I killed him! When I was talking to you in the garden I saw there was no time to waste—and I went straight in and saw to things.

The aeroplane that came over gave me my chance. I went into the study, sat down by Henry who was writing and said: 'Look here, old man—' and shot him! The noise of the plane drowned the sound. Then I wrote a nice affecting letter, wiped off my fingerprints from the revolver, pressed Henry's hand round it and let it drop to the floor. I put the key of the study in Henry's pocket and went out, locking the door from the outside with the dining-room key which fits the lock.

I won't go into details of the neat little squib arrangement in the chimney which was timed to go off four minutes later.

Everything went beautifully. You and I were in the garden together and heard the 'shot'. A perfect suicide! The only person who laid himself open to suspicion was poor old Nicholson. The ass came back for a stick or something!

Of course Bobby's knight errantry was a bit difficult for Moira. So she just went off to the cottage. We fancied that Nicholson's explanation of his wife's absence would be sure to make you suspicious.

Where Moira really showed her mettle was at the cottage. She realized from the noise upstairs that I'd been knocked out, and she quickly injected a large dose of morphia into herself and lay down on the bed. After you all went down to telephone she nipped up to the attic and cut me free. Then the morphia took effect and by the time the doctor arrived she was genuinely off in a hypnotic sleep.

But all the same her nerve was going. She was afraid you'd get on to Evans and get the hang of how Savage's will and suicide was worked. Also she was afraid that Carstairs had written to Evans before he came to Marchbolt. She pretended to go up to a London nursing home. Instead, she hurried down to Marchbolt—and met you on the doorstep! Then her one idea was to get you both out of the way. Her methods were crude to the last degree, but I believe she'd have got away with it. I doubt if the waitress would have been able to remember much about what the woman who came in with you was like. Moira would have got away back to London and lain low in a nursing home. With you and Bobby out of the way the whole thing would have died down.

But you spotted her—and she lost her head. And then at the trial she dragged me into it!

Perhaps I was getting a little tired of her . . .

But I had no idea that she knew it.

You see, she had got the money—my money! Once I had married her I might have got tired of her. I like variety.

So here I am starting life again . . .

And all owing to you and that extremely objectionable young man Bobby Jones. But I've no doubt I shall make good!

Or ought it to be bad, not good?

I haven't reformed yet.

But if at first you don't succeed, try, try, try again.

Goodbye, my dear—or, perhaps au revoir. One never knows, does one?

Your affectionate enemy, the bold, bad villain of the piece,

Roger Bassington-ffrench.

CHAPTER 35

News from the Vicarage

Bobby handed back the letter and with a sigh Frankie took it.

'He's really a very remarkable person,' she said.

'You always had a fancy for him,' said Bobby coldly.

'He had charm,' said Frankie. 'So had Moira,' she added.

Bobby blushed.

'It was very queer that all the time the clue to the whole thing should have been in the Vicarage,' he said. 'You do know, don't you, Frankie, that Carstairs had actually written to Evans—to Mrs Roberts, that is?'

Frankie nodded.

'Telling her that he was coming to see her and that he wanted information about Mrs Templeton whom he had reason to believe was a dangerous international crook wanted by the police.

'And then when he's pushed over the cliff she doesn't put two and two together,' said Bobby bitterly.

'That's because the man who went over the cliff was Pritchard,' said Frankie. 'That identification was a very

289

clever bit of work. If a man called Pritchard is pushed over, how *could* it be a man called Carstairs? That's how the ordinary mind works.'

'The funny thing is that she recognized Cayman,' went on Bobby. 'At least she caught a glimpse of him when Roberts was letting him in and asked him who it was. And he said it was Mr Cayman and she said, "Funny, he's the dead spit of a gentleman I used to be in service with."'

'Can you beat it?' said Frankie.

'Even Bassington-ffrench gave himself away once or twice,' she continued. 'But like an idiot I never spotted it.'

'Did he?'

'Yes, when Sylvia said that the picture in the paper was very like Carstairs he said there wasn't much likeness really—showing he'd seen the dead man. And then later he said to me that he never saw the dead man's face.'

'How on earth did you spot Moira, Frankie?'

'I think it was the description of Mrs Templeton,' said Frankie dreamily. 'Everyone said she was "such a nice lady". Now that didn't seem to fit with the Cayman woman. No servant would describe her a "nice lady". And then we got to the Vicarage and Moira was there and it suddenly came to me—*Suppose Moira was Mrs Templeton?*'

'Very bright of you.'

'I'm very sorry for Sylvia,' said Frankie. 'With Moira dragging Roger into it, it's been a terrible lot of publicity for her. But Dr Nicholson has stuck by her and I shouldn't be at all surprised if they ended by making a match of it.'

'Everything seems to have ended very fortunately,' said Bobby. 'Badger's doing well at the garage—thanks to your father, and also thanks to your father, I've got this perfectly marvellous job.'

'Is it a marvellous job?'

'Managing a coffee estate out in Kenya on a whacking big screw? I should think so. It's just the sort of thing I used to dream about.'

He paused.

'People come out to Kenya a good deal on trips,' he said with intention.

'Quite a lot of people live out there,' said Frankie demurely.

'Oh! Frankie, you wouldn't?' He blushed, stammered, recovered himself. 'W-w-would you?'

'I would,' said Frankie. 'I mean, I will.'

'I've been keen about you always,' said Bobby in a stifled voice. 'I used to be miserable—knowing, I mean, that it was no good.'

'I suppose that's what made you so rude that day on the golf links?'

'Yes, I was feeling pretty grim.'

'H'm,' said Frankie. 'What about Moira?'

Bobby looked uncomfortable.

'Her face did sort of get me,' he admitted.

'It's a better face than mine,' said Frankie generously.

'It isn't—but it sort of "haunted" me. And then, when we were up in the attic and you were so plucky about things—well, Moira just faded out. I was hardly interested in what happened to her. It was *you*—only you. You were simply splendid! So frightfully plucky.'

'I wasn't feeling plucky inside,' said Frankie. 'I was all shaking. But I wanted you to admire me.'

291

'I did, darling. I do. I always have. I always shall. Are you sure you won't hate it out in Kenya?'

'I shall adore it. I was fed up with England.'

'Frankie.'

'Bobby.'

'If you will come in here,' said the Vicar, opening the door and ushering in the advance guard of the Dorcas Society.

He shut the door precipitately and apologized.

'My—er—one of my sons. He is—er—engaged.'

A member of the Dorcas Society said archly that it looked like it.

'A good boy,' said the Vicar. 'Inclined at one time not to take life seriously. But he has improved very much of late. He is going out to manage a coffee estate in Kenya.'

Said one member of the Dorcas Society to another in a whisper:

'Did you see? It was Lady Frances Derwent he was kissing?'

In an hour's time the news was all over Marchbolt.